Cranes in the Sky

Connect With Me

EMAIL >> durtylittlesecrets@gmail.com

TWITTER >> www.twitter.com/keishaervin

FACEBOOK >> www.facebook.com/keisha.ervin

INSTAGRAM >> @keishaervin

SNAPCHAT >> kyrese99

YOUTUBE >> www.youtube.com/ColorMePynk

"I done had too many heartbreaks." – Dawn Richard, "Hey

#1

Messiah

"Messiah, I know you hear me." Her mother, Etta, turned around in her seat and shook her knee.

"I hear you... damn!" Messiah angrily snatched her leg away. *"Leave me alone, please,"* she begged.

"Who in the hell do you think you talkin' to?" Bill, her dad, yelled as he maneuvered his way down the dark, slick, winding road. *"Curse again and see what happen."*

"Bill, honey, calm down. We're all tired and on edge. We've been driving for hours. We haven't eaten. Just...just calm down. Messiah knows we're only doing this to help her." Etta tried her best to smooth over the situation.

"Yeah, whatever." Messiah sucked her teeth and looked out the window at the rapidly falling snow.

"Disrespect your mother again and I swear to God, I'm gonna pull this freakin' car over," Bill warned, having had enough of his daughter's attitude.

"What don't y'all get? Y'all are not helpin' me! You're ruining my life!"

"We're ruining your life?" Etta snapped in disbelief. *"You're the one who's pregnant at 16, not us. You're ruining your own damn life. Your father and I are only doing what we feel is best for you. One day when you get older, you'll understand that. Now,"* Etta took a much-needed breath. *"You're going to go to Tuscaloosa with Aunt Mae for the last few weeks of your pregnancy. You'll*

*give the baby up for adoption, as we discussed, then you'll
come back to Saint Louis, finish school, go to Juilliard and
move on with your life. We'll put this whole ordeal behind
us, as if it never happened."*

*"I have told you a million times, I'm not giving my
baby up for adoption. Bryson and I are going to get
married and raise this baby together. I love him and he
loves me; so deal with it. He's not going anywhere and
neither is this baby," Messiah spat, rubbing her belly.*

Her baby boy had just kicked.

*"Messiah, you're delusional if you think that boy is
going to marry you. Bryson is only out for himself. That
boy don't give a damn about you for real. Plus, he's 16
years old. No 16-year-old boy wants to get married, let
alone be tied down to a wife and child," Etta reasoned,
rolling her eyes.*

*"You don't know how he feels about me. Bryson
loves me." Messiah spat.*

*"You're a teenager. What the hell do you think you
know about love?" Bill chuckled indignantly. "You know
how ridiculous you sound? Never in a million years did I
think my daughter would grow up to be so damn naive.
Why can't you be more like your sister? Lake has a good
head on her shoulders. She's in college. She's working. She
just won her fifth beauty pageant. She's about to compete
for Miss America. You should aspire to be more like her."*

*"Oh, my god." Messiah groaned, waiving her
father off. "We all know Lake is the golden child, but guess
what? I'm not her. I'm Messiah, and guess what else? I'm
16 and I'm pregnant. I know this isn't what you envisioned
for me but I'm not ashamed of being pregnant - or my
baby. I'm gonna be a great mother; so, you can drive me*

5

down to Alabama all you want to, but I'm keeping my damn baby."

"Curse again! I dare you!" Bill cautioned as sleet pelted the windshield of the car.

He could barely see the road; the weather was so bad.

"Are you really sure you wanna keep this baby?" Etta asked again.

"Oh, my god." Messiah groaned, rolling her eyes. "How many times do I have to tell you? Yes!"

"Messiah, what has happened to you? Ever since you got with this li'l boy, you've changed. You're defensive, you're argumentative and outright disrespectful," Etta grimaced, confused.

"Ain't nothin' wrong with me. This is who I've always been. You and Dad just want to control me."

"No, you have changed. This isn't the daughter I raised. What happened to the girl that wanted to go to Juilliard? You've been studying ballet since you were a year old. You were on the cusp of receiving a scholarship. Now you don't even dance anymore. You're only 16, Messiah. How are you going to raise a child, 'cause your father and I are not going to help you?"

"You don't have to help me. Bryson and I are going to raise our son together. We'll get jobs. We'll do whatever it takes. Even if it means me getting on welfare. We'll figure it out." Messiah stated confidently.

"You hear your child?" Bill asked Etta. "'Cause this for damn sure ain't my daughter. No child of mine would sound this dumb. Messiah, you sound like a damn

6

fool." Bill's nostrils flared as he gripped the steering wheel.

"No, you're the fool for driving eight hours for nothing! Nothing you're gonna say or do is gonna make me change my mind! Now, for the last time; I'm keeping my baby, and if you and Mom can't accept that, then the both of you can kiss my ass as far as I'm concerned!" Messiah shot, wishing she could take back the words as soon as she said them.

"That's it! I have had enough of you and your smart-ass mouth!" Bill barked, turning around in his seat to scold her without thinking. "You disrespectful li'l brat!"

"Bill, what are you doing? Keep your eyes on the road!" Etta yelled.

"No, Etta! She gon' learn today. I don't give a damn if she is pregnant! She ain't too old to get an ass whoppin'!" Bill tried his best to grab Messiah with one hand as he drove the car with the other.

"No! Daddy, stop! I'm sorry! I didn't mean it!" Messiah scooted away from him.

"BILL, HONEY! THE ROAD! WATCH OUT!" Etta shrieked at the top of her lungs, as he veered off the road.

"OH, MY GOD! DADDY, WATCH OUT!" Messiah screamed, jumping out of her sleep.

Panting heavily, sweat poured from her body. Instinctively, she reached down and touched her stomach to make sure her baby was safe. Messiah quickly remembered that she'd had another bad dream and that her baby was dead. Running her clammy hands down her face, she shook her head and tried her best not to cry. Every day she got to wake up to live another day, she regretted being the only survivor of the horrific car accident that claimed the lives of both her parents and her unborn son. Six years had passed but Messiah still carried the burden of feeling that the accident wouldn't have ever happened if it weren't for her immature behavior.

"Oh, my god, Messiah. Pull it together. You gotta shake this shit." She stressed, running her hands down her face.

Once she caught her breath, she looked around the empty room and tried to remember where she was. It quickly dawned on her that she was inside her new, one-bedroom apartment in the Lennox Square complex. The place was nice, but it was nothing to run home to your mama about. It was clean, affordable, spacious enough and two blocks away from her night job at Joe's Diner. Somehow, she'd fallen asleep on the floor while resting her head on a stack of towels.

Messiah never imagined that this was what her life would be like, at the age of 21. She thought she would have the picture-perfect, fairytale lifestyle she always envisioned. She thought that she and Bryson would be happily married and raising their son. Instead, here she was, alone, moving into a place she could barely afford. Messiah was in so much debt it was swallowing her whole.

After her parents and baby died, she sank into a deep, dark depression. She was so traumatized that she wouldn't leave her room or the house for a year. She had to see a therapist to deal with the aftermath of the accident. Once her father lost control of the car, he crashed into a tanker truck. The vehicle overturned and everyone was thrown from the car. Her parents were killed on impact. Police found Messiah on the side of the road barely breathing. Her baby boy was found a few feet away from her with his umbilical cord still attached. He, too, was pronounced dead after paramedics tried to resuscitate him.

Messiah was rushed to the hospital. Everyone thought she was going to die. Miraculously, after doctors performed emergency surgery to stop the internal bleeding and close her stomach, she survived. Messiah didn't want to live though. She wanted to die along with everyone else. It wasn't fair that she'd have to be the one to live with the horrifying memories.

She was so overwhelmed with grief that she didn't even finish high school. Her older sister, Lake, never said it out loud but she blamed Messiah for their parents' death. Messiah could see it in her eyes whenever she looked at her. Lake did the bare minimum to make sure Messiah was ok. She was too busy living her life as a beauty queen. Their aunt, Mae, was assigned as Messiah's legal guardian until she turned 18. She tried to do all she could to get Messiah out of her funk, but the only person Messiah felt she could lean on was Bryson. Then one day, she looked up and realized she'd missed her senior year of school and Bryson had gotten accepted to Temple University in Philly on a partial scholarship.

Depressed with no high school diploma and her first love leaving, Messiah didn't know what she was going to do. She wanted to be selfish and beg him to stay. She needed him like she needed her limbs to function. Bryson didn't want to leave her either. He loved Messiah immensely. The accident had fucked him up too. Their son was only a few weeks away from being born. He'd bought clothes, bottles and a crib. Even though he was young, Bryson was going to make sure his baby and Messiah were good.

Now that there was no baby, he couldn't stay stuck in sadness forever. He had to push through the anger and

9

hurt. While Messiah excluded herself from the world, he put all his focus on school. He and Messiah made a pact that he would go off to school and come back to visit her as much as he could. Once he graduated, he'd find a job in his field and send for Messiah. He'd work and then she'd go to college herself.

Since Bryson only had a partial scholarship, finding money for him to finish paying for school was hard. His parents didn't have much and couldn't pay for him to go to school, so Messiah gave him the life insurance money her parents left, which totaled out to be $15,000. She also took out a loan for 10 g's and maxed out a $7,000 credit to help. Bryson swore once his career took off he'd pay Messiah back every red cent. She believed in Bryson and wanted to see him succeed in getting his MBA in accounting, so she didn't mind helping him out. Besides, he was the love of her life and her future husband. She would do whatever it took to make him happy, even if it meant putting herself in debt.

Between paying off the loan, credit card bills, rent, utilities, getting her car out of the shop and paying her car insurance, she barely had enough money left over to eat. She hadn't been getting regular oil changes on her car because she couldn't afford it. The result of that caused her car to lock up and now she needed a new engine. Messiah didn't want to catch the bus back and forth to work, but she had no choice. She was deeply in love and willing to do whatever to hold her man down - even if that meant sacrificing her own livelihood.

He'd held her down the six years they'd been together. He'd loved her when she had no one. Outside of Bird, her best friend, Bryson was the only person who acknowledged her pain. Talking to Lake was useless. Up until her death, Aunt Mae had been a source of love and encouragement; but now that she was gone, Messiah had little to no one.

Messiah spent most her time coasting through life, pretending to be happy, when really, she was dying on the inside. The only slice of happiness she had was when Bryson called or visited. Soon, they'd be together permanently. He was in his last year of school. Messiah counted down the days till she got to wake up to his handsome face every day. Bryson was supposed to come down and help her move but his first semester classes started earlier than expected. Messiah was disappointed. They hadn't seen each other in two months. It was the longest they'd ever been apart. Having a long-distance relationship was pure hell but Bryson promised he'd come see her soon.

"Siah!" Bird charged through the door, excited.

Messiah looked down at her watch. It was a little after 3 pm. Bird should've been back with more boxes and lunch two hours ago.

"Bird, where the hell have you been?" Messiah grimaced as she walked into the living room with nothing but a McDonald's cup in her hand.

They'd been friends since as far back as she could remember. They were total opposites in every way imaginable but their differences were what connected them. Bird brought Messiah out of her shell. She was everything Messiah feared and envied. Bird was loud, brassy, extremely sexual and overly confident. She was a pint size powerhouse. Her mocha skin, big, brown eyes, voluptuous lips, A-cup breasts and size two frame was very modelesque, except, she was only 5'3.

She had black roots and blonde tips with a deep side part. Bird loved to wear all black. She was an all-around bad bitch. Nothing or no one could tie her down. She lived life by her own rules. If you didn't like the way she lived her life, then you could kiss her ass.

"I had to make a li'l stop real quick." She blushed, compressing her legs together.

"You mean to tell me, instead of going to get more boxes, you went and got more dick!" Messiah exclaimed.

"Girl, I got yo' li'l punk-ass boxes. They in the car," Bird snarled.

"Where my food?"

"That's in the car too." Bird tried to stifle a laugh. "Yo' fries might be cold."

"Ya think? I swear you are good for nothin'." Messiah eased off the concrete floor. "And who you go fuck, anyway? Please, don't let it be ole girl with the Tisha Martin head."

"Uh… no," Bird rolled her eyes. "That bitch will never get to lick this clit again. I went to see Armon."

"Hell, that's even worse. I thought we got rid of him."

"Child, please, don't hate. That dick is magically delicious. He's back and we're fuckin' like two lieutenants after lights-out."

"I can't with you." Messiah chuckled, trying to make her way out the door.

"Hold up." Bird stopped her. "I just saw on Facebook that they're having a Wu-Tang tribute tonight at Blank Space. Everybody is supposed to be there."

"Ok… and?" Messiah shrugged her shoulders, unimpressed.

"And… we're going."

"You out yo' damn mind. I'm not going nowhere. I have to finish unpacking and cleaning up."

"Stop being such a sour puss. Bitch, we going; so once we get this shit in the house, go through them boxes and find you something cute to wear 'cause we kickin' it tonight."

"No… we're not."

"Yes… we are. Just 'cause you're engaged to be married don't mean you can't have a social life." Bird curled her upper lip.

Messiah looked down at her left hand and admired her engagement ring. It wasn't extravagant by any means necessary. Bryson had gotten her a simple, 10k, white gold, 1/10 carat ring with smaller accent diamonds surrounding the center stone. Even though the diamond was minuscule, Messiah loved her ring and wore it with pride

"Ok, we'll see about that," Messiah challenged.

"We will," Bird spat back.

"How we met must've been fate." – Nas,
"K-I-SS-I-N-G"

#2

Messiah

Messiah stood off in the cut with her back pressed up against the exposed brick wall. Blank Space was filled to capacity. It seemed like the whole South Side was in there. It was hot from all the body heat and lack of air conditioning. A single fan spun 'round and 'round on the ceiling but it only circulated hot air. Messiah used her hand to fan her face. She hated to sweat. It was so unladylike and gross.

Why did I let Bird talk me into coming here tonight, she thought. She should've been home unpacking instead of in a blistering hot, sweaty club. The atmosphere was thick with sexual hedonism and hate. Summertime in St. Louis brought out the crazy in people. Anything could pop off at any moment. Messiah scanned the crowd. Bodies were pressed up against one another like sardines.

Messiah wanted to get out of there. It was hot as fuck. Her naturally thick, curly hair was sticking to her moist face. She wished she had a rubber band to tie her hair back. This was one of those times she wished her car was fixed. Being at the mercy of Bird was not her idea of fun. When Messiah was ready to go, she was ready to go.

She knew she probably looked ridiculous sulking in the corner. Especially since everyone else was having a ball. Drinks were being passed, hands were in the air, heads were bobbing and hips swayed to the hypnotic beat of Wu-Tang's *C.R.E.A.M.* The one good thing about Blank Space was the eclectic crowd. You could find hipsters, thugs, skateboarders, around the way girls, artists and soul singers. That night there was a mixture of them all.

Messiah searched the dark room for her friend. Bird was grinning up in some girl's face. No matter where they went, she was always the life of the party. Messiah wished she could be confident and carefree like her best friend but the accident had changed her. She was cold and often distant. Messiah was a loner, for the most part. The only time she had any fun was when she was with Bryson or Bird. Other than that, she found no joy out of life.

"I just wanna go home," she groaned, like a little kid.

Messiah honestly felt like she'd wasted a cute outfit, makeup and 10 dollars getting into the club. She didn't have money to be wasting. Ten dollars was a lot of money for a broke-ass chick like her and she didn't like getting dolled up for nothing. The bold, sexy, red, matte lipstick that decorated her Bratz-doll-like lips could've been saved for another occasion. The silver, tribal, statement necklace, bohemian style, V-neck, bell sleeve romper and strappy heels she wore captured the essence of her boho-chic style.

Messiah knew she was pretty but wasn't the type to trip off her looks. People often compared her to Blackish star Yara Shahidi. Like her, she had flawless, honey-colored skin. Black, silky curls cascaded past her shoulders. She had thick, perfectly-arched brows, almond-shaped, brown eyes, razor sharp cheekbones, full, pouty lips and a dimpled chin.

She was on the petite side. She had 34C cup breasts, a flat stomach, small, curvy hips and a li'l booty with a li'l bounce to it. Messiah wasn't your typical beauty. She was something special. She wasn't like most girls.

Unbeknownst to her, she stood out amongst the Instagram baddies: Kylie Jenner, Beyoncé and Nicki Minaj wannabes. She had her own, unique swag. Messiah didn't have much money but she made her thrift store and Forever 21 finds look like a million bucks.

Maybe that was why Shyhiem hadn't been able to take his eyes off her. Since he'd laid eyes on her, she'd kept him wanting more. He wasn't the type of dude to sweat no chick but Messiah had captured his heart without saying a word. She didn't even know she'd seized his undivided attention, or that he was filming her. She was completely oblivious to his presence. Shyhiem didn't mind. He liked watching her from afar, without her noticing him.

She was the prettiest, caramel-colored girl he'd ever seen. He prayed the camera on his phone did her justice. Her ruby lips called his name in the dark. Entranced by her beauty, he leaned back against the bar and took a sip of his beer. If he never saw the angelic beauty again, he was at peace with knowing he'd have the video of her forever. Shyhiem was somewhat of an amateur film maker on the low. After being locked up for three years, he liked to keep mementos of poignant moments in life. The beauty across the way was a memory worth capturing. She took his breath away.

Love wasn't what he came to Blank Space for but it felt good. For the first time in years, he felt his heart beat erratically. None of the other women he'd ever encountered made him feel this way. He had to have her, but the angry expression on her face made him feel like a chick like her would never go for a nigga like him. She was Coachella chic and he was a menace to society. It was a good thing she hadn't noticed him. If he got his hands on her, he'd probably ruin her.

Shyhiem was always known for going after what he wanted without hesitation, but this girl had him on edge. He'd heard people talk about love at first sight; and up until that moment, he never found it to be true. Somehow, he'd fallen in love with her without even knowing her name. Then, a blessing came down from God. Shyhiem watched as she sauntered slowly across the room and over to the bar. To his surprise, she landed right next to him. It was then that he pressed stop and ceased recording. There was no way he wasn't going to bask in the essence of being in her presence.

Oblivious to her surroundings, Messiah rested her forearms on the bar and tried to get the bartender's attention. The enthralling, panty droppin' smell of Tom Ford cologne floated up her nose. Messiah followed the scent and looked up to find a mocha chocolate god eye-fuckin' the shit outta her.

Instantly, she felt naked under his mesmerizing gaze. He was enchanting. Never had she seen a man that made her gasp for air. He was mystical, black magic wrapped up in 6 feet of African wonder. He donned a low-cut Caesar with a part, like the rapper Nas. A smooth set of eyebrows hovered over his coal black, diamond-shaped eyes. A well-groomed beard outlined his kissable, brown lips.

He looked to be about 180 pounds of pure muscle. He reminded her of the actor Kofi Siriboe that played Ralph Angel on Queen Sugar. Messiah skimmed her eyes over his physique. He wore a thin, gold chain, white, longline t-shirt, ripped, denim jeans, clean, white, Nike Roshe sneakers and a gold watch. He was fly as fuck. For years, Messiah had only had eyes for Bryson, but this dude giving her goosebumps was of a different breed. On sight, he had her willing to risk it all.

"Hi." He finally said.

"Hi," she replied, softly with a slight smile.

Her heart felt like it was going to fall out of her chest.

"What's your name?" His deep, raspy voice sent chills up her spine.

"Messiah." She held out her left hand for a shake.

"Shyhiem." He gently took her hand in his.

A spark of electricity shot through Messiah's veins as the palms of their hands connected. Everything in her was screaming, *look away; he's no good*, but her eyes stayed fixated on him. She couldn't look away if she tried.

Shyhiem swallowed the lump in his throat and looked down at her hand. *Damn, she's married,* he furrowed his brows, incensed. It seemed like he always had crushes on chicks he couldn't have, but the woman standing before him was the girl of his dreams. Whoever her man was, it didn't matter. He could tell by the look in her eye she didn't give a fuck either. He wanted her and he was going to have her.

Say something, you shy muthafucka, she's waiting, he thought. Shyhiem wasn't afraid of anything but this girl made him nervous. She was different from the women he was used to. Her swag was on another level. She was special and different. This girl was a rarity. She was way out of his league, but he knew if he got her in his grasp, she would be all he'd ever need.

Just as he was about to part his lips to ask if she wanted a drink, shots rang out in the air. Messiah jumped, startled from the bang of the gun. Feeling the need to protect her, Shyhiem swiftly covered her body with his and

19

made her crouch down. Messiah closed her eyes tightly and covered her face with her hands, as glass shattered around them. After the seventh shot, an eerie silence swept over the room. The music had stopped. Suddenly, a blood curdling scream filled the air and a stampede of people started running for the door. Abruptly, Messiah's survival instincts kicked in and she called out for Bird.

"Stay down!" Shyhiem yelled.

"No! I have to find my friend!" She tried to get up.

"Messiah!" Bird appeared out of thin air and grabbed her hand. "Come on!" She pulled her towards the exit.

Not used to running in heels, Messiah tried her best to keep up as they ran but people were pushing and acting reckless. Somehow, Messiah got pulled away from Bird. Tears scorched her cheeks as she searched frantically for her friend. By the time, she made it to the door, she was stopped dead in her tracks by the sight of a dead body on the floor covered in blood. The visual instantly took her back to the accident.

"Move, bitch!" A girl shouted, pushing her out the way.

Realizing she'd been standing frozen stiff, Messiah came back to reality and ran outside as another blast of a gun sent shockwaves throughout her body. Afraid for her life, she looked over her shoulder to make sure the gunman wasn't behind her. Not paying attention to what was happening in front of her, she was run over by Shyhiem. He was running so fast, he accidentally tackled her to the ground.

As she fell, everything seemed to move in slow motion. Her arms and legs flailed in the air. She had no time to brace herself for the fall. Her head hit the concrete with a thud. Shyhiem didn't realize who he'd run over until he looked down and spotted her innocent face.

"My bad. You a'ight?" He asked, helping her off the ground.

Messiah nodded and rubbed the side of her head.

"Yo, Shy, come on!" His brother, Mayhem, pulled up.

Shyhiem hesitantly looked at Messiah. He didn't want to leave her but he had to.

"Messiah! What the hell are you doing? C'mon!" Bird rushed over, looking at her like she was crazy.

Seeing she was cool, Shyhiem took one last look at her and hopped inside his brother's ride. Messiah continued to massage her head as Shyhiem sped off. As Bird escorted her to the safety of her car, Messiah couldn't help but wonder if she would ever see the beautiful man who'd protected her again.

"Beep me, boy, or at least give me a call." –
Missy Elliot feat. 702, "Beep Me 911"

#3

Messiah

The day was September 6th, 2016. Messiah held her hair back, closed her eyes, made a wish, and then blew out the single candle. It was her 22nd birthday. Bird had bought her red velvet cupcakes and sushi for a small b-day turn up during lunch. Messiah hated working at Charter Communications. She worked in the call center department during the day. Thank God Bird worked there too. Having her bestie by her side made the day go by faster. For the most part, her coworkers were cool. There were a few people that got on her nerves, but on that day, Messiah was determined not to let anyone steal her joy.

A few weeks had passed since the shooting at Blank Space that left one person dead. The gruesome event had Messiah shook for a minute. Everywhere she went, she was on high-alert. The incident reminded her just how precious life was. She couldn't take a day for granted. Tomorrow wasn't promised. She was going to cherish each day as if it were her last day on earth. Done blowing out the candle, Messiah opened her eyes as Bird and their coworker, Twan, clapped excitedly.

"Happy birthday, boo." Bird kissed her cheek and handed her a pink, glittery box.

Tears stung the brim of Messiah's eyes. No one ever went out their way to do anything nice for her. Her birthdays were normally uneventful; but each year, Bird made it her business to get her a gift.

"Thanks, Bird." Messiah held back her tears.

Crying in public wasn't a part of her repertoire. Messiah wasn't a fan of public displays of emotion. She wasn't an overly emotional or affectionate person. She kept her feelings close to her chest - always. Being vulnerable opened the door for pain. She couldn't risk it. Opening the box, she found a gorgeous, gold, statement necklace with pearl and rhinestone accents. The necklace was exquisite.

"You like it?" Bird asked nervously.

"Girl, yes. I love it." Messiah held out her hand for a five.

"No, bitch, give me a hug." Bird wrapped her arms around Messiah tightly.

Messiah begrudgingly hugged her bestie back.

"Ok, that's enough." She pushed Bird away.

"Yo' thug-ass," Bird laughed. "Bitch, you gon' love me."

"Mmm... these cupcakes are the bomb!" Twan licked icing off his index finger. "Who made these? This icing taste like sex."

"My homegirl, Mo. Follow her on IG. Her IG name is CakeDust," Bird replied.

"That's what's up. I'ma have to place an order with her."

Messiah would never admit it, but Twan was one of her favorite people in the world. He constantly had her cracking up with his over-the-top antics. He was 20, 5'9 with ombre, honey blonde locs that touched the middle of his back. The man had a body that would put most females to shame. He had a fatty and a small waist. Twan wasn't the type to wear female clothes, but was known to step into a feminine frock on occasion. He loved dick and pushing people's buttons.

What Messiah admired about him was that he was 100% comfortable in his own skin. He owned his sexuality and flamboyant personality. He and Bird loved to be the center of attention, while Messiah preferred fading into the background. Growing up mixed was a challenge. She was too black for the white kids and wasn't black enough for the black kids. Messiah felt like she didn't fit in anywhere.

Being an African American, Jewish, Native American girl who loved ballet, Japanese animate, comic books and wrestling caused her to stick out like a sore thumb. It was a blessing when she befriended Bird in the 3rd grade. Messiah didn't know what she'd do without her.

"Why do I smell smoke in here?" A coworker by the name of Colleen questioned.

"Messiah just blew out the candle on her cupcake," Bird answered.

"Having a lit candle is a fire hazard. I'm going to have to tell Tom about this," Colleen insisted.

"You know snitches get stitches," Twan held up a plastic knife.

"Tom!" Colleen raced out of the break room to tattle.

"I can't stand her ass," Twan rolled his eyes.

"Me either," Bird agreed. "We going out for drinks after work. You coming?" She asked Messiah while devouring a cupcake.

"I gotta work at the diner tonight," Messiah replied, regrettably.

It sucked that she had to work both her jobs on her birthday.

"Play hooky, Cookie." Twan played with a strand of her hair.

"I can't. These bills ain't gon' pay themselves." She arched her brow.

"Boooooooo!" He gave her a thumbs down.

"Even if she didn't have to work, you know she wasn't gon' go, wit' her boring-ass," Bird twisted her lips to the side.

"Look at what happened the last time I went out wit' you. Somebody died!" Messiah stressed, getting up from the table.

Her break was over.

"You two whores need to take a page out of my book and stay y'all asses at home." She said, heading back to her desk.

"Child, please, it's too much good dick out here to be wasting my time sitting in the house," Twan replied, following her out of the break room.

In the privacy of her cubicle, Messiah checked her phone to see if Bryson had called. To her disappointment, he hadn't. It wasn't like him not to call and at least say good morning, let alone, happy birthday. *Maybe he's got a surprise for you,* she thought, getting excited. As Messiah settled into answering calls, her mind drifted off to the chocolate cutie she met at Blank Space. Since their encounter, he'd invaded her mental space often. She couldn't shake him. The spark he'd ignited burned slow in the pit of her belly. She wondered what she'd do if she ever got the opportunity to see him again.

"Nothing." She spoke out loud. "You're engaged to be married, girl."

"Excuse me?" The caller on the other end of the line said.

"My bad… I mean, I'm sorry, ma'am." Messiah straightened up and remembered where she was. "You said your DVR isn't working, correct?"

"Said you never leave me lonely. Fly tenderoni but you phony." – Method Man feat. D'Angelo, "Break Ups 2 Make Ups"

#4

Shyhiem

"Daddy, Daddy!" Shyhiem's six-year-old daughter, Shania, shook his arm profusely.

"Daddy's sleep, Baby girl." He mumbled with his face planted in the pillow, half asleep.

Shyhiem had been peacefully dreaming about the caramel shorty he met at Blank Space. She'd invaded his memory bank and taken up space there. He couldn't get her off his mind. He'd watched the short video he'd captured of her on his phone at least 10 times.

"What is it?"

"We hungry." Shania poked out her bottom lip.

"It's we're hungry; and what you mean you hungry?" Shyhiem opened his eyes, confused. "Hold up. Why ain't you at school?"

"Mama said we ain't have to go."

"Where is your mother?" Shyhiem turned over on his side.

"She gone to get her nails done."

"What?" Shyhiem screwed up his face.

The sun was shining brightly, stinging the hell out of his eyes. Once his vision was straight, he looked at the clock. It was 12:30pm.

"She told us to tell you to fix us something to eat when we get hungry. Well, we hungry, so, Daddy, get up." Shania tried to pull her father out of bed. "Me and Brother want some French toast and bacon. Will you make us some? Pleaaaaaaase, Daddy!" She begged, jumping up and down.

Shyhiem wiped the cold out of his eyes, looked at his daughter and laughed. She stood on the side of the bed dressed in a too little, Elsa pajama set he'd bought her when she was four. Her cute, little, chubby stomach poked out of the bottom of the shirt and the legs of the pajama pants ended at her knees. Shania's natural, long, thick, black hair was matted into a ponytail but she was still as cute as a button. She had Shyhiem's radiant ebony skin but looked just like her mother. Every time Shyhiem looked at Shania, she made him smile. No matter how much her mother pissed him off, Shyhiem could never take it out on Shania or his son.

"Yeah, li'l mama. Daddy got you. Give me a minute tho'. I gotta make a phone call real quick." He swung his long legs over the side of the bed and placed them on the floor.

"Thank you, Daddy!" Shania jumped up and kissed the side of his face, before running out.

"Close the door, baby."

"Ok, Daddy." Shania pulled the door closed behind her.

Angry beyond belief, Shyhiem grabbed his iPhone off the nightstand and called his kids' mother. Keesha was always doing stupid shit like this to piss him off. She knew damn well the kids should've been at school. It was the first day. They had no reason to be home. They weren't sick. Plus, it was Shyhiem's day off and he was tired as hell.

Being a UPS delivery driver was a taxing job and he needed all the rest he could get. Keesha knew that.

"Hello?" She giggled, answering on the third ring.

"Why the fuck ain't the twins at school?" He barked into the phone.

"Good morning to you too, Shy," Keesha sighed, rolling her eyes.

"Yo, I'm not in the fuckin' mood. Why ain't the kids at school?"

"'Cause they ain't feel like going. It's the first day of school, anyway. Don't nothing important happen on the first day."

"Do you hear how dumb you sound? You know damn well they need to be at school. Yo' ass was just too lazy to get up and take them to the bus stop," Shyhiem shot.

"It's only one day, Shyhiem. Damn… calm down. They ain't missing nothing."

"I swear to God you's a silly-ass broad. I wish I never met you." He ran his hand down his face, exasperated. "All you gotta do is get up and take them down the street to the bus stop. That's all I ask you to do, but nah, that's too much work for you. But you can get up and take yo' ass to get yo' fuckin' nails down. What kind of birdbrain shit is that?"

"You couldn't possibly be talkin' to me 'cause I ain't no fuckin' bird," Keesha spat.

"Just hurry up and get home. I got some shit I need to do." He ended the call before she could say another word.

After only three hours of sleep, there was no way that Shyhiem could listen to the nonsense coming out of Keesha's mouth. He was vexed, to say the least, but it was all good. He loved spending time with his kids. It was past noon. There was no telling how long they had been awake with no food in their little bellies. Shyhiem jumped out of bed, threw on a t-shirt, and headed towards the front of the apartment.

He and Keesha had been living at the Lennox Square apartment complex for three years. Shyhiem hated every second of it. After serving time in jail, he needed an address on record for his P.O. Shyhiem didn't want to, but he had no other choice but to move in with Keesha, unless he wanted to be homeless. Now that he was back on his feet, Shyhiem wanted desperately to get away from her, but she'd threatened on more than one occasion that she would get the courts involved and file child support if he left. Shyhiem couldn't have the government taxing his pockets. It was cheaper for him to suffer in silence than have half his check taken each month. On top of that, Keesha was unfit as hell. He couldn't leave his kids around her alone.

She refused to get a job, hated cleaning, smoked weed all day, cursed too much, didn't know how to save money and was known to lie and fight. Shyhiem wanted to get full custody of the twins and raise them on his own but he was a known felon. No judge in the state of Missouri would give him custody because of his extensive rap sheet. Shyhiem had to figure something out quick 'cause living with Keesha was driving him insane.

Shyhiem walked to the front of the apartment, and just as he'd expected, the living room and kitchen were a mess. The twins' toys were sprawled all over the floor. Dishes were piled up in the sink, the countertop hadn't been wiped down, the floor hadn't been swept or mopped and the trash hadn't been taken out. Keesha had been at home the entire day before and hadn't bothered to clean up shit. He wouldn't have been so mad if she had a job or school as her excuse, but Keesha's lazy-ass was a quote, unquote, stay at home mom.

"Morning." He walked further into the living room and spotted his son, Sonny, playing Barbies with his sister.

Shyhiem's heart dropped but his face stayed stone. This wasn't the first time he'd caught his son on some girly shit. Once, he'd caught Sonny making his male WWE figurines kiss. Shyhiem didn't know what to make of it. Deep down, he knew his son was different but accepting his truth was a different story. As soon as Sonny saw his father, he immediately threw the doll down. His father never told him not to play with dolls but his mother had. He'd gotten several whoopings from her because of it. Shyhiem swallowed hard and acted like he hadn't seen anything.

"Morning, Pop," Sonny responded apprehensively.

"Ay, come help Daddy clean up while I fix y'all something to eat," he ordered.

"Aww, man, the Descendants is on," Sonny whined.

"Ain't that a musical?" Shyhiem frowned.

"Yes, and it's amazing." Sonny replied with dramatic flair. "Everybody sings and dances and wears sickening outfits. Oh, my god, I wanna be a princess when I grow up."

"Jesus, help me." Shyhiem said a silent prayer.

"Can we finish watching this first, Pop? Please?" Sonny begged.

"What I tell you about whining? Chill with all that and c'mon."

"Alright." Sonny got up and turned off the TV.

"Shania, pick your dolls up," Shyhiem pointed.

"Ok, Daddy," she said happily.

Shyhiem loved the hell out of his little girl, 'cause no matter what he said, it was always *ok, Daddy*. It took them almost an hour to get the living room and kitchen spotless. Once everything was clean, Shyhiem and the twins sat around the dining room table eating French toast and bacon, just as requested.

"So, Pop, when you gon' get me the new Madden?" Sonny asked, taking a sip of milk.

Shyhiem laughed at the milk mustache on his lip and replied, "If your report card is good, I'll get it for you then."

"That's what's up." Sonny nodded.

Shyhiem's son was a trip. He looked and acted just like him, except when it came to his love of musicals and baby dolls. Sonny was six with deep brown skin, eyes the shape of the moon and dimples. He really didn't say too much, but when he did, it was always something hip or flamboyant.

"I can't wait to go to school tomor and show off my new book bag." Shania danced in her seat.

"You should've went to school today," Shyhiem said under his breath.

"Yeah, Daddy, why didn't we go to school today?" Sonny asked.

"Yo' mama told me y'all ain't wanna go."

"Na uh… she told us we ain't have to go," Sonny shook his head profusely. "We wanted to go to school today."

"Oh, word?" Shyhiem arched his brow as he heard Keesha placing her key in the door.

"Mommy's home!" She walked through the door with a handful of bags.

"Mommy!" Shania screamed, running over to her mother.

Although she was fine as fuck, Shyhiem barely wanted to look at Keesha. He couldn't stand the sight of her. Every time he looked at her, she made his stomach hurt. Sometimes Shyhiem would sit up at night and wonder why he ever got with her dizzy-ass in the first place. Then he would look over at her fat ass and instantly remember why. The year was 2009. He was 20. She was a 19-year-old around the way girl that everybody wanted.

It was one of those hot, sticky, summer nights. Everybody was outside. He and his boys were posted up in front of the liquor store. Keesha and her girls were riding through when they spotted him and his crew. She claimed they only stopped because they were thirsty and wanted a drink but he knew better. As soon as Keesha stepped out the car, his eyes were glued to her curvaceous hips. Keesha's body was sick. She had smooth, honey-colored skin, slanted eyes, a bunny nose, heart-shaped lips and full, 42-DD boobs. She was by far the baddest chick in the neighborhood. The belly shirt and denim, booty shorts she wore showcased the fact even more.

"Where yo' sexy-ass going?" Mayhem tried to grab her hand as she walked by.

"Boy, gone!" She smacked his hand away, with an attitude.

"Forget you then. You need to be happy a nigga like me even noticed yo' big, watermelon-head-ass." He responded, salty that she'd turned down his advances.

"Whateva, I don't need you to notice me. I only want Shyhiem's eyes on me anyway." Keesha batted her false lashes and swayed her leg from side-to-side.

Every girl in North County wanted him. Shyhiem was the shit. He was fine, dangerous, cocky as fuck and getting money. Keesha was willing to do any and everything to get him to be her man.

"As a matter-of-fact, I was just thinkin' about you the other day."

"Is that right?" He eyed her lustfully.

"Yep," Keesha smiled wickedly. "You know I miss seeing you around, Goodnight."

Shyhiem hung his head and chuckled. It always made him laugh when people called him that. He'd gotten the nickname Goodnight 'cause he was known for knockin' niggas out with his lethal right hook.

"Come show a nigga some love then." He replied, as she sauntered close.

Shyhiem took a long pull off the blunt and tried his best to ignore the twitch in his dick. Keesha's titties were practically resting up against his chest, she was so close.

"Where you been? I ain't seen you around lately." She admired his tantalizing lips.

"Gettin' money." He boasted pulling out a wad of cash.

36

"That's what's up." Keesha gazed down at the stack of cash. "I was thinkin'," she placed a small kiss on his chin. "You should call me sometime. Maybe we can go to the movies or something."

"What you gettin' into right now?"

"Nothin," she smirked.

"Come take a ride wit' me." Shyhiem grabbed her by the waist and squeezed her butt cheek.

"A'ight," Keesha bit her bottom lip. "Let me tell my girls I'm rollin' wit' you." She skipped back towards the car happily.

"Man, you really finna fuck wit' that dusty ho?" Mayhem scowled, still angry.

"Now she a dusty ho? C'mon, man, she wasn't dusty when you were just tryin' to get on her," Shyhiem laughed.

"You my brother. I'm just tryin' to warn you; watch that bitch."

"A'ight, nigga," Shyhiem gave him a dap. "I'ma get up wit' you later."

Shyhiem and Keesha never made it to the movies that night. Shyhiem fucked her doggy style in the back seat of his ride with no rubber. Like most dudes at that age, he thought he could pull out before bustin' but was dead wrong. Two months later, Keesha called and said she was pregnant. Shyhiem's life, as he knew it, was over. Whenever he thought back on that fateful night, he always remembered what his deceased mother would always say. "Boy, you betta stop messin' wit' all these li'l fast tail girls. One day you gon' meet one you can't get rid of. You watch and see."

Shyhiem figured Keesha would be an occasional fuck. Someone he kicked it with from time to time - not his baby mother. She wasn't wifey material. He knew that at the age of 20 but he was stuck. In the beginning of their relationship, Shyhiem tried his best to make things work. He wanted his kids to grow up in a household with both of their parents. It was something he didn't have growing up, but they argued about everything imaginable.

From the outside looking in, it seemed as if they had everything. He was getting money, selling dope and she was pretty arm candy. Little did everyone know, Shyhiem was beyond unhappy. Having sex with Keesha was the only joy she brought to his life. Things went from bad to worse when he caught a three-year bid behind a gun charge.

Keesha swore she would hold him down but she barely placed money on his books and hardly brought the kids to see him. Shyhiem hated not being able to see his kids. Missing out on the first three years of their lives nearly killed him. Little did he know, but serving time behind bars gave Shyhiem a whole new aspect on life. He no longer wanted to be a D-boy. There was nothing cute or lucrative about selling crack cocaine. It destroyed lives and he no longer wanted to be a part of the destruction of the black community. He wanted to be a better example for his kids. They deserved to have a father that was present in their lives.

When he got out of jail, Shyhiem was determined to turn his life around. Keesha, on the other hand, was content with being a dope boy's girlfriend. She loved that his name rang bells in the streets. She loved the fast money, fast cars, shopping sprees and trips. She hated that he didn't have unlimited funds anymore. Keesha didn't know the concept of budgeting or saving.

When Shyhiem told her his dream of moving to California and going to film school, she laughed in his face. Keesha planned on living and dying in Saint Louis. It was home to her. She never wanted to leave the streets alone. Shyhiem, however, never wanted to live out his days in St. Louis. There was too much violence, hate and jealousy. He wanted to be out in the middle of nowhere creating visual art and living his life in peace.

"Hey, sweetie pie." Keesha kissed Shania on the nose, lovingly. "Mommy got you a present."

"Oooooh... what you get me?" Shania jumped up and down.

"I got you some more Monster High dolls." Keesha held up a Walmart bag.

"Yay!" Shania clapped her hands.

"Here. Take the bag in your room and go play."

"You get me some too, Mama?" Sonny asked hopeful.

"Hell naw! I ain't get you no goddamn dolls! Don't ask me no shit like that." Keesha fumed.

Sonny's face went flat.

"Boys don't play with dolls. You hear me?" Keesha squeezed his cheeks tightly.

"Yes, ma'am." Sonny held back his tears.

He knew that if he cried it would only make things worse.

"Now gone and get out my face before I spank yo' li'l butt." Keesha pushed his face away.

Shyhiem could tell Sonny was hurt, but like his father, he wasn't going to show it.

"Don't even trip. Daddy got you. I'll bring you back something later today. Ok?" Shyhiem wrapped his arm around Sonny's shoulder and pulled him close.

"Thanks, Pop." Sonny forced a smile on his face, before sulking off to his room.

"You like my nails?" Keesha held out her hand, trying to spark up a conversation with Shyhiem.

He continued to clean off the table, as if she wasn't there.

"You still mad at me?" She poked out her bottom lip and tried wrapping her arms around Shyhiem's neck, as he cleaned off the table.

"You know better." He snapped, pushing her arms away. "Don't fuckin' touch me."   "Huuuuuh... why you actin' like that?" Keesha pouted, stomping her foot.

"Go 'head wit' that. You know exactly why I don't fuck wit' you." Shyhiem threw the dish towel in the sink and walked away.

"Are we ever gon' get past this? I thought you had forgiven me?" She followed him down the hall.

"Who told you that lie?" Shyhiem chuckled.

"How many times do I have to say I'm sorry for you to forgive me?"

"Once was enough."

"But it wasn't even nothin' like that between me and dude," Keesha pled.

"It was something! You was giving that nigga my money!" Shyhiem seethed with anger.

While he was locked up, Keesha spent every red cent of the $200,000 he had stashed. He learned that she'd spent the money on clothes, weed, weave, and some nigga she was fuckin'.

"Instead of holding me down while I was in jail, you was out here trickin' off my money on a nigga that didn't even wanna claim you," Shyhiem continued.

"I know what I did was stupid but you were gone and I was lonely. That was three years ago, anyway. Since you've been home you barely show me any attention. Only time you talk to me is when it got something to do with the kids. We don't do nothin' with each other no more. I mean, damn, Shy, we barely even have sex," she said in a hushed tone. "You act like you barely wanna be around me."

"Whaaaat? You not as dumb as I thought." Shyhiem shot sarcastically while making up the bed.

"Whatever. You just being ignorant now." Keesha swung her long, blue weave over her shoulder.

"What you go to the store today and buy?" Shyhiem changed the subject.

"Some toys for Shania," she replied, caught off guard by his question.

"Who was all that other shit for?"

"Me."

"That's what I thought." Shyhiem resumed making up the bed.

"What I do wrong now?"

"You out here spending my fuckin' money like it grow on trees. Why don't you get off yo' ass and get a job? Go back to stripping or something."

"Umm, excuse you? I wasn't a stripper. I was a waitress at the strip club." Keesha corrected him.

"You were a topless waitress at the Pink Slip which is even worse. It just means you couldn't dance."

"Anyway," Keesha waved him off. "Why would I work? That's what I got you for," she smirked.

It took everything in Shyhiem not to spit in her face and call her a bitch. This was exactly the reason why he could never get past the dirt she'd did. Keesha wasn't remorseful. She knew exactly what she was doing. She used their kids as leverage against him. If he left her, she'd never let him see the twins. She'd make his life a living hell. Shyhiem loathed her. The beast inside of him wanted to knock her upside her head; but for the twins' sake, he kept his composure.

"Keep fuckin' wit' me," he warned. After a brief pause, he asked, "Why you ain't buy Sonny anything?"

"'Cause he don't need nothin'."

"Neither do you! I don't know why you always doing him like that. Is it because he's—"

"I don't do him like nothin'!" Keesha yelled, covering her ears. "And I don't know what you finna say, but he ain't that! Shania is a little girl. She's supposed to be spoiled."

"You are fuckin' delusional. You sound like the bum bitch you are." Shyhiem shook his head, repulsed.

"Bum? Nigga, I'm far from a bum. I wasn't a bum when you decided to nut up in me."

"Yes, you were. You were a bum then and you're a bum now." He moved her out of his way, as his phone began to ring.

"Boy, please." Keesha screwed up her face. "Yo' mama's a bum," she whispered under her breath.

Thankfully, for her sake, Shyhiem didn't hear a word she'd said. Ignoring her existence, he answered the phone and placed the call on speakerphone.

"Yo, Shy, where you at?" Mayhem shouted.

"At the crib. Why? What's up?"

"Get dressed. I'm comin' yo' way."

"A'ight." Shyhiem ended the call.

"So, I guess you gettin' ready to leave?" Keesha spat with an attitude.

"Nobody ever told you not to ask questions you already know the answer to?" Shyhiem grabbed a crisp, white tee and jeans from the closet.

"Well, since you leaving, I need some money." Keesha put her hand out.

"I just gave you three hundred dollars the other day. What the fuck you do with it? Oh, I forgot. You went shoppin'. You need to stop tryin' to outdo them raggedy bitches you hang out wit' and get a job."

"You know I can't work. Somebody gotta be here with the kids."

"Man, please. Don't try to play mama now. We both know you'll fail miserably," Shyhiem quipped.

"Fuck what you talkin' about. Are you gon' give me the money or not? 'Cause I need to get my hair done. Me and Tracy going out tonight." Keesha stood back on one leg with her hand out.

"Man, if you don't sit yo' ass down somewhere. It's Tuesday. You just went out Friday, Saturday and Sunday," Shyhiem stressed.

"And?" Keesha looked at him like he was dumb.

"I gotta get the fuck up outta here!" Shyhiem went into the master bath and slammed the door behind him.

Keesha stood outside the door and said, "Sooooooo... is that a yes or a no?"

"Some lessons ain't worth learnin'." – SiR, "Tricky"

#5

Shyhiem

"I don't even see why you still fuck wit' her stupid-ass." Mayhem shot, getting onto the highway.

"She's the mother of my kid's, man. What the fuck am I supposed to do? If I leave, she ain't gon' let me see the twins. You know I can't have that," Shyhiem explained.

"I don't know what to tell you then, homeboy. But uh, fuck that bitch. I ain't tryin' to talk about Keesha raggedy-ass all day. What you need to be focusing on is gettin' you a new bitch."

"I did meet this fly-ass shorty when we were at Blank Space. She was a nice, little, fine ting," Shyhiem spoke in a Jamaican accent.

He'd been thinking about Messiah nonstop. Their brief encounter made him feel alive again. She was home and he wanted to live in her smile. Shyhiem hoped and prayed to God he'd get the chance to see her again.

"Why you ain't get on her?" Mayhem looked over at him.

"'Cause you decided to spray the whole place, nigga. That's why," Shyhiem laughed.

"Aww… yeah." Mayhem laughed too. "I forgot all about that shit. I told ole boy when I saw him it was gon' be on sight. You know I don't do no talkin." He said with a sinister glare.

Shyhiem looked at his half-brother with deep concern. It was well documented that Shyhiem would beat a nigga's ass but he wasn't on no killing shit. Mayhem would shoot a nigga without flinching. Taking another man's life was nothing to him. Mayhem only had love for a few people, and that was his mother, father, Shyhiem, his niece and nephew. If you crossed him, irritated him or pissed him off, you could catch a bullet.

Michael Simmons aka Mayhem was a feared man. People knew not to fuck with him unless you wanted to end up dead. He and Shyhiem grew up in separate homes. He was raised in the same household as his mother and father. Whereas, Shyhiem was raised by his mother - alone. For reasons, unknown to neither Mayhem nor Shyhiem, their father was a constant figure in his life and not Shyhiem's. This sometimes-caused friction between the two half-brothers, but for the most part, they got along well. There was a mutual love and respect between the two.

They looked out for one another. Born only six months apart, the two brothers were like twins. The even looked alike. Mayhem was the spoiled, mouthy, cocoa brown, street nigga that got whatever he wanted. Their father, Ricky, was a hustler that turned his street money into a lucrative house flipping business. He had property and real estate all over Saint Louis. Mayhem never had to want for a thing growing up. Shyhiem, on the other hand, had to lie, cheat and steal just to help his mother keep the lights on.

The two boys knew of each other from the few times Ricky would go pick up Shyhiem. They didn't truly form a bond until junior high when they attended Normandy Junior High together. From then on, they were inseparable. Shyhiem never said it out loud, but he was low-key jealous of the life Mayhem had. He got to have the love and admiration of their father. He also got to bask in the spoils of all his riches.

Every time a new pair of Jordan's came out, Mayhem had them. Shyhiem would be so hurt when Mayhem would go on family vacations to Disneyland or New York City because he was never invited. It was hard for him to watch his brother get a brand-new Benz when they turned 16 - while he was still on the bus. Shyhiem couldn't figure out for the life of him why his father wanted nothing to do with him. He acted as if he never existed. The more he saw his mom struggle to keep a roof over their heads, the more Shyhiem resented his father.

Little did he know, but Mayhem was jealous of him too. Mayhem didn't have Shyhiem's drop-dead good looks. It took him 20 years to grow into his face. The girls went crazy over Shyhiem. They never gave Mayhem the time of day. Girls used to tease him and call him Godzilla. It didn't help that he was black, ugly and scrawny as hell. Mayhem got picked on all the time and wasn't much of a fighter. He'd constantly get beat up because of his mouth and arrogant attitude.

When he and Shyhiem became close, Shyhiem began to fight all his battles. Shyhiem was the one who could fight and had street cred. He'd been taking boxing lessons since he was a kid and was known to knock a nigga out. He knocked dudes out so much that he got the nickname Goodnight. The older they got, Mayhem realized he couldn't always depend on his brother to be around to protect him. This notion became crystal clear the night he got sliced in the face, so he picked up a gun.

The first-time Mayhem shot someone was a pure rush of adrenaline. He never had to be afraid again. Carrying a gun gave him the sense of confidence he always yearned for. Now things were starting to get out of hand.

He had so many bodies under his belt, it was hard for him to keep count. Shyhiem knew his brother was out of control but there was no controlling the animal he'd become.

Mayhem wasn't to be fucked with. He'd put on weight in the gym and become cocky and swole. He was a 6 foot 2, 230 pound, chocolate monster with spinning waves, Colgate smile and abs of steel. He was the biggest D-boy on the Northside of St. Louis. Women couldn't stay off his dick, but underneath the menacing persona, still lie the scared, little, insecure boy he once was.

"Yo, on the real, fam, you need to chill wit' all the gunplay." Shyhiem tried to talk some sense into him.

"Man, fuck what yo' scary-ass talkin' about. A nigga step to me incorrect, he gettin' clipped. End of story." Mayhem got off the highway.

"Yeah, a'ight, talk all that shoot 'em up, bang bang shit all you want to. Nigga, I know you. Never forget," Shyhiem chuckled.

"What that mean? Nigga, you can get it too." Mayhem pulled up his shirt and revealed his gun.

"Man, if you don't put yo' shirt down. Niggas gon' think we on some fag shit up in here." Shyhiem barked, as they pulled up in front of a house on Vernon Avenue.

"Yo, you know I don't even play that. I done got more ass in one week than you have your whole entire life," Mayhem quipped.

"Picture that." Shyhiem twisted his mouth. "Yo, where we at?"

"Don't worry about it. I gotta make a run real quick." Mayhem replied.

Shyhiem quickly realized that they were at one of Mayhem's trap houses.

"What the fuck I tell you? Stop making runs while you around me. You know I can't be nowhere near this shit no more!" Shyhiem stated pissed.

Mayhem knew his black ass was on papers. It was bad enough he was risking his life just being around his brother. If he even got caught associating with a known felon, he was sure to be put away. The only reason he still associated with Mayhem is because he was his brother. He was his best friend. They'd gotten locked up together, smoked trees together, fucked bitches and sold dope together. There wasn't anything Shyhiem wouldn't do for him, but sometimes Mayhem could be on some dumb shit.

He knew his brother had sat down for three years, and on top of that, given a five year back up plan. If he got in any trouble, he could go back to jail and serve the remainder of his eight-year sentence. Shyhiem wasn't trying to go back to jail for nobody. Being away from his kids was pure hell, so when he got out, Shyhiem vowed to never hustle again. So far, he'd been able to keep his word. Working as a UPS deliveryman wasn't the glamorous life he was used to. The pay was cool but it wasn't nearly as much as he made selling dope. What kept Shyhiem on track was that he could keep a roof over his head and buy his kids whatever they wanted.

"Nigga, yo' punk-ass need to get back into business wit' me. I got a huge supply coming in that's gon' make me a lot of money. I mean, retirement type money."

The thought of retiring at the age of 27 enticed Shyhiem. With that kind of money, he could pay Keesha to give him the kids. He could move out of town and live happily ever after. Then, Shyhiem remembered that nothing good ever came from making fast money. The risk of going back to jail wasn't worth his livelihood.

"I ain't fuckin' wit' it." He waved Mayhem off. "That's all you, playboy."

"Yo' lame-ass. Just tell me you'll think about it."

"I'll think about it. Now, hurry the fuck up." Shyhiem shot pissed.

"Here, hit this and relax." Mayhem passed him a freshly rolled blunt then hopped out.

Shyhiem got out too and surveyed his surroundings. Growing up, Pine Lawn was a cesspool of low-income housing, gang members, young mothers and fatherless sons. As far as Shyhiem could see, nothing had changed. It had gotten worse. The neighborhood was still broke down and raggedy than a muthafucka. Shyhiem wanted to get the fuck outta there. He didn't feel comfortable. The police could swoop down at any moment. Needing something to calm his nerves, he took out a lighter and lit the blunt. The potent smoke was exactly what the doctor ordered.

Shyhiem knew he had no business smoking weed. He'd have to see his P.O. soon and would probably have to take a drop. If he failed, he'd be right back in jail. Plus, his job could randomly drug test him, and if he failed, he'd immediately be fired. But with all the stress in his life, Shyhiem needed something to ease his spirits. Dealing with Keesha, his racist-ass boss and P.O was too much to digest at times. It was either smoke weed from time to time or unleash the beast that was dying to be released inside. Just as he was about to take another pull from the blunt, Shyhiem noticed his pot'nah, Tricky, driving up the street.

"Errrooop!" He made the noise a police siren would make with his mouth.

Tricky looked at Shyhiem and thought about driving right past him but quickly remembered that wouldn't be wise. Reluctantly, he slowed down his car and let down the driver's side window.

"What's good, Shy?" He smiled brightly, trying to hide his nervousness.

Tricky owed him $400 after losing in a dice game. He'd been promising to pay his debt but hadn't.

"Nah, nigga, what's good wit' you? Where my money?" Shyhiem leaned over into the car.

"On everything I love, I got you, for real. Shit just been tight."

Shyhiem ice-grilled him and blew smoke in his face.

"Fuck that. You been duckin' and dodgin' a nigga for over a month now. What's up wit' you? I'm really tryin' not to put my hands on you but you makin' it hard."

He was known for having a short fuse. Lately, niggas had been trying to test him 'cause he wasn't in the life anymore, but Shyhiem would fold a nigga up if need be.

"A lot of shit been happening." Tricky wiped sweat from his brow. "I got laid off from my job, plus my girl pregnant—"

"What the fuck that got to do with me?" Shyhiem cut him off.

"C'mon, Shy. You know I'm good for it. Look, let me give you my number. Hit me up tonight so I can set up some kinda payment arrangement wit' you or something."

"Nigga, what the fuck I look like, a bill collector? Yo, my man, you know a man shouldn't gamble if he can't pay his debts." Shyhiem apprehensively handed him his phone.

"I swear on my unborn child, I got you."

"You bet not be on no bullshit. I'ma hit you up tonight, a'ight? I want my money." Shyhiem warned.

"C'mon, Shy, don't do me like that. You know I got you. I'm good for it, I swear."

"Yeah a'ight. Get the fuck outta here." Shyhiem waved him off.

"Hit me up!" Tricky yelled, speeding off.

"You know you just got ganked, right?" Mayhem laughed, coming down the steps.

"Yeah right. Tricky gon' give me my money," Shyhiem professed.

"That's the same thing you said a month ago."

"It was weird how we met, huh?" –
Chingy feat. Jason Weaver, "One Call
Away"

#6

Messiah

Messiah's feet were on fire by the time she made it home that night. To say she was tired was an understatement. She was exhausted. A nice, hot, steamy bath and her queen size, comfy bed was calling her name. It felt like she had no time to breathe. Life and responsibilities were drowning her slowly. She was constantly stressed out over her jobs, bills and collectors calling her phone nonstop every day. Most days, she wanted to lay down and die. She begged God to reunite her with her parents and son, but no matter how much she begged, her prayers went unanswered.

The only thing that kept her going was her love for Bryson. She knew it wasn't healthy to depend on a man for happiness but he was the only shining light in her dimly-lit life. Ballet used to bring her joy but she hadn't put on a pair of ballet slippers in years. She needed Bryson by her side but all she got from him was sympathy via the phone. She needed more; but him finishing school so they could finally be together was the main priority.

She couldn't deny that it was pretty fucked up she hadn't heard from him all day. It was her birthday for God's sake and he hadn't bothered to call once. Messiah was beyond hurt. It was bad enough they barely got to see one another. His phone calls meant the world to her. They kept her going. The fact that he hadn't hit her up to say happy birthday was like a gut punch to the stomach.

She'd been blowing up his phone since that morning and still hadn't gotten one reply. It wasn't like

Bryson to fall off the face of the earth. Messiah's stomach was in knots. Something had to be wrong. She thought about calling his parents to see if they'd heard from him but quickly thought against it.

It was late and they didn't care for her too much. They thought she was no good for their son and accused her of getting pregnant on purpose, which was a lie. If she hadn't heard from him by the following morning, then she'd pick up the phone and give them a call. Until then, she'd calm her nerves and try to get a good night's sleep. She couldn't let her whole birthday be an entire waste.

Messiah tried her best not to fall apart and walked tiredly into her apartment building. The smell of freshly washed clothes filled the hallways. Messiah rummaged through her ratty, old purse for the mailbox key. She knew the only thing inside was junk mail and bills she didn't have the money to pay for but decided to check anyway. Maybe Bryson had sent her a gift. The thought lifted her spirits some. As she continued to dig in her purse, the sound of a pair of flip flops coming up the steps caught her attention. Messiah looked towards the basement steps and saw a girl on her cellphone coming her way.

The chick was the personification of hood glamour. She had 32-inch, aqua blue weave flowing down her back, perfectly-arched brows, long, thick, fake lashes and sun-kissed skin. She had on a too little tank top and shorts that resembled underwear. The barely there outfit emphasized her big breasts and bountiful ass. Her pussy print, thighs and legs were exposed for anyone to see. The girl obviously didn't have any qualms about showing off her physique. She held a little girl's hand while talking annoyingly loud on the phone. Messiah hated when people were loud for no reason, and this girl was loud as fuck.

There was no reason she should know her entire phone conversation.

"So, you know I had to check the shit out that bitch, right? Since she wanted to talk shit, I posted on Facebook, *'before you say I do, make sure your nigga ain't involved in a seven-year fuckship that's never ending. Just be humble, sis. The other woman probably picked out the ring you love so much; but don't listen to me. I'm just the side chick',*" Keesha cackled into the phone. "Old bitch."

"Girl, no you didn't!" Her friend Breshawna exclaimed.

"Yes, I did. I don't give a fuck. She need to keep my fuckin' name out her mouth. It ain't my fault her nigga in love with me."

"And you in love with him too. I don't know why you and Mayhem just won't be together."

"Girl, Mayhem ass ain't shit, but that dick… mmm," Keesha relished the thought of their last rendezvous, as she spotted a girl staring at her. "Hold on." She stopped dead in her tracks. "What the fuck you lookin' at? You got a problem?"

Caught off guard, Messiah blinked repeatedly. She wasn't a punk but didn't want any problems with the girl. She looked like fighting was her favorite hobby. The chick looked like she fucked up a few niggas in her time and boxed with bulls.

"Umm… hi… no, I was just… umm… your son, he's… crying." Messiah pointed anxiously.

Keesha rolled her eyes and looked over her shoulder at Sonny.

"Huhhhhh," she sighed exasperated. "What you cryin' for?" She yelled irritated.

"It's too heavy." Sonny sobbed, struggling to lift the laundry bag full of clean clothes.

The bag was bigger than him. Messiah felt so bad for the little boy. He looked to be around the same age her son would be, if he was still alive.

"Boy, quit all that damn cryin' and pick up the bag! It ain't that heavy! Quit being so fuckin' dramatic all the time! Ooooh," Keesha groaned, placing the phone back to her ear. "He get on my damn nerves. Act like a li'l ass girl."

"Who?" Breshawna asked.

"Sonny. Wit' his faggot-ass," she hissed. "He act like his punk-ass daddy." Keesha shot the girl at the mailbox a death stare and unlocked the door to her apartment.

Messiah wanted to help the little boy but didn't want to offend his mother any more than she already had, so she quickly grabbed her mail and headed to her apartment on the fifth floor. Inside her place, she slipped off her shoes and breathed a sigh of relief that she was home. Her apartment was her sanctuary. Her safety net. Messiah's one bedroom, one bath apartment had an eclectic Urban Outfitters feel.

Her bedroom was her favorite space. On the wall above her bed was a black, fringed scarf that mimicked a headboard. The comforter set on her bed was dark and sexy. It was black, white, rust orange and brown. Soft, fairy lights twinkled over her bed like fireflies. On a built-in shelf on the wall were a few succulent plants, books, her first pair of ballet shoes and a picture of her parents on their wedding day. A nice size black and white print area rug gave warmth to the otherwise sterile concrete floor.

Unenthusiastically, she sat on the edge of her bed and went through the stack of mail. To her dismay, there was a disconnect notice from Ameren. She'd missed her budget billing payment the month before and if she didn't pay the minimum balance due of $200, they were going to cut her lights off. Thankfully, she had two weeks till the payment was due. Finished with the mail, she turned on her tablet and went directly to her Tidal app. Messiah couldn't afford many perks, but listening to music was a must.

Music was life for her. It transported her to another dimension and soothed her senses. Stevie Wonder's *Summer Soft* serenaded her ears. Getting lost in the lyrics, she turned the hot water on and squirted a little dishwashing liquid into the tub for a ghetto bubble bath. Messiah quickly stripped down naked, lit two candles, turned off the lights and got into the tub. The scolding hot water stung her bottom, but soon, her body adjusted to the temperature.

Messiah closed her eyes and sank down so that only her head peeked through the suds. Relaxing her worn out body was the best birthday gift she could've ever received. Her neck and feet were killing her after working a six-hour shift at the diner. She hated waitressing and sucked at it but needed the extra money. She'd worked her body to the bone. A vacation would've been great, but Messiah couldn't afford the time off. Every month she played Russian Roulette with her bills.

She desperately wanted to ask Bryson for help but he'd just get mad and say she needed to be patient until he finished school. Her hard work would eventually pay off. She and Bryson would be living the high life. She'd finally be able to sit down and think about what she wanted to do with her life. Needing to hear his sexy voice, she picked up her phone and called him again. Like all the other times she called, he didn't pick up. Messiah hung up and let out a heavy sigh.

"Where the hell is he?" She asked herself.

Messiah tried to shake the nervous jitters that seeped through her veins but they wouldn't go away. Something was up. She prayed to God Bryson was alive and well. With each hour that went by, she started to imagine the worse. During times like this, she hated that they lived so far apart. Then suddenly, her phone rang and all the anxiety she felt vanished. Relieved, she answered after the first ring.

"Where have you been? I've been trying to reach you all day." She answered without bothering to look at the screen.

"Uhhhh… speak to Tricky." Shyhiem asked confused.

"Who?" Messiah took the phone away from her ear and looked at the screen.

She didn't recognize the number.

"Is Tricky there?" Shyhiem asked again.

"You got the wrong number." Messiah ended the call, disappointed that it wasn't Bryson.

As soon as she got back comfortable, the phone rang again. Annoyed, she picked up the phone only to see the same number.

"Hello?" She answered with an attitude.

"My bad, Baby girl, I don't mean to bother you. My pot'nah gave me this number. This is 555-4678?"

"Yeah, but this not yo' friend phone." Messiah corrected him.

"Damn, that nigga got me," Shyhiem chuckled.

"Yep, he did. Is that it?" Messiah questioned.

"Yeah, thanks." Shyhiem hung up then called right back.

"Oh, my god, what?" Messiah answered pissed.

"Yo, you sure I got the wrong number?" Shyhiem asked quizzically.

"Yessssss!" Messiah laughed.

"I'm just askin' 'cause the nigga said he had a girl."

"Why would I lie to you? I don't even know you." Messiah replied, somewhat intrigued by his smooth, deep voice.

"You don't but I can hear the hesitation in your voice. You ain't gotta be afraid. When I see him I won't hurt him," Shyhiem lied.

He knew damn well the next time he saw Tricky he was going to bust his ass.

"I don't care what you do to him when you see him 'cause this is not his phone," Messiah confirmed. "Whoever *he* is."

"So, Tricky ain't yo' man?"

"No!" Messiah laughed.

"If he ain't ya man, then who is?" Shyhiem found himself asking.

He didn't know what had gotten into him but this girl had him intrigued.

"Excuse you?" Messiah tried to steady her voice.

The sound of his voice sent chills down her spine.

"That's none of your business, sir. For all I know, you could be a serial killer."

"Since you won't answer, that must mean you got a man."

"Agggg… wrong," Messiah decided to play along. "I'm single."

"You lyin' but a'ight."

"How you know I'm lying? You don't know my life."

"'Cause anybody sounding this good gotta have a man," Shyhiem flirted.

"Well, I don't, stalker," she joked.

"First, I was a serial killer. Now, I'm a stalker," Shyhiem smiled, smoking a blunt. "Tell the truth."

"You're right; I do have a man. As a matter-of-fact, I'm happily married with 13 kids."

"Now I really know you lyin'."

"How?"

"'Cause no one with 13 kids is happily married," Shyhiem joked.

Messiah couldn't help but crack up laughing. Not only did this guy sound good but he was funny. *What the fuck am I doing,* she thought. *You don't have no business talkin' to this man. This is a new low. Even for you,*

Messiah. For some reason, she didn't want to end the call. The guy on the other end had piqued her interest.

"So, who is this Tricky guy that you're tryin' to track down?"

"A dude I know. He owes me $400 after losing a dice game. I ran into him today and he gave me this number so we could set up a payment arrangement. And before you say anything, I know… it sounds crazy. I feel stupid repeating this dumb shit."

"In the words of DJ Khalid, *you played yourself,*" Messiah teased.

"Aww, you got jokes, Miss…" He probed for her name.

"Uhhhhhh… Lake." She gave him her sister's name. "And yours?"

"Goodnight." Shyhiem gave her his nickname.

For all he knew, she could be crazy. On top of that, he didn't go around giving out his government name to random people.

"What kind of name is Goodnight?" Messiah scoffed.

"You don't even wanna know," Shyhiem smirked.

"Goodnight." Messiah let his name roll off her tongue. "I like that," she ran her index finger across her bottom lip.

She wondered how Goodnight looked. He was probably ugly as fuck in real life, but over the phone, she imagined him to be tall, dark and handsome with a commanding gaze.

"Well, I hope you find this Tricky person."

"I'ma run into him sooner or later," Shyhiem assured, confidently.

For a second, they both held the phone unsure of what to say.

"Let me ask you a question. You don't find it weird that you're on the phone with a stranger?" Messiah asked.

"This is some straight creep shit," Shyhiem chuckled. "But you seem cool. You think it's weird?"

"Yeah, but for some reason I don't want to get off the phone."

"Me either," Shyhiem replied, loving the sweet sound of her voice.

"Well, I got some news that could brighten up your day," Messiah beamed.

"What?"

"Today's my birthday." She spoke with glee.

"Word? Happy birthday!" Shyhiem smiled.

"Thank you." Messiah said, feeling sad.

This was not how she should be spending her birthday. Instead of talking to a man she didn't know, she should've been wrapped up in Bryson's arms.

"How old you turn?"

"Didn't your mother ever tell you not to ask a woman her age?"

"No. My mother's dead." Shyhiem said regrettably.

"I'm so sorry. I had no idea." Messiah sat up.

"Yeah, 'cause you don't know me, remember," Shyhiem laughed. "Let me find out this is Tricky phone," he kidded.

"You know what I mean. If it's any consolation, my mother's dead too."

"Wow, that's crazy." Shyhiem flicked the ashes from the blunt into an ashtray.

He tried his best not to think of his mother. The mere thought of her made him depressed.

"How'd she die?" Messiah found herself asking.

"Breast cancer. Yours?"

Just as Messiah was about to answer, her other line clicked. She looked at the phone and saw that it was Bryson. Her heart instantly skipped a beat.

"Hold on." She clicked over without waiting for a reply. "Hello?"

"Hey, babe." Bryson spoke in a low tone.

"Thank God you're alright. I thought something was wrong."

"My bad. I got caught up studying," he whispered.

"Oh."

"What you doing?"

"Taking a bath. Why are you whispering?" Messiah quizzed.

"'Cause I'm wit' my study group. I just stepped off to the side to call and tell you happy birthday. I didn't want you to think I forgot."

"I was wondering," Messiah giggled.

"I would never forget your birthday. You know how much I miss you."

"Aww, I miss you too. Babe, I'm so overwhelmed with everything. Sun Loan keeps calling me. You know I almost missed a payment this month. And I hate to ask this with everything you got going on but, baby, I really need—"

"Bryson!" Messiah heard a girl call his name.

"Here I come." He replied in a regular tone. "Look, babe," he resumed whispering. "I gotta go."

"What you mean you gotta go? I haven't talked to you all day," Messiah scowled. "And who the fuck was that bitch callin' yo' name?"

"My lab partner," Bryson lied.

"Yo' lab partner? Nigga, you must think I'm a fool. You ain't got no science classes in yo' grad program." Messiah raised her voice.

"Look, I'ma call you in the morning." He ignored her sarcasm.

"Are you fuckin' kidding me?" Messiah yelled.

"Calm down. I'll call you in the morning, alright?" He shot sternly. "Have a good night."

Before Messiah could protest, Bryson hung up. Speechless, she held the phone in her hand until she remembered she had ole boy on the other end. Messiah tried to click back over but realized he'd hung up too. Sad, she placed the phone down on the side of the tub and rolled her eyes.

"What a fuckin' birthday."

"Me and you, this ain't nothin'." – Justine Skye, "Strangers"

#7

Shyhiem

The next day, all Shyhiem could think about was the mystery girl he'd talked to over the phone. Memories of her sweet, soothing voice ran through his mind. He thought about hittin' her up but that would be creepy. He was far from a creep and didn't do weird shit like talk to a chick he'd never met before. That was some straight sucka, cornball shit; but this girl had him willing to make a complete fool out of himself.

He wanted to talk to her again... See how her day went... Make her laugh so he'd have a reason to smile. He yearned to know more about her. For some reason, he felt like this girl could be the missing piece to the puzzle that was his life. He was drawn to her like a moth to a flame. Shyhiem just didn't know how to go about the situation. He thought about asking Mayhem for advice but he'd just make fun of him. He wasn't in the mood to be a bunch of punk, pussy-ass niggas. Mayhem wouldn't understand his feelings. Hell, he didn't either.

Shyhiem needed to talk to someone that would give him sound advice. Unfortunately, there was no one in his life that he could turn to. Outside of his brother, he was a lone wolf. Times like this, he wished he still had his mother. These were things a son went to his mother for. Growing up, his mom was his best friend. He told her everything. She never judged him.

She always tried to lead him in the right direction and give him sound advice. Shyhiem didn't listen most of the time. His mother, Joann, told him to stay out of the streets. She often told him that fast money wasn't good money but Shyhiem was caught up in the life. He liked living in the fast lane.

He had everything he'd ever dreamt of. You couldn't tell him shit. The days of going to bed hungry or being freezing cold 'cause the heat was off were over. He'd gotten a taste of the good life. It was nothing for him to hop on a flight to Mexico or buy out the Gucci store. There was no way Shyhiem was ever going to suffer again. He'd gotten him and his mother out the hood and would be damned if he ever went back.

It wasn't until he was sentenced to eight years in prison that he wished he'd listened to his mother. Her words really hit home when she died of breast cancer while he was locked up. If he'd never sold a drug, he would've got to be there when she passed. It ate him up that his mother died with no one by her side. No one should ever have to suffer that way. Now, he had to live the rest of his life knowing he never got the chance to say goodbye.

Shyhiem would give his last breath just to hear her voice again. He missed her with every fiber of his being. Thinking of his mother gave him the realization that nothing in life was certain. He had to do what made him happy; and if calling a stranger made him happy, then fuck it. What did he have to lose - except his mind?

It was mid-afternoon as he pulled up to his apartment complex and parked his Cadillac CTS-V sedan. Shyhiem had just gotten off work. He couldn't wait to get in the house and change out of his uniform. Even though he had no regrets on leaving the street life behind, Shyhiem hated walking around in the doo-doo brown outfit. He felt like it took away some of his street cred when he wore the monkey suit.

Looking down at his phone, he checked the time and wondered if he should hit ole girl up again. The thought of contacting her still didn't sit well in his stomach. He didn't want her to think he was some crazed, maniac, stalker but she kept poppin' up in his head. Nervously, he located her number in his call log. His heart beat a mile a minute, as his thumb hovered over her number. Shyhiem was so caught up in the tug-of-war going on in his brain that he wasn't paying attention as he walked into the building. Before he knew it, he'd ran chest first into someone and caused the bag of trash they were carrying to spill all over the floor.

"My bad." He quickly apologized.

"Oh, my god!" Messiah huffed, angrily. "Watch where the fuck you going!"

There was trash all over her feet. She was already having a shitty day. This only made it worse. Pissed, she rolled her eyes and began to pick up the trash. As she bent down, Shyhiem caught a good look at her face. Time instantly stood still. Crouched down on the floor before him, picking up dirty paper towels and old takeout boxes, was the girl from Blank Space. Shyhiem couldn't believe his eyes. He thought he'd never see her again but here she was live in the flesh. She was pissed as hell, but even angry, she was still cute as a button.

Her hair was pulled up in a messy ponytail. She wore no makeup but her face was still flawless. There wasn't a blemish in sight. Her silky, caramel skin glistened under the orange radiance of the afternoon sun. Shyhiem wanted to ease the frown lies on her face and make her smile but she hadn't looked up at him once. She was so mad she could spit. Slowly, he bent down to help her.

"Messiah?" He said her name cautiously, as if she wasn't real.

Caught off the guard by the sound of her name, she stopped and looked up. As soon as her eyes linked with his, her heart dropped down to her knees. Suddenly, a smile graced the corners of her lips. Her day had instantly gotten 10 times better. Messiah studied his face and realized she missed everything about him. He was beautiful. The sweet nectar of his lips called her name.

"Hi." She spoke, barely above a whisper, as his hand brushed against hers.

The way Shyhiem was looking at her made her feel naked under his gaze. The seat of her panties promptly became wet. Messiah didn't know what kind of cruel joke the universe was playing but she did not have time to be looking a hotmess.com in front of this fine specimen of a man. She'd just gotten off work and was still dressed in her waitress uniform. It was nothing but a black t-shirt, jeans and apron, but there were grease and tomato sauce stains all over her. There was a big chance she smelled like ass too.

Messiah planned on running outside and coming right back in the house. But no, here she was crouched down on the floor picking up old chicken bones and used period pads. *My pads,* Messiah thought, mortified. With the speed of lightning, she quickly threw them back into the garbage bag and prayed to God Shyhiem hadn't seen. He hadn't. Anxiously, she admired his chocolate face. Shyhiem was next level fine.

"I wanna sit on your face." She caught herself saying out loud.

"What was that?" Shyhiem asked, noticing she worked at Joe's Diner.

"Umm," Messiah panicked. "I said, I wonder what happened to the rapper Mase." She rose to her feet.

"Yeah a'ight." Shyhiem chuckled, standing up.

"What you doing here? Let me find out you stalkin' me," Messiah joked.

Shyhiem looked at her quizzically. Flashbacks of his conversation with Lake entered his mind. She'd jokingly called him a stalker too. *Is it her,* he wondered. *Nah, it couldn't be.*

"Never that." He finally answered. "I live here."

"You lyin'." She said shocked.

"I do, for real. Don't tell me you live here too?"

"Yeah, I just moved in a few weeks ago." Messiah confessed, feeling like she was in a whirlwind.

"That's crazy 'cause I've been thinkin' about you ever since that night," Shyhiem confessed.

"Lies but ok." Messiah waved him off.

"I ain't got no reason to lie to you. I'm tellin' the truth. I missed you." Shyhiem stared deep into her eyes.

"Now you really buggin'. You don't even know me to miss me." Messiah looked away nervously.

"I'd miss you even if I never met you," Shyhiem replied truthfully.

Messiah looked him square in the eyes and knew that he wasn't lying. Their chemistry was crazy. It was so explosive it couldn't be contained. Shyhiem felt the same. Now that he had her right there before him, he never wanted to let her out of his sight. It was urgent that he have

73

her. Shyhiem didn't have to be convinced. Messiah was the woman he was going to spend the rest of his life with. She was made just for him. Messiah had him in the palm of her hand and didn't even know it.

Shyhiem had to approach her right. God had given him a second chance at greatness. There was no way he was going to fuck this up. He had to be on his best behavior. He didn't want to scare her away with his brash behavior and bad attitude. He could be a nightmare at times. He'd calmed down a lot over the years, but the demon he'd tried to suppress still lingered. Messiah wasn't like the other women he'd dealt with in the past. She deserved nothing but the best of him.

"Let me ask you a question," he said.

"Shoot."

"Is it ok if I call you sometime?" He pulled out his phone.

"Shyhiem, right?" Messiah tucked a piece of her hair behind her ear.

"Yeah."

"You seem like a nice guy. You really do; but I'm engaged." She held up her left hand and wiggled her ring finger.

Shyhiem looked at the ring. The diamond was barely visible. A woman like Messiah shouldn't be walking around with a diamond the size of a pebble. Her man obviously didn't know her worth and neither did she.

"Put ya hand down, ma, I don't want you embarrassing yourself."

"Excuse you?" She scoffed. "My ring is nice." She examined her hand.

"Sure it is," Shyhiem laughed.

"Whatever. You don't know me like that to talk about my ring." She screwed up her face.

"I know one thing."

"What?" Messiah cocked her head to the side.

"You don't love that man."

"You are one cocky muthafucka." Messiah folded her arms across her chest causing her titties to press together. "You don't know what I love."

"Keep lyin' to yourself, ma. You don't love that nigga," Shyhiem stressed, eying the outline of her luscious breasts.

"Why? 'Cause I love you?" Messiah fell right into his trap.

"You said it. I didn't," He smirked, proud of himself.

"Whatever." Messiah hit him playfully on the arm.

"I'm just sayin'… if you really loved that nigga, you wouldn't be standing here talkin' to me. If you were my girl, another man wouldn't even be able to get a second of your time."

"That's just it." She poked his chest with her index finger. "I'm not your girl."

"Not yet." Shyhiem took her hand in his. "Unlike you, I know how this story is gonna end."

"And how is that?" Messiah unknowingly held her breath.

Shyhiem pulled her close. Her breasts were pressed up against his broad chest.

"Wit' you being my wife." He stated confidently.

Messiah gazed up into his eyes. A part of her believed him but she had to remind herself that she loved Bryson. Hesitantly, she released her hand from his and stepped back. Shyhiem reluctantly let her go.

"I gotta go." She turned to walk away, completely bewildered.

"The dumpster is that way." Shyhiem pointed towards the front entrance, noticing she was going the wrong way.

"I know." She played it off, turning around.

"Hold on tho'." He stopped her. "Before you go. Put your number in my phone." He handed it to her.

Shyhiem wasn't going to let her get away that easy. From the looks of him, Messiah knew Shyhiem wasn't the type to take no for an answer. Since they lived in the same building, she figured she'd give him her number and never answer his calls. Prayerfully, after a few unanswered calls, he'd get the hint that she was committed to her fiancé.

"You can put it in yourself. It's 555-46—"

"78," Shyhiem said in unison.

Messiah eyed him skeptically.

"Lake?" He eyed her confused.

"No, it can't be." Messiah's eyes grew wide. "Goodnight?" Her heart stopped beating.

"Holy shit." Shyhiem covered his mouth with his hand, shocked.

"This is crazy." Messiah shook her head in disbelief.

She couldn't believe that Shyhiem was the guy she'd talked to the night before on the phone.

"This is too much of a coincidence. I'm really starting to think you stalkin' me for real now." Messiah said shook.

"Nah, this is fate, baby girl." Shyhiem reached out and held her hand.

For a brief second, Messiah believed him. That was until the door to apartment 1A opened. Keesha stood in the doorway and looked at them. Her face immediately burned red. Shyhiem was all up in the girl's face from the mailbox. He didn't even notice she was standing there. He gazed into the girl's eyes, as if she was best thing on earth.

Jealousy ached throughout Keesha's body. He'd never looked at her that way. Keesha wanted to run over and snatch the bitch up but kept her composure. She didn't know anything about the girl but hated her on sight. The chick was naturally pretty. She was the total opposite of her. What ate Keesha up the most was that she reeked of elegance and class. She was everything Keesha wanted to be but was too lazy and ignorant to achieve. Not feeling their little love connection, she decided to put an end to it before it began.

"Twins! Yo' daddy home!" She said loudly, placing her hand on her hip.

At the same time, Shyhiem and Messiah glanced towards the direction of her voice. Keesha shot Messiah a look that could kill. Messiah quickly put two and two together and realized that not only was the loud girl his baby mama but that they lived together.

"Daddy!" The kids ran out looking filthy.

It looked like they'd been playing outside in the dirt and Keesha hadn't bothered to bathe them. Shyhiem was embarrassed, to say the least. Disgusted, Messiah snatched her hand from his. She should've expected for him to be on some typical nigga shit. He was too fine and put together not to have a bitch. Messiah had no business even considering talking to him anyway. She was engaged to be married to her high school sweetheart.

"Oh, hell naw." She glared at Shyhiem with disdain.

"It's not what you think." Shyhiem tried to explain, as the kids ran towards him.

"Get the fuck outta here. You tryin' to holla at me and you live with a chick. Boy, bye. Do us both a favor. Lose my number." Messiah bypassed him heatedly.

Shyhiem wanted to run after her but decided now wasn't the best time. Heated, he looked at Keesha with contempt in his eyes. He knew she'd sent the kids out on purpose. The pleased expression on her face said it all. Keesha smiled brightly. She would be damned if Shyhiem ever left her for someone else. If she couldn't have him, no one could.

"Shit just got real. Things are getting intense now." – PartyNextDoor feat. Drake, "Come and See Me"

#8

Messiah

Joe's Diner, located on North Grand Blvd., was a South City staple. If you were leaving the club, got the late-night munchies, or worked the overnight shift and wanted a filling meal, then Joe's Diner was the place to be. Upon entry, the décor was fun and vibrant. The vibe was 1960's Doo-wop. There was black and white checkerboard floors, a jukebox, colorful, neon lights, album memorabilia and black, vinyl seats.

Messiah had only been working there a little over a month. She'd never waited tables before but was getting the hang of the hectic job. Working at the diner, she never really got a chance to breathe. The place was always packed with families, out-of-towners, hipsters, businessmen and couples. It was after 8pm and she was already on her last leg. She still had four more hours to go. Messiah didn't know if she was gonna make it. Her neck, shoulders, back and feet were aching. She'd been going hard, nonstop, since six that morning.

After working an eight-hour shift at Charter, she left there and came straight to the diner to work another eight hours. Messiah didn't know how she found the strength to work both jobs. It was taxing on her mind, body and soul. She barely got any sleep or relaxation. She knew her body was eventually going to give out on her if she didn't get some rest soon.

On the low, she was thankful for the lack of sleep. No sleep equaled no nightmares. Not having to dream about the car accident was a blessing. Working two jobs also kept her mind off thinking about her parents and her dead son. She couldn't go back to the dark, depressed place she was in after their deaths. She'd finally gotten her life back on track. There was a sense of normalcy to her every day routine again. That didn't stop the hole in her heart from getting bigger.

Messiah floated around the diner taking orders, numb to the smiling faces and laughter around her. She didn't know what it felt like to be happy anymore. She hadn't been genuinely happy since that fateful day. Messiah didn't feel she'd have true happiness till she and Bryson were finally together and somehow was able to have a family. Holding a plate of smothered chicken, mash potatoes and string beans, she tried to pretend that her feet didn't feel like shards of glass were stuck in them as she walked.

"Here you go, sir, but please be careful; the plate is hot." She placed the scolding hot plate down in front of a middle age, silver-haired, white man.

"Took you long enough." He huffed, rolling his eyes.

Messiah paused and looked at him.

"Let me know if you need anything else." She plastered a fake smile on her face.

As soon as she walked away, the smile vanished. At the counter, she stole a quick moment to text Bryson. Things between them had been weird lately. They still talked every day, but she peeped that it was because she was the one reaching out. When they spoke, Bryson was always sweet and loving, but Messiah couldn't shake the feeling that something was off. Maybe it was her guilt of flirting with another man that had her shook. It had been a few days since she ran into Shyhiem.

She'd blocked his number immediately after finding out he was a lying, cheating bastard. And yes, she was dumbfounded how fate seemed to be drawing them together, but none of that mattered. She didn't want any parts of him or his ratchet-ass baby mama. She had enough strife in her life to add anymore. She was wrong as hell anyway for entertaining the thought of even giving him a chance to get close to her. It would never go anywhere. She belonged to someone else and so did he.

Besides that, Messiah loved Bryson with all her heart. She could never see her life without him. He was the only man she'd ever kissed, had sex with, gave her heart to and loved. They'd been through hell and back, together. He'd nursed her back to life when she wanted nothing more than to die. There was no chance of Shyhiem entering her heart. He'd had a slight chance and failed miserably. Messiah never went backwards, only forward. She never wanted to talk to or see Shyhiem again. Quickly, she texted Bryson before she got caught taking an impromptu break.

Messiah: I was just thinkin' about u

He responded right back.

Bryson: Look at you being sweet.

Messiah: WYD?

Bryson: Studying

Messiah: Ok get back to work. I just wanted to say hi and I love you.

Bryson: ☺

Messiah grinned at the smiley face emoji but wished he would've said I love you too. She needed the reassurance.

"Excuse me!" The white man yelled, getting her attention.

Messiah slid her phone in her back pocket and forced another fake smile on her face.

"Yes, sir?"

"Are you deaf? I've been calling your name for the last five minutes! This food is ice-cold! Take it back!" He shoved the plate into her hand.

Messiah glared at him with venom in her eyes. She wanted to slap the shit out of him but kept her composure. He wasn't the first asshole customer she'd have to deal with and he wouldn't be the last.

"I'll get that warmed up for you right away." She promised, with a smile.

To Messiah's surprise and dismay, as soon as she turned around, Shyhiem's sexy-ass was standing right there. She was so shocked to see him that she didn't even notice he'd filmed her reaction. All the air in her lungs escaped. A guy like him should wear a warning. He couldn't just pop up on her like his mere presence wouldn't turn her world upside down. Shyhiem was dangerous and she loved it. She would never admit it, but she was addicted to him. Messiah could play tough like she wanted nothing to do with him when he wasn't around, but face-to-face, there was no hiding her attraction to him.

Tall and black as night, he stared so deep into her eyes she swore he saw the depths of her soul. His hair was freshly lined and cut to perfection. His dark, majestic skin reminded her of black, Indonesian sand. He wore a black Adidas sweatshirt that showed off his muscular arms, black, fitted, ripped jeans and a crisp pair of shell toe Adidas. Messiah wanted nothing more than to lick his face.

Then, she remembered his baby mama and kids who were probably at home wondering where he was. Not in the mood for whatever he was selling, she stomped past him and said, "I'ma get a restraining order on yo' crazy-ass."

Shyhiem looked at her with an amused expression on his face and placed his phone inside the pocket of his pants. She knew damn well he wasn't crazy. He was, a little bit, but that wasn't the point.

"Bobby, can you reheat this for me? The man at table 15 said it was cold." Messiah handed the cook back the plate.

"What? That plate was piping hot." Bobby took the plate from her, annoyed.

"I know," Messiah agreed. "I don't know what his problem is." She folded her arms across her chest and pretended like Shyhiem's cologne wasn't driving her insane.

He stood watching her every move, without saying a word. After a few seconds of silence, Messiah couldn't take his domineering presence anymore.

"What?" She snapped, giving him her full attention.

Shyhiem found her attempt at being mad cute. She was far too pretty for him to take her little attitude seriously.

"Let me holla at you for a second." He pulled her to the side so they could be alone.

"Did I say you could touch me?" She looked down at his hand on her arm.

"If you give a nigga a chance, you gon' want me to do way more than just touch you."

Messiah inhaled deeply, as her panties became wet. This crazy, intoxicating, allure he had would be the death of her. Visions of him holding her legs, while sliding his dick in and out her wet slit as she called him daddy, invaded her mind.

"How did you know I worked here?" She asked curiously. "If you think you about to Michael Ealy me, you got another thing coming. I ain't Sanaa Lathan, nigga. I will fuck yo' fine-ass up."

"Oh, you think I'm fine, huh?" Shyhiem grinned.

"You a'ight." Messiah acted unfazed. "How you know I work here?"

"You had your uniform on when I saw you in the building, remember?"

"Aww... yeah," Messiah grimaced.

"Why you ain't answer none of my phone calls? I tried callin' you a few times." Shyhiem quizzed.

"'Cause I blocked your number, psycho," Messiah shot.

"Stop being ridiculous. Give me your phone." Shyhiem demanded, holding out his hand.

"No," Messiah scoffed.

Hating to be disobeyed, he took it upon himself to locate her phone. Aggressively, Shyhiem placed his hands on her round hips and pulled her close. Messiah gasped for air, shocked. Shyhiem used his thumbs and caressed her front pockets. Not finding what he was looking for, his hands traveled around to her backside. Messiah swallowed hard. Her pelvis was pressed firmly against his dick. Shyhiem wanted her to feel all 10 inches of him.

Never once taking his eyes off her, he squeezed his left hand into the back pocket of her jeans, causing her to inch closer to his broad chest. Her sweet breath tickled his collarbone. Messiah looked up into his mysterious, brooding eyes, helplessly. She was stunned that he had the gall to manhandle her, but enjoyed every second of it. She was turned on to the fullest. Shyhiem pulled the phone out her back pocket. Within seconds, he located his number in her call log and unblocked it.

"Don't do that shit no more." He placed the phone back into the pocket of her jeans. "You gon' make me mad."

Wet beyond belief, Messiah's cheeks burned crimson red. Shyhiem loved the effect he had on her. She had no idea what else he had in store for her once she stopped fighting the inevitable.

"You got a lot of nerve." She said in disbelief of his behavior.

Shyhiem placed his right hand on the wall above her head, slightly trapping her in, and leaned in close.

"What time you get off?"

"None of your business." Messiah screwed up her face.

"You drive to work or walk?" Shyhiem ignored her sarcasm.

The diner was around the corner from their building.

"I walked." She rolled her neck.

"How yo' so-called fiancé got you out here walkin'? Between that, and that Cracker Jack special you call an engagement ring, it's obvious he don't give a damn about you."

Messiah felt a crack surface on the face of her heart. Her feelings were hella hurt by his comment 'cause every bit of it was true. She knew Bryson should've done more to help her. She gave him the world and seemed to get nothing in return. Messiah didn't want to face the truth though.

"You gon' quit talkin' about my ring." She scowled. "And the only reason I walked to work is because my car is in the shop."

Not paying attention to a word she said, Shyhiem traced her bottom lip with his thumb. He wanted her in the worst way. With her permission, he wanted to spend the night burying his face between her thighs. Messiah unknowingly arched her back, pushing her pelvis into his stiff dick. She wanted to tell him to stop but couldn't find the words to speak. Her pussy was throbbing for him to enter her slit.

"You know, ever since I met you that night, I wondered what it would be like to kiss your lips." Shyhiem continued to explore her succulent mouth with lust.

"I don't think your girlfriend would appreciate that." Messiah finally found her inner strength.

Furious, Shyhiem abruptly stopped caressing her lips and glared at her.

"I'ma say this once so you know exactly where I stand. Me and Keesha, my baby mama, stay together; but it's strictly for the sake of my kids. I don't fuck wit' her. I barely even like her dumbass. We haven't fucked around in years. I like you." He pointed at her chest.

"A lot. I've never met a woman that makes me feel the way you do. And the way everything has gone down between us so far, lets me know that God got His hand in this. I see us being together forever, but for that to happen, you gotta stop fighting me."

Messiah narrowed her eyes. *This nigga really is crazy,* she thought. Yet she found herself believing every single word that came out of his mouth.

"Miss! Do I have to call your manager?" The white guy snarled, getting her attention. "Where the fuck is my food? I'm waiting here! You can talk to your li'l boyfriend later! Jesus Christ! What do you have to do to get good service around here?"

Messiah inhaled deeply and dipped under Shyhiem's arm.

"Bobby, is that plate ready for table 15?" She tried her best to keep her cool.

"Here you go, sweetheart."

Messiah took the plate over to the white man and placed it down before him.

"Sorry for the wait, sir. Hopefully, that's hot enough for you."

"For your sake, it better be." He frowned, picking up his fork.

Messiah folded in her lips and kept quiet. *Remember, you need this job.* Shyhiem peeped how she handled the situation and admired her grace under pressure.

"Listen, I have to get back to work—" She tried to explain before she was rudely interrupted by the customer again.

"OH, MY GOD!" The white man threw his fork down in revulsion. "This tastes like nothing but salt! I know you did something to my food, bitch!" He slammed his hand down on the table.

Messiah hadn't touched his food but Bobby had. He'd doused it with salt as payback for the man's rude behavior. Just as Messiah was about to go handle the situation, Shyhiem pulled her back and stormed over to the guy. He didn't utter a word. Shyhiem walked up, grabbed the man by the back of his head, and slammed his face down onto the table with so much brute force the sound of the bones breaking in his nose echoed throughout the diner. The man screamed out in agony. With malice in his eyes, Shyhiem gripped his hair and yanked the man's head back. Blood spewed from his nose and dripped down his chin, like running water. Messiah jumped and gasped for breath out of fear. She didn't know what to do. Everyone in the diner was afraid.

"Call her a bitch again," Shyhiem warned.

He would be damned if anybody disrespected Messiah in front of him. Hopefully, now she would believe him when he professed his affection for her. Repulsed by the ignorant man's presence, he pushed him away like he was nothing.

"Somebody, help me! This man just attacked me!" The man held his nose. "Where's the manager? This mutt bitch's boyfriend attacked me!" He screamed as blood gushed all over his hand and onto the floor.

"Why did you do that? I'm good as fired now." Tears welled in Messiah's eyes. "I needed this job!" Her bottom lip trembled.

"You not gon' get fired, trust me," Shyhiem assured, trying to calm her down with his touch.

"You don't know that!" She jerked away, upset.

Shyhiem felt like shit. He hadn't wanted her to see this side of him so soon. He had a quick temper that was hard to control. He prayed to God it wouldn't scare her away.

"What the hell is going on out here?" The owner, Mr. Johnson, came from the kitchen.

He was an older, black man with no hair and a potbelly. Mr. Johnson had a limp in his walk that made it difficult for him to get around. He was a no-nonsense man that didn't play around when it came to his restaurant.

"This fuckin' psychopath just assaulted me! I want him arrested immediately!" The man pointed his finger at Shyhiem frantically.

Mr. Johnson looked at the culprit and realized immediately who he was. Although he hadn't seen him in a while, Mr. Johnson recognized Goodnight's face instantly. He used to terrorize the streets of St. Louis heavy back in the day. He'd run up on pedestrians to rob them, as well as local businesses. Then, he and his brother got into the coke business and started flooding the community with poison. Everyone feared them, including Mr. Johnson. He was old, but he knew that being on Goodnight's bad side was not where he wanted to be.

"Goodnight," Mr. Johnson's voice quivered. "Please, I don't want no trouble. Whatever this gentleman did, I personally apologize on his behalf."

"What?!" The man shouted. "Are you fucking kidding me? Look at what he did to my nose!"

"SHUT UP!" Mr. Johnson yelled so loud the glass on the tables shook.

The man stood frozen, afraid to move. Once Mr. Johnson saw that the man would remain quiet, he faced Goodnight, and with pleading eyes said, "Please, Goodnight, I don't want no trouble."

Messiah didn't know what was going on or why Mr. Johnson was so afraid of Shyhiem. The only thing she was concerned about was keeping her job.

"Mr. Johnson, I'm so sorry. I didn't know he was going to do that. Please, don't fire me. I'll work overtime to make things right," she begged.

"She won't have to do that. Will she, Mr. Johnson?" Shyhiem stood firm.

"No," Mr. Johnson shook his head profusely. "No. Messiah, you're alright. You're not getting fired. I just want to put this ordeal behind us. Act like it never happened."

"We good," Shyhiem guaranteed Mr. Johnson. "Listen, I'm about to jet. What time you get off?" He asked Messiah.

"What?" She looked up at him bewildered.

He'd just broken a man's nose and wasn't fazed by his actions at all.

"Her shift ends at 12." Mr. Johnson replied for her.

"I'll be back to pick you up then." Shyhiem left before she could respond.

As soon as Shyhiem left out the door, Mr. Johnson let out a sigh of relief. Messiah, on the other hand, was more confused as ever. *Who the fuck is this guy,* she asked herself, still on edge. *And what the hell have I gotten myself into?*

"Fall into the sea of possibility." – John Legend, "Start"

#9

Shyhiem

Just as promised, Shyhiem was waiting outside when she got off. Messiah exited the diner door, unsure how she felt about seeing him again. After the stunt he'd pulled, she wasn't so sure if she wanted to be around someone with such a violent temper. Seeing him act so viciously scared her. But as she watched him lean against the passenger side door of his car, all her fears washed away. His right hand was clasped over the other, as he stood in a typical hood-boy stance.

Shyhiem watched as she stepped cautiously into the cool, night air. He couldn't get over how breathtaking she was. Even in a simple, black tee, skin-tight jeans and dirty, white, Converse sneakers, she was the baddest chick he'd ever seen. Shyhiem watched with hunger in his eyes as she walked slowly in his direction. His eyes stayed glued to her curvaceous hips, as she untied her apron from around her waist and placed it inside her purse. Shyhiem couldn't wait to get his hands on her. She'd be his sex slave in a matter of no time. And yes, he wanted to explore the hidden treasures her body possessed, but his desire to make her his woman outweighed his sexual affinity for her.

It didn't take a rocket scientist to see she hadn't been exposed to a real man. Messiah was the kind of woman who deserved the sun, moon and stars. Shyhiem wanted to be the man that showed her what real love looked like. Even though he'd never been in love, he was sure that this was what it felt like. He'd never pursued a woman before. Women normally flocked to him, but

Messiah wasn't an easy lay. He'd have to work extra hard to get her to open up to the possibility of them being one.

Messiah bit the inside of her lip as she approached the curb. Being around Shyhiem was a bad idea, but she couldn't walk away. He had her hook, line and sinker. Shyhiem pushed the weight of his body off the car and stood up straight. Messiah stood before him. He toward over her small, 5 foot 5 frame. Spiral tendrils of hair fell carelessly over her forehead, covering her eyes. Shyhiem brushed the soft curls to the side, revealing her almond-shaped eyes and long lashes. If given the blessing, he could stare at her face for the rest of his life and never get bored.

"You didn't have to come back." Messiah spoke, barely above a whisper. "I could've walked home."

"Stop frontin' like you ain't wanna see me." Shyhiem grinned, opening the passenger side door.

"Ah uh." She wagged her index finger in his face.

"What?" Shyhiem paused, confused.

"We need to talk about what happened earlier. You damn near killed that guy."

"He disrespected you." Shyhiem shrugged his shoulders.

"Shyhiem… you can't go around beating up everyone that says something you don't like."

"Who told you that lie?" He chuckled. "Where I come from, that's how you do things."

"But wouldn't you rather be loved than feared?"

"No, when people fear you, they respect you."

"Respect is to be earned not taken," Messiah rebutted.

"I disagree. When people fear you it's the most intoxicating sensation a man can possess."

"Oh, my god." Messiah sighed, put off. "Well, you need to learn a different way. 'Cause that wasn't cool. I don't like stuff like that. It really scared me."

Shyhiem saw the fear in her eyes. He never wanted her to question her safety around him.

"Listen," He stepped up on the curb. "I'll admit, I could've handled it a different way. It's hard tho'. My whole life, I've had to be aggressive. I don't know another way. For you... I'll work on it; but know, I'm a man and I protect what's mine."

Messiah drew her head back.

"How many times do I have to tell you? I'm not yours."

"That's what your mouth say... but your body is tellin' me different." He watched as her breathing slowed to a snail's pace. "You want me just as much as I want you."

Messiah couldn't deny, he was telling the truth. She wanted to decorate him with her love so everyone would know he was hers.

"Cat got your tongue," he teased.

"No!" Messiah playfully pushed him away.

"C'mon, get inside so I can take you home." Shyhiem ushered her in the car.

Messiah didn't make it a habit of getting into cars with strange men she barely knew, but Shyhiem made her feel safe. If he did try some slick shit, she'd finally get to practice the self-defense moves she'd learned years ago on YouTube. Inside his car, she nestled into the plush, leather seats. She hadn't been in a nice car in ages. Her usual form of transportation was Bird's 2012 Malibu, the bus or MetroLink. Being in his ride made her miss her hooptie. It would be another month before she could get her car out the shop.

Shyhiem hopped inside and turned the radio on but didn't start the engine. He wasn't in a rush to get her home. This was his chance to get to know her better. Leaning to the side, he observed her cheekbones. They reminded him of two sharp knives.

"My God, you're beautiful." He found himself saying out loud.

Messiah ran her hands down her thighs nervously and blushed.

"I'm a'ight." She downplayed her looks.

It wasn't every day she was told she was beautiful. Unlike other girls her age, she didn't have much. She couldn't afford to get her hair and nails done. She shopped at thrift stores. To Messiah, she was plain Jane. She didn't see what Shyhiem saw in her. She was the complete opposite of his baby mama. Keesha wore the best weave and had a body that would put most video chicks to shame. She wore her sexuality with pride. Messiah didn't have much experience in the sexual department. If Shyhiem got to know her better, he'd soon learn she was a lame and his infatuation with her would be over.

"You have no idea how dope you are?" He eyed her quizzically.

"You act like I'm some kind of work of art. I'm cool," she laughed, uncomfortably. "I am no Beyoncé."

"Do me a favor." Shyhiem asked, seriously.

"What?" Messiah avoided looking him in the eye.

"When you're around me, don't downplay yourself."

"That's kind of hard to do, when you've been through some of the stuff I've been through." She thought of the accident.

"We all got a past."

"True, but some are worse than others." Messiah envisioned her parents lying dead on the cement ground. "My past has dictated my future."

The fatal accident had left her unable to bare anymore children. Messiah didn't have to look at him for Shyhiem to notice the sadness written on her face. She was broken in places he wasn't sure he could fix, but he damn sure wanted to try.

"You know you have complete control over your destiny, right?"

"That's cute. Where'd you get that from Obi-Wan Kenobi? A Hallmark card?" She said sarcastically.

"No… from my mother." Shyhiem replied, solemnly.

"Fuck." Messiah slapped her hand against her forehead. "I'm sorry. I just keep on fuckin' up."

"You cool."

"No, I should go." She tried to open the door, mortified.

"I said you're good." He pulled the door closed, before she could get out.

Shyhiem wasn't going to let her off the hook that easy. He was determined to find out where the source of her pain came from. Seeing that he wasn't going to let her escape, Messiah sat perfectly still and gazed out the window. It'd begun to rain. Rain drops trickled down the window with ease.

"I take it you don't believe in much?" He spoke in a low, mellow tone.

"No." Messiah stared aimlessly out the window at the rain. "That's a lie. You know what I believe in?"

"Tell me."

"I believe in the sound of Stevie Wonder's voice. I feel like that's the closest I'll get to believing in God," Messiah answered truthfully.

The day the three most important people in her life died, she stopped believing in God. To her, He was nothing but a mythical figure people prayed to, to make themselves feel better.

"That's a shame… 'cause I believe in God and in you."

"Cut the bullshit, Shyhiem, Goodnight, Morning… whatever your name is. You don't even know me to believe in me. If you knew the things I've done, you wouldn't even look at me the same." Messiah snapped, facing him.

She did not have time for him to be running game on her. It wasn't necessary or needed. Shyhiem saw the spark of anger in her eyes but wasn't going to back down.

"All that unhappiness, that feeling like you've… landed in the wrong life… everybody feels that way. You don't know it yet, but all that anger and bitterness bottled up inside of you will one day become the anecdote you need to push forward. Trust me, I know. I've been there," he promised.

"What could you have possibly gone through to make you so optimistic?"

"I was locked up for three years," he confessed.

If Shyhiem having a criminal past was going to scare her away, it was best he told her now.

"What did you go to jail for?"

"I got caught up on a gun charge." Shyhiem played with the leather on the steering wheel.

He wasn't ready to tell her he was an ex drug dealer. Messiah was a good girl that seemed not to know anything about the streets. He didn't want to paint a negative image of himself. She'd already seen how savage he could be.

"Wow," Messiah looked away, shocked. "It seems like jail didn't mess your life up too much. I mean, look at you. You're doing well. Most felons come home to nothing and end right back in jail."

"That's because I made up my mind that I was going to make the necessary changes to make my life better. Having my son and daughter motivated me to be a better man."

Messiah let his words sink in and then asked, "Why are you being so nice to me?"

"What you mean?"

"You act like you know me."

"I like you, and for us to get married, I have to like you, right?" Shyhiem arched his brow.

"You are insane." Messiah shook her head. "I'm perfectly willing to warn you to forget all about me. If I were you, I wouldn't have anything to do with a girl like me. I'm no good. I'll only end up hurting you in the end," she warned.

"Messiah, you don't scare me," he smirked. "I'm digging the fuck outta you. I would straight put a baby up in you."

"Oh, my god," she laughed.

"No matter how much you try to fight it, we gon' be together. You gon' be my wife one day." He started up the car.

A few minutes later, they stood in front of her apartment door, drenched from the rain. She lived in apartment 2E on the fifth floor. Pieces of her black hair were stuck to her face and neck. She looked sexy as hell standing before him all wet. Her t-shirt clung to her full breasts. It took everything in Shyhiem not to have his way with her right there in the hallway. He hated that they had to part ways. He wanted more time with her. He hadn't gotten his full of her yet.

"Thank you for bringing me home." Messiah slicked her hair back with her hand.

"Anytime." Shyhiem placed his hands inside the pocket of his jeans.

He hoped she couldn't hear his heart beating. He'd never let her know it, but Messiah made him nervous. He couldn't control himself around her. Unsure of what to do next, Messiah reached inside her purse for her keys. Locating them, she pulled them out. Before she could blink her eyes, Shyhiem took the keys from her hand and unlocked the door. Messiah pressed her lips together and tried to conceal her smile.

"Here." He handed her back the keys.

"Thank you." She said in awe of his chivalry.

In a state of madness, Shyhiem placed his hand on the back of her neck and pulled her close. He couldn't go a second longer without tasting her honey-coated lips. He had to have her. Shyhiem fisted her hair and rotated between kissing her top and bottom lip. It was apparent, by the way she kissed him back, that she wanted him as bad as he wanted her.

Messiah had no idea, but she had his heart. Shyhiem had fallen hard. He'd landed on another planet but it felt like home to him. He hoped and prayed to God she didn't end up hurting him. He'd never been this vulnerable with a woman. Shyhiem couldn't focus on any potential pain. All he wanted was for her to continue to kiss him softly.

Wrapped up in his magic, Messiah held on for dear life. Her legs felt like jelly. She had no time to think as his lips pressed up against hers. Every ache and pain she'd felt that day had magically gone away. Shyhiem's sweet kisses were heaven-sent. He had her trapped and no one could save her. Minutes passed before either of them came up for air.

"What you doing Friday night?" He cupped her cheeks with his hands.

"Nothing." Messiah's chest heaved up and down.

"Let me take you out."

"I want to but…"

"C'mon, Messiah, I just want to spend a little time with you."

Messiah hesitated. Saying yes would open a door she wasn't sure she was ready to walk through.

"Ok," she finally replied.

"For real?" Shyhiem asked excited.

"Yes," Messiah giggled.

"Bet. I'ma call you tomor, a'ight?" Shyhiem caressed her cheek with his thumb.

"Ok." Messiah replied, unable to think straight.

Shyhiem stared deeply into her eyes and placed one last kiss on her lips.

"Have a good night." He said before jumping on the elevator.

Messiah watched as the elevator doors closed and he disappeared. She wanted to ask him to stay but didn't want to come across thirsty. Plus, she was engaged.

Alone on the elevator, Shyhiem smiled, pleased at how the night ended. He knew getting Messiah to fall head over heels in love with him would be an uphill battle. The girl was complicated. Her heart was made of a house of mirrors. It was up to him to break down her walls. Their first date would be his chance to get her to see all the possibilities of what their love could be. He just had to get her to hold on tight as they became one and set sail to their island underneath the sun.

"What am I supposed to do when I can't help how I feel?" – Elle Mai, "I Wish"

#10

Messiah

Friday came faster than Messiah wanted or expected. She was a nervous wreck over her date with Shyhiem. Her conscious kept telling her she was making a huge mistake, but her heart yearned to see him. Pushing the negative thoughts out of her mind, Messiah sat on a comfy, white, tufted couch and crossed her legs. A chilled glass of champagne rested in her hand, as she waited for her sister to come out of the private dressing room.

They were at The Ultimate Bride boutique trying on wedding dresses. Well, Lake was. She was engaged to marry Cardinal's pitcher, Austin Rhodes. They'd only been together a little over a year and planned to wed on New Year's Eve. Messiah tried not to be, but she was salty her sister was getting married before her. Bryson had proposed to her three years prior and they still hadn't set a wedding date.

It seemed like Lake always had better luck than her. She had the perfect life. She was an accomplished beauty queen who'd made it all the way to the Miss America pageant. Unfortunately, she didn't win. Lake made it into the top 10. After the Miss America pageant, she went on to become a C-list actress. She had bit parts on the Bold and the Beautiful, Vampire Diaries and Hit the Floor. She even starred in a few Lifetime movies, such as: The 19th Wife, Marriage of Lies, An Amish Murder and The Craigslist Killer.

Despite her lack of acting ability, Lake's beauty, charisma and poise kept her in all the right social circles. At a Samsung event in Miami, she met Austin. He was 6 feet tall, muscular, fine as hell and white. Let Lake tell it, from the moment they met, it was love at first sight. Maybe for Austin it was, but Messiah wasn't a fool. She knew her sister better than anyone. Lake loved Austin's fame and 200-million-dollar contract.

She was an equal opportunity gold digger. She didn't discriminate when it came to her next, big come up. She's dated all kinds of men in her 28 years on earth. Men were happy to have her on their arm. She was a showpiece and liked to be shown off.

Messiah checked her watch and sighed. It was taking Lake forever to come out in her fifth dress. Messiah didn't have all day to be waiting on her. She had to get home in a little while to get ready for her date. It would take Lake almost an hour to drive her all the way back down to the South Side. Messiah was just about to get up and see what the holdup was, when Lake came out in the most stunning dress she'd ever seen.

It wasn't your typical, white wedding gown. It was a Romona Keveza, blush & French violet, printed, silk organza, ball gown with a draped, one-shoulder bodice. The dress was amazing. The blush-colored dress faded into purple at the hem. Floral accents cascaded down the skirt. The ball gown was a lot of dress, but it didn't overpower Lake. Her beauty outshined the dress.

Lake smiled gleefully as she stepped onto the podium and checked herself out in the mirror. She took her own breath away. Messiah sat up on the couch and stared at her sister like she was a Disney princess. Everyone said she and her sister looked just alike, but Messiah thought Lake was far prettier. She and the actress Gugu Mbatha-Raw were often mistaken for one another. Lake hated it. Her naturally curly, auburn hair framed her picture-perfect face. Lake's sun-kissed skin, arched brows, round, brown eyes and beauty mark above her plump lips made her every man's wet dream.

She had a long neck, was 5'7 and wore a size 4. She was exquisite. Messiah felt like a mutt around her. When Lake entered a room, she commanded your attention. She had an air of sophistication about her; but for those who knew her well, Lake was a complete bitch. She and Messiah barely got along. They tolerated each other. Lake loved her sister but had a hard time forgiving her for the death of their parents. Since becoming pregnant at 16, Messiah had made one bad decision after another. Lake didn't understand what her little sister was doing with her life.

"I think this might be the one." She beamed with glee.

"It's beautiful." Messiah agreed, wishing the dress could be hers.

She could never afford such an extravagant gown though. She would be glad if she could swing a dress from the clearance rack at David's Bridal.

"It's spectacular, isn't it?" A bridal consultant by the name of Nenita gleamed.

"Obviously, I picked it out." Lake ran her hands across the bodice.

"More champagne?" Nenita asked, holding up a bottle of Veuve Clicquot Ponsardin Brut.

"Of course," Lake said without hesitation.

With all the money she was potentially going to spend with the boutique, she wanted the VIP treatment. Nenita filled her and Messiah's glasses.

"Thank you." Messiah said, feeling a little bit tipsy.

She was on her third glass.

"So, Lake, are you gonna say yes to the dress?" Nenita asked, placing her hands gently on Lake's shoulders.

Lake looked at herself again in the mirror and swayed from side-to-side.

"Mmm, I don't know." She wrinkled her nose.

"Girl, you done lost your mind." Messiah looked at her like she was crazy.

"I'm just not sure." Lake held the glass of champagne up to her lips in contemplation.

"It's the prettiest dress you've tried on today. What else are you looking for? This is it. You'd be a fool not to get it," Messiah assured.

"I agree with your sister," Nenita spoke up. "The dress is beautiful on you and it's a one-of-a-kind. There isn't another dress in the world like it."

"Nabet, right?" Lake screwed up her face.

"It's Nenita." The bridal consultant corrected her.

"Tibet, Babette, Soon Yi—"

"Soon Yi is a Korean name. I'm Filipino," Nenita cut her off, insulted.

"Whatever." Lake waved her off. "I know you're desperate for commission but I won't be pushed into a purchase if I'm not ready. And Messiah, darling… I appreciate your help, but you know nothing about fashion.

You walk around dressed like Cree Summers... Who is not a great fashion reference, mind you."

Messiah looked down at her outfit. She liked the way she looked. She hated looking like everyone else. Lake didn't know what she was talking about. She always got compliments on her style.

"I'm sorry, if you thought I was tryin' to pressure you. That wasn't my intention." Nenita apologized, looking like she wanted to cry.

"Mmm hmm. Leave us, please." Lake shooed her out the room.

"I'll be right outside if you need me," Nenita left the dressing room in a hurry.

Messiah felt so bad for the woman. She didn't deserve to be spoken to that way. As a person in the customer service industry, she knew exactly how Nenita felt. People often treated public servants as if they were nothing.

"Your racist-ass did not have to talk to that girl like that," Messiah shot, embarrassed by her sister's behavior.

"I'm mixed. I can't be racist. Plus, I love Filipinos. They're Asian but not cocky about it," Lake smirked.

"You're ridiculous." Messiah rolled her eyes.

"I'm a realist." Lake spun around and faced her. "Unlike you, who refuses to get off her ass and do something with her life. How long are you going to wait on Bryson to get his shit together before you get yours? You barely have money to buy a pack of noodles, yet your engaged to a man who doesn't even live in the same state as you. It's pathetic."

109

"I didn't come here for you to dissect my life," Messiah countered.

"Somebody needs to. You're my sister, for heaven's sake. ACT LIKE IT!" Lake threw her hands up. "Haven't I taught you anything? You could have any man you want, Messiah. Just put a little effort into yourself. I'll even help you. Let me give you a makeover. I swear you'll be wife'd up in no time."

"Lake, go suck a hot fart out yo' butt," Messiah groaned. "You can't tell me shit about marriage or relationships. Be happy you found a man that is willing to marry you, despite how many industry dicks you've sucked."

Lake's mouth dropped open. She didn't know Messiah had it in her for such a witty comeback. Quickly, she regained her composure and said, "Touché but you know I'm right. Bryson is not good enough for you. He's a user! You just don't want to see it. In my opinion, you love him way too much. Remember what mama used to say. Find you a man that loves you more than you love him."

"He loves me and I love him. You just don't understand our relationship."

"What relationship? The negro lives in Philly. You're in St. Louis—"

"And we're engaged," Messiah quipped.

"Girl, please." Lake took a sip of her champagne. "That thing you call a ring is nothing but a false sense of hope. You need to get you a man with some cash that's gon' spend it on dat ass! I'm so tired of seeing you look homeless. Mary Kate and Ashley can barely pull the look off. What makes you think you can?"

"For your information, I'm not as stuck on Bryson as you think. I have a date tonight." Messiah blurted out to shut Lake up.

"Hallelujah! Look at Blue Ivy! Won't she do it?!" Lake leaped off the podium and plopped down next to her sister. "Tell me everything about him." She squeezed her arm.

Messiah glared at her sister before speaking.

"Ok, calm down. You're doing the most. His name is Shyhiem and he's gorgeous. He's tall, dark, has an athletic build and is charming as fuck. The man looks like he walked out of the pages of a magazine." Messiah blushed.

"Really?" Lake replied, intrigued. "Continue."

"We have this crazy chemistry, and the way we met was like some shit straight of a fairytale. He seems to really like me. I don't know why, but he does. He's very confident but in a sexy, arrogant kind of way. Honestly, he scares me a li'l bit. But he's sweet, so that makes up for his aggressiveness. When I'm around him, I can't think straight—"

"Ok, I get it. He's fine and he makes your puss wet. Let's get to what matters the most. Does the negro have a job?"

"Yes, he works for UPS."

"What?" Lake looked at her like she was dumb. "Girl! Don't be wasting my time with this bullshit." She struggled to sit up in the huge dress.

"What?" Messiah eyed her sister clueless.

"The nigga work for UPS. He ain't got no money!" Lake rolled off the couch and stood up. "Here I was thinking you finally got a goddamn clue."

"Unlike you, I don't date men for their money, whore."

"And that's why you sittin' there in yo' five dollar fashions, wit' no money in yo' purse, catching the bus. While I, on the other hand, am about to buy a $20,000 wedding gown and marry a ball player. You need to get like me, baby girl."

"Whatever, Lake." Messiah downed the last of her champagne.

She was beyond ready to leave at that point. She and Lake were entirely two different people.

"All I'm saying is, if a nigga can't give you no cash, he don't deserve no ass. Stop giving your heart to men who can't afford to take care of it. And I mean that literally, not figuratively."

"Do you even love Austin at all?" Messiah eyed her sister with disdain.

"Of course, I love Austin," Lake swayed her hips from left to right. "But I love his money even more. One thing you need to learn about men is that no matter how much they say they love you, they'll get bored of you sooner or later. Men always want something young, shiny and new. So, when that day comes, when his eyes wander elsewhere, instead of crying and feeling blue, you remember the clause in your prenup that states if he ever cheats the prenup is null and void. That's when you take his ass for everything he's got. Love is cute, little sis. It's fun for a while, but it will always let you down. Money, on the other hand... always makes you happy."

"Remind me to put that on your headstone," Messiah replied dryly.

"Tell me this. Does he have any kids?"

Messiah sat quiet. She was over the conversation.

"I take that as a yes," Lake laughed. "Messiah, please, get it together. You can't go from one bum to another. Ain't you tired of struggling? Mommy and Daddy didn't raise you to be like this." She shook her head.

"What should I expect from you? You never listened to them anyway. That's why they're dead now," Lake said underneath her breath.

Messiah inhaled deeply and willed herself not to cry. Lake had basically kicked her in the stomach with a steel toe boot. She couldn't believe that she'd went there. She could deal with Lake making fun of her life, but when it came to the death of their parents, she knew that was a sore spot. Lake stared at her sister through the mirror and rolled her eyes. She hated when Messiah got all emotional and in her feelings. If it hadn't have been for her getting knocked up at 16 and defying their parents, they would still be alive. Lake tried not to blame her sister for their death but it was hard not to.

"Sorry." She spat empathically.

"No, you're not, so don't even pretend like you are." Messiah crossed her arms over her chest.

"Whatever, li'l girl. Nabet!" Lake called out for the bridal consultant.

"Yes." Nenita scurried into the room.

Messiah could tell she'd been crying.

"I think I'm going to say yes to this dress." Lake smiled, gleefully.

"I told you, boy, this ain't good for ya but ya didn't wanna listen to me." – Ella Mai, "Wanted"

#11

Messiah

The ride home from the bridal salon was strained, to say the least. Messiah hadn't uttered a word to her sister since the remark she made about her killing their parents. As far as Messiah was concerned, she could choke on a dick and die. Lake should've been glad she hadn't slapped the dog shit out of her. After the way she'd spoken to her, Messiah would be damned if she helped or participated in her fake-ass, overpriced wedding. Heated, she was on her phone scrolling through Instagram when a call came in. Bryson was calling. A smile graced the corners of her lips before she answered the phone. Hearing his voice was exactly what she needed to lift her sour mood.

"Hey." She spoke sweetly.

"What you doing?" His deep voice resonated into her soul.

"On my way home. What you doing?"

"On my way to see you."

"What?" Messiah's eyes grew wide.

"Yeah, my flight lands in two hours so be ready. We're going out."

"Where?" Messiah's mind raced.

"Out to eat, so wear something nice."

"Alright, I can't wait to see you."

"Me too… Messiah?" Bryson called out her name before she hung up.

"Huh?" She replied, overwhelmed with his unplanned visit.

"I miss you," he confessed.

"I miss you too." She whispered, feeling her heart swell.

"See you in a few."
"Bye." Messiah ended the call.

She looked out the passenger window and tried to figure out what she was going to do. She was due to meet Shyhiem in a few hours. She really wanted to spend time with him and didn't want to cancel their date but had no choice. Bryson was her fiancé. He came first. And sure, she had a connection with Shyhiem that couldn't be explained, but she barely knew him.

Bryson coming into town must've been a sign from God that she was fucking up. Messiah knew even considering going out with Shyhiem was a bad decision. She'd felt like shit about saying yes since he'd asked her. Kissing him was even worse. God was trying to remind her that Bryson was her reality. Shyhiem was nothing but a fantasy. He was there to fill the void of not having her fiancé around.

And yes, she liked the attention she got from him. He made her feel wanted but her heart belonged to Bryson. She loved him abundantly. They were going to build their lives together. All they had to do was make it through his last year of school and they'd be able to start their lives as one. Messiah had to cut things off with Shyhiem. Shit was starting to get real. She'd almost messed up her entire relationship; and for what, a dinner and a movie? Losing Bryson wasn't worth the trouble. She and Shyhiem could be nothing more than friends. Now, she had to figure out how she was going to tell him that.

Messiah's heart raced as she found Shyhiem's number in her phone. She should've given him the common courtesy of calling, but she didn't have balls enough to say her peace with her mouth. Messiah bit her bottom lip and wondered what she should text him and say. She didn't know it would be so hard to tell him she couldn't see him. After a few minutes of contemplation, she finally came up with:

Messiah: Hey, I know it's last minute, but I'm not going to be able to make it tonight. I don't feel good.

Messiah sat with baited breath, praying he wouldn't respond, when a text bubble popped up on the screen. She hoped he was busy and wouldn't be able to respond right back.

Shyhiem: You ain't gotta lie, li'l mama... You scared.

He said more as a statement and not a question.

Messiah: I swear, I'm not. I think I caught the flu or something. My whole body aches, my throat is sore and my nose is stopped up.

Messiah felt like such an asshole for lying. She just couldn't find the strength to tell him the truth.

Shyhiem: Damn, that's fucked up. I hope you feel better.

Messiah: Me too.

Shyhiem: You need me to bring you anything?

Messiah: Nah, I'm just going to take some meds and go to sleep.

Messiah rolled her eyes to the sky. She was a piece of shit for not telling him she couldn't see him at all on an intimate level.

Shyhiem: A'ight, well get some rest.

Messiah: Thank you, I will.

Once the conversation was over, Messiah let out a sigh of relief that he'd believed her lie. Her next dilemma was figuring out what she was going to wear. Nothing she had at home was suitable enough for a romantic date. She wanted to rock something sexy and new. The problem was - she had no money. Well, she had the two-hundred bucks she needed to pay her light bill. Messiah knew it was risky to spend her bill money on a new outfit but she had to. She hadn't seen Bryson in months. She wanted to look like a sex goddess for him. She had to knock his socks off.

Fuck it, you only live once, she thought. Messiah's mind was made up. She'd use the bill money to get a new outfit and shoes. After an amazing dinner and mind-blowing sex, she'd ask Bryson to give her two-hundred dollars to pay Ameren. She hardly ever asked him for anything, so it wouldn't be a problem. Well, at least it shouldn't be. It was a win-win situation. She'd get to look like a sexpot *and* keep her lights on.

"Aye." She turned to Lake.

"What?" Lake kept her eyes on the road.

"Can we make a quick stop at the mall? I need to buy a dress."

"You had me at the word mall," Lake grinned.

Bryson would be arriving any minute. Messiah anxiously stood in front of her full-length mirror, examining her look. She never bragged on her looks, but that night, she looked damn good. She prayed to all the miscellaneous gods in the sky that he liked it. He better. She'd spent the last of what she had on it. In true Messiah fashion, she wore a rose gold, sheer, V-neck, long sleeve, sequin romper. It showed just enough boob and a lot of leg.

Since the outfit was a statement piece, she wore her hair in a wild, curly afro. Cute, strappy, rose gold heels that cost $100 decorated her freshly-painted toes. Messiah had never paid so much for a pair of shoes in her life. Not an expert in wearing heels, she'd scuffed the bottoms so she could walk without falling. Her body was dipped in gold, shimmer lotion that she'd bought from Forever 21. Pink, shimmer shadow, mascara and pink lip gloss highlighted her angelic face. For the first time in a long time, Messiah felt good about herself. The $200 was money well spent.

Suddenly, there was a knock on the door. Messiah jumped at the sound. The butterflies in the pit of her stomach were on overdrive. Bryson had a strange effect on her. She knew he'd be the man she married from the first moment she laid eyes on him. The day they met danced around in her head often. It was one of her favorite memories.

The two met their junior year in high school. Messiah was late for class. She searched frantically inside her locker for her Geometry book when he approached. Messiah didn't even notice him standing there.

"What's up, beautiful?" He leaned against the locker next to her.

"Huh?" Messiah stepped back to see his face.

"I said... what's up, beautiful?" Bryson eyed her lustfully.

"Not you." Messiah tucked the book under her arm and slammed the locker door shut.

She tried to act like her heart hadn't stopped beating but she was attracted to Bryson from the jump. He was six foot three with skin the color of raw honey. His eyes were small but pierced deep inside the parts of her she tried to hide. Hating the effect he had on her, she spun around on her heels to walk away.

"Where you going?" He grabbed her by the hand.

"I gotta go. I'm late for class." Messiah whined, trying to break loose.

"Hold up. Let me holla at you for a second." Bryson pulled her back.

"What do you want?" She groaned, not in the mood.

"I'm tryin' to get at you. If you would chill for half a sec."

"I'm good." Messiah tried to walk away again.

"You good?" Bryson screwed up his face, loving the challenge she proposed.

"Yeah."

"Damn, it's like that? You just gon' break a nigga heart and leave?"

"Bryson, please. You can have any girl in this school. Why me?" She cocked her head to the side.

"Why not you?" He played with a strand of her hair.

Messiah's entire body turned to Jell-O. She'd never heard anything sweeter. Bryson was a smooth-talker that knew exactly what to say to win her heart. Unable to resist his charm, she gave in and gave him her number. Bryson had her from the minute he said hello.

From then on, Messiah couldn't tell which way was up and which way was down. The two of them were inseparable. Instead of attending school, she spent her days skipping with him. Instantly, his world became hers and she loved every minute of it. She was fascinated by Bryson's mind, how intelligent he was, his wit and persistence. School, ballet and family were all put on the back burner.

Spending every waking moment with him was all she cared about. All of that changed once her parents found out she'd missed 20 days of school and hadn't gone to ballet class in months. Bill and Etta couldn't believe that their daughter was living so recklessly. She'd completely changed. Messiah was lying all the time and sneaking around. All the trust she built with her parents had completely gone out the window.

Bill and Etta tried to warn, lecture and punish her but it was too late. Messiah was already pregnant and determined not to abort the baby. Nothing anyone said mattered. She loved Bryson and their baby. There was nothing anyone could do about it. Messiah fought her parents to the end. She was determined to prove to all the naysayers that she and he were meant to be. Her parents' plan was to send her to Tuscaloosa until she had the baby. Once she did, Messiah would give it up for adoption and return to St. Louis. Her parents hoped that once she returned, Messiah would have Bryson out her system.

Unfortunately, they would never get the chance to know if their plan worked or not.

Messiah skipped over to the door, excited to see Bryson's face. Swiftly, she opened the door and found him standing there. It took everything in her not to jump into his arms. Bryson was a dream. He looked even finer than he had the last time she saw him. Over the years, he'd grown into his boy-next-door good looks. He rocked a bald head, full beard and a body full of muscles she wanted to devour. *What the hell were you thinkin'? You were about to cheat on this,* Messiah licked her bottom lip.

"Hi." She beamed, wrapping her arms around his neck.

"Hey." Bryson gave her a one-arm hug. "I'm tired than a muthafucka." He quickly let her go and walked inside.

Messiah wished he would've held onto her longer. It had been months since she held him in her arms. Bryson placed his bag down and then took off his jacket.

"You got something to drink?" He asked, plopping down onto her couch.

"Yeah, you want a bottle of water?" Messiah walked to the fridge.

"That's all you got?" He grimaced.

"That's all I can afford," Messiah quipped.

"I'll take it," Bryson huffed, exhausted. "Aye, babe, I'm shot. Can we go out to dinner tomorrow?"

Messiah's heart plummeted. *He can't be serious,* she thought. She'd gotten dolled up for nothing. It was bad enough he hadn't even mentioned how hot she looked. He

123

hadn't even really looked at her. Messiah was dumbstruck. Her feelings were shattered. She'd spent money she didn't have to spend for nothing. Keeping a straight face, she handed him the water.

"You mad?" Bryson finally looked up at her.

"It's cool." Messiah avoided eye contact.

"I promise, we'll go tomorrow," he assured.

"Mmm hmm." Messiah sat opposite him and crossed her legs.

"My flight was crazy. It was delayed twice. I was supposed to be here hours ago." Bryson chugged down the water.

"Well, I'm happy you came."

She was truly disappointed that they weren't going out. She never got to do anything fun. Her feelings were hurt that he hadn't even bothered to get her anything for her birthday. Dinner would've made up for it. And sure, he'd said they'd go out the following day, but knowing Bryson, it was unlikely to happen.

"The place looks nice." He looked around. "It's a little cramped but nice."

Messiah bit her tongue. Their reunion was not going how she envisioned at all. She couldn't believe he was dissing her apartment. Her apartment wasn't the most extravagant thing ever but it was hers. She didn't have much in life to claim as hers. She was proud of her crib.

"You might need to dust in here too. My allergies are flaring up." He coughed, rubbing his nose.

"Well, since we not going nowhere, let me go take off my clothes." Messiah rose to her feet, pissed.

If she didn't leave, she was liable to cuss Bryson's ass out. He was being rude as fuck. Her entire night was ruined. At that point, she low-key wished she would've gone out with Shyhiem instead. He wouldn't have treated her like dirt. Whenever she was with him, he made her feel like number one.

"Wait a minute. Where you going?" Bryson grabbed her hand and pulled her down onto his lap.

Messiah felt his hard-on as soon as she sat down.

"We're not going out so I'm going to take my clothes off," Messiah spat with an attitude.

"Nah, let me look at you for a minute." Bryson played with the neck of her romper. "I like this li'l thing you got on."

"Thank you." Messiah held her breath.

When Bryson touched her, she lost all sense of self.

"It'll look even better off of you." He kissed her neck.

Messiah let out a soft moan. She watched as his hand slid down her torso and landed on the face of her pussy. Messiah inhaled deeply, as his fingers began to circle her clit through her clothes. It was the sexiest shit she'd ever witnessed. No matter how much Bryson angered and let her down at times, whenever she was in his presence, she became weak. He'd been her lifeline for the past six years. Her world didn't exist unless he was in it. They were best friends. He knew all the layers that made up her existence. Messiah often chalked his unsympathetic attitude up to him being an immature, only child. She figured once they got older he'd change.

But Messiah couldn't focus on any of Bryson's hang-ups. He'd ripped off her romper and left her in nothing but her heels. Messiah gasped for air. There was no way she could take it back now. With her back pressed up against the couch, Bryson stood between her shimmery legs. The sight of her thighs open with her stilettos on turned him on to the fullest. Her pussy was freshly-shaven and ready to be devoured.

Messiah watched with hungry eyes as he took off his shirt. Her tongue ran across her lower lip as she admired his chiseled abs. Bryson's body was out of this world. He stayed in the gym. There wasn't an ounce of fat on him. Messiah couldn't wait to place a trail of wet kisses over his abs and down to his dick. Bryson liked how she ogled his physique. He was the apple of Messiah's eye and he knew it.

Slowly, he unbuckled his belt and slid it through the loops of his jeans. Hard as a rock, he held the belt by his side. Messiah's taut, caramel frame was calling his name. Nasty thoughts of what he would do with the belt filled her mind. She wanted him to bend her over the couch and spank her until she couldn't take it anymore. Messiah and Bryson had great sex but it could be better. Messiah was a quote, unquote, good girl; but when it came to sex, she liked a little kink. The dirtier the sex the better. Bryson was cool with different sex positions but that was where he drew the line. He wasn't down for role play, bondage, spankings or toys.

After falling in love with Christian Grey, Messiah wanted to try some new shit. Now was the perfect time for him to indulge her fantasies. Messiah looked up at him shyly and extended her arms. She wanted to feel the leather belt tighten around her wrists as he fucked her into outer space.

Bryson looked at her hands, shook his head and threw the belt down to the floor. He wasn't about to tie her up with his belt. It might leave a bruise on her skin and he didn't want to hear her mouth about it later. Plus, he didn't want anyone to think he'd hit her. Instead, he unzipped his jeans so his dick could spring loose. Messiah tried to hide her disappointment but it was hard to conceal. The eager look in her eyes had vanished. Instead of having earth-shattering sex filled with pleasure and pain, they'd have boring, missionary sex on the couch.

Messiah wanted more. Her body craved more. She wanted to be controlled and taken to new heights of ecstasy. Completely naked, Bryson stood before her, stroking his cock. His dick was erect and dying to enter her slit. Although she was pissed he wouldn't grant her bondage request, Messiah couldn't deny that him pleasuring himself was a major turn on. Bryson was more than well endowed. His dick stood at full attention, saluting her. She watched with desire as his hand slid up and down his shaft. The thought of him cumming on her chest made the walls of her pussy contract. She had to have him now.

Sitting up, she replaced his hand with hers and then wrapped her lips around the tip of his dick. Bryson closed his eyes and allowed his head to fall back. Messiah's warm mouth on his throbbing cock was too much for him to bear. His hand fisted a handful of her hair as she ran her tongue from the head of his dick down to his balls. On the brink of cumming, he begged her to stop. He didn't want to cum that way. He wanted to cum inside the place he called home.

Gently, he lay Messiah back on the couch. Before he gave her all eight inches of him, he had to taste her. The first lick sent electric shocks throughout her body. Messiah ran her hands over his bald head and moaned. Bryson was torturing her with his tongue. The man knew how to give Oscar-worthy head. He would rotate between flicking his tongue across her clit to sucking it like it was a pacifier. His freak level might've been a four but he sure knew how to get her off. Messiah was always guaranteed an orgasm, no matter what.

"Fuck!" She wailed, cumming.

Bryson watched as her body shivered. Once she calmed down, he licked her juices off his lips and climbed up her body. His dick was perfectly aligned with her vagina. For six years, he'd been fucking her pussy raw. Each time felt like the first. Bryson felt like the man knowing he was the only one to have her. Messiah's pussy was the best and it was all his. He'd taught her everything she knew.

Dizzy from climaxing, Messiah held onto his back. Bryson looked down into her eyes as he entered her slowly. He'd never get tired of this. That weekend, he planned on losing himself in her pussy. Messiah was the first woman he'd ever loved. She was perfect. She loved him unconditionally and put up with his bullshit. He didn't deserve her and he knew it. He owed her the world. Sometimes, she'd loved him more than his own people. She'd given up her life for him.

He never wanted to hurt her and hated when he didn't live up to her expectations. Bryson loved Messiah dearly. She was his baby. He'd give her the world if he could. Grinding his hips in a circular motion, he buried his face in the crook of her neck. Messiah was so wet, he could barely keep from slipping out.

"Tell me you love me!" He demanded, squeezing his eyes tight.

Bryson was on the brink of exploding.

"I love you." Messiah replied, breathlessly.

The room had begun to spin. Another orgasm was around the corner. Messiah tried her best to hold on, but the deeper Bryson crashed into her, the more she couldn't contain herself. Bryson could feel her walls tighten around his dick. The feeling was sensational. Rising on his elbows, he studied Messiah's face. He loved to watch her cum. Messiah couldn't hold out any longer.

"Bryson, fuck!" She screamed, biting his shoulder. "Oh, my god! I love you."

"I love you too." He groaned, cumming long and hard inside her.

For a few minutes, they lay there spun. Neither could utter a word, they were so exhausted. Bryson lie on top of Messiah as she caressed his back. He was hot and sweaty but she didn't mind. She would take hot and sweaty Bryson any day. Moments like this, where she got to hold him in her arms, she cherished the most. It would probably be months before she got to see him again. She couldn't take a second with him for granted.

"Damn, I miss my pussy." He kissed her collarbone repeatedly.

"Your pussy?" Messiah laughed.

"This shit mine and you know it," Bryson grinned, slapping her thigh.

"Yeah, okay. If you say so." Messiah held him tighter.

"We gotta get up," Bryson mumbled, sleepily.

"No, we don't. Let's just lay like this." Messiah kissed his forehead.

"Nah, let's get cleaned up. Come hop in the shower wit' me." He rose.

Messiah poked out her bottom lip and pouted. She enjoyed having his semi-hard dick inside her as he lay on top of her.

"I'll join you, if I can get a round two," she bargained.

"You ain't said nothin' but a word." Bryson winked his eye and headed to the bathroom.

As Messiah sat up to follow him, there was a knock at her door. Her forehead wrinkled. She wasn't expecting any guests. Confused as to who it could be, she grabbed Bryson's shirt and wrapped it around her. Her heels clicked against the concrete floor as she made her way across the room.

"Who is it?" She asked.

"It's me... Shyhiem." His deep voice boomed through the door.

Messiah's entire body went ice-cold. She'd completely forgotten about him. She totally forgot that she'd lied and said she was sick. Never in a million years did she think he'd show up at her door unannounced. *What the fuck am I gonna do,* she thought. Bryson was in the back. She had enough time to see what Shyhiem wanted and shoo him away without anyone getting their feelings hurt. Quietly, she cracked open the door and stuck her head out.

"Hi." She spoke, trying to sound like she was asleep.

"Hey." Shyhiem smiled. "My bad, was you sleep? I ain't mean to wake you."

130

"It's ok; but what are you doing here?"

"I ain't tryin' to come off like no weirdo or nothin'. I just wanted to bring you some soup and flowers since you weren't feeling well." He held up a bag of food from Panera Bread and a dozen pink roses.

Messiah's heart sank. She felt like shit. It didn't help that he looked good enough to eat. Shyhiem donned a black, Yeezy, dad hat with a black hoodie. On top of the hoodie was a brown and black checkerboard flannel. A pair of black, fitted jeans and brown, suede boots completed the rough and rugged streetwear. Unexpectedly, tears welled in her eyes. Shyhiem was being so sweet to her. She didn't deserve his kindness.

"What's with the tears? You a'ight?" He asked, trying to push the door open.

"I'm fine." Messiah held the door steady. "Just sicker than I thought."

"That's why I'm here - to take care of you."

"I would let you in but I don't wanna get you sick," she lied, faking a cough. "Plus, I don't want you seeing me like this. I look a mess."

"You could never look nothing short of beautiful to me," Shyhiem replied, truthfully.

Even with the bead of sweat on her forehead and disheveled hair, she was magnificent. Sick and all, he wanted to place his thumb in her dimpled-chin and kiss her like she'd never been kissed before. Shyhiem was willing to risk his health just to have a few seconds with her.

"You sure you don't want me to come in?" He slid his hand down the side of her face.

Messiah closed her eyes and relished the touch of his rough hand on her skin.

"Shyhiem, I—" She began, before Bryson's voice overshadowed hers.

"Aye, babe! What's taking you so long?" He called from the hallway.

Shyhiem glared at Messiah's face. His hand instantly dropped down to his side. He couldn't believe she'd lied to him. Suddenly, she'd become a monster.

"Shyhiem, I—"

"Yo' nigga in there?" He asked furrowing his brow.

"I'm sorry." Messiah pulled the door open, forgetting Bryson's shirt was wrapped around her.

Shyhiem hung his head low and chuckled in disbelief. He never felt more like a sucker in his life. Here he was thinking Messiah was of a different breed, when really, she was just like any other raggedy bitch he'd ever dealt with. He thought they were headed to the promise land. He thought he'd found his Ruth. And yeah, she'd told him she had a man, but she ain't have to lie and say she was sick to get out of kickin' it with him. She could've kept it 100.

He felt like a fuckin' idiot. He'd never be able to look at Messiah the same. He was stupid for thinking she would keep it real with him. She couldn't even keep it real with herself. From the sorrowful look in her eyes, he could see her feelings for him were stronger than she let on. Yet, here she was, wearing another man's shirt. They'd obviously just finished fuckin'. Shyhiem wanted to choke the shit out of her then bury her man six feet deep.

Messiah couldn't take the look of pure disappointment and sadness on his face. It made her feel worse than she already did. The memory of how he looked at her in that moment would always be etched inside her brain.

"Please, just let me explain," she begged.

"Be good, shawty." Shyhiem said before walking away.

Messiah wanted to call after him but couldn't. She couldn't let Bryson know she was at the door falling apart over a man other than him. Messiah would pretend like the incident never happened. She didn't owe Shyhiem anything. He knew she was engaged to be married. He had no right to be mad. They had a crazy connection and shared an amazing kiss... That was it. Messiah would put Shyhiem and his spellbinding eyes and tender kisses behind her and act like he never existed.

"Baby, who is that at the door?" Bryson asked.

"Nobody." She closed the door behind her.

"I opened up, she let me down. I won't feel that no more." –Omarion, "Ice Box"

#12

Shyhiem

The ice around Shyhiem's heart was just starting to thaw. Now, the wall he'd built was back up and padlocked closed. He didn't know where the road he and Messiah walked on would end, but he didn't think they'd end up here. Drowning his sorrows wasn't the answer to his problems but he found himself at Windy City anyway. Windy City was a hole-in-the-wall bar that played the blues and sold stiff drinks.

It was small, secluded and quiet. It was just what he needed. He didn't want to be around anyone he knew. Mayhem had been blowing him up but he'd get with him later. Shyhiem needed to tend to the open wound in his chest. He was bleeding out at a rapid pace. Only alcohol would numb the pain. Messiah shouldn't have control over his feelings. Yet, she was to blame for his foul mood. He hated the hold she had on him.

A cold-hearted nigga like him wasn't used to caring. If this was what love felt like, he didn't want any parts of it. He normally didn't give a fuck about much, besides his kids and brother. He had no reason to open his heart to anything else. The only woman he'd ever loved was buried six feet deep. Until he met Messiah, Shyhiem thought he'd never meet a woman worthy of his love and affection. He didn't think he was capable of giving his heart to a woman. Messiah, however, opened his mind to love and its endless possibilities.

He wanted to give her the world but she'd shitted on him. Maybe she didn't take his advances seriously? Maybe she wasn't attracted to him? Shyhiem laughed at the thought of Messiah not being attracted to him. There was no way on God's green earth that she wasn't. He noticed how her chest rose and fell every time he came near. When he touched her soft skin, she could hardly think straight. She became a nervous wreck. He found her desire for him adorable 'cause she had the same effect on him.

None of that mattered now. He was alone, burning his throat with Hennessy, while she laid up with her fiancé. The thought of her with another man made him sick. She should've been with him. The nigga she was fuckin' with wasn't a man. He was a boy playing dress up. He didn't deserve to have a loyal chick like her by his side. It was obvious he didn't treat her right. If Shyhiem had the world in his hand, it'd be hers. He'd always find new ways to love her more. If she was with him, Messiah would never have to want for a thing.

Shyhiem had to remind himself that all the wishing and hoping in the world wouldn't change reality. She wasn't his girl. He was foolish to think that she could be the one. He should've backed off when she told him she was taken. He should've just walked away and acted as if that night at Blank Space and the phone conversation they shared never happened. Cupid had fucked up and shot the wrong arrow. No matter how much the universe tried to push them together, it just wasn't meant to be. But he couldn't get her out of his veins. Shyhiem was obsessed with her for reasons even he couldn't understand.

It pissed him off that she'd played the shit out of him and he still wanted her. Maybe that was what he liked about her so much. Messiah wasn't an easy capture. She made him work for her affection. Getting women usually came easy to him. Messiah wasn't easily persuaded by his good looks and charm. She fought his advances tooth and nail.

Shyhiem was beyond fucked up in the head. The liquor wasn't helping any. A million thoughts crammed his head. No woman had ever played him to the left. Shyhiem felt like a complete idiot for pining after her. He had to get over her - and quick. The sting of her dismissal would fade in time. He just had to get through the night and everything would be alright.

The fact that they couldn't be together didn't stop him from fantasizing about tonguing her down. He wanted to stay buried in her pussy for hours on end. Shyhiem yearned to see her climax while he had her pinned down to the bed. That would never happen though. The conclusion made Shyhiem drink more. He had to get her out his brain. She took up too much space.

Shyhiem hated not being in control of his emotions. It was uncharted territory that he'd never explored. He had to resolve the problem ASAP. If Messiah didn't want to fuck with him, then fuck her. There were plenty of hoes that were dying for his attention. It was a chick a few seats down from him that had been eye-fuckin' him since he walked through the door.

She was cute and had a nice rack but all Shyhiem could think about was Messiah's brown, magnetic eyes. He wanted to take up residence in the dimple on her chin. God couldn't have placed a prettier feature on her face. It sucked that he'd have to forget about her alluring smile. Whatever they had was over before it started. Yet her name still danced on the tip of his tongue.

Five glasses of Hennessy later, Shyhiem's belly was full. The lids of his eyes hung low and his balance was off-kilter. It was time for him to head home. It was a little past midnight when he walked through the door. To his surprise, Keesha was lying on the couch watching The Rap Game with the lights off. A blanket covered her.

Normally, on a Friday night, she'd be in the club spending money she didn't have. What shocked him even more was that the house was clean. Shyhiem drunkenly rubbed his eyes to make sure he was in the right apartment. He didn't know what brought on her sudden desire to tidy up but was pleased with the results. The place smelled of lavender-scented candles. None of the twins' toys were sprawled on the floor. The kitchen was spotless and the living area was presentable enough to sit in.

Shyhiem tossed his keys down on the counter and noticed the flowers he'd bought Messiah on the dining room table in a vase. He wondered how they'd gotten there. He'd thrown them in the kitchen trash. Shyhiem looked over at Keesha. She'd been watching his every move. Keesha pulled the blanket from her body and rose to her feet. She wore one of his wife beaters, that barely covered her ass, and a neon pink thong. The light from the television illuminated her heart-shaped lips as she stalked her prey. Shyhiem normally didn't pay Keesha any mind, but that night he was drunk, the kids were gone and she was looking right.

"Thanks for the flowers, baby." She ran her rhinestoned, stiletto-manicured hand down his chest.

"So, that's why you cleaned up?" Shyhiem chuckled, taking off his shirt.

"Yeah, I figured you were tryin' to do something nice for me and got mad 'cause of how the house looked, so I decided to make it up to you."

"Sorry to burst your bubble, but the flowers weren't for you." He pushed her out of the way.

He needed a beer. Seeing the flowers only made him think of Messiah more. He couldn't escape her no matter how hard he tried.

"Who they for then?" Keesha stood back on one of her legs and folded her arms.

"Not you." Shyhiem popped the top off a beer and took a huge gulp.

"Let me find out they for that mop head bitch in 2E," Keesha challenged.

"They were." Shyhiem said nonchalantly.

He wasn't fazed by Keesha's hissy fit. She wasn't his woman. She was strictly his baby mama. He didn't owe her a damn thing and could care less about her feelings.

"Ugh... what you see in her lame-ass? She ain't even that cute."

"You mad 'cause she look better than you?" Shyhiem pulled his hoodie over his head.

"Nigga, please," Keesha fumed, feeling like he'd spit on her. "On her worst day, that bitch can't look better than me."

Shyhiem laughed. Keesha was so predictable. He knew she'd flip her lid when he said another chick was cuter than her. She prided herself on being the baddest bitch.

"It's best day." He corrected her.

"What?" Keesha replied confused.

"Nothing." Shyhiem shook his head.

He didn't have time to explain analogies to her.

"How you gon' bring flowers for another bitch in my house? That's disrespectful, Shy. You know I love you." Keesha stepped inside the kitchen.

"You so full of shit. I'ma buy you Pull-Ups." Shyhiem smirked, bypassing her.

"No, I'm not! I'm tellin' the truth. You know what it is and how I feel about you." She grabbed his arm and pulled him back.

"Keesha, it's late. I've had a fucked-up day. I'm drunk. I don't feel like arguing wit' you." Shyhiem pled, with his back against the wall.

If she pushed him too far, there was no telling what he might do. Shyhiem wasn't in the mood for her shenanigans. All he wanted to do was go to bed and forget about the day's events.

"No, listen to me." Keesha begged, getting in his face. "I love you and I want us to be a family again. I miss the way we used to be. You don't like that bitch for real. She wack as fuck. She can't understand you like I do. Me and you, we're cut from the same cloth. Her county-bound-ass don't know shit about struggling. She will never be wit' a nigga like you."

Shyhiem swallowed hard. Keesha was saying everything he'd been trying to ignore. A part of him felt like he wasn't good enough for Messiah. She was the kind of girl that needed to be on the arm of a politician. She deserved to have the finer things in life. She needed a refined man with a college education, not some ex-convict who delivered packages during the day.

"You know I'm right, that's why you ain't sayin' nothin'. Why you throw away the flowers 'cause she ain't give you no play?"

Shyhiem adverted his eyes and didn't respond.

"I'm right, ain't I?" Keesha smiled, pleased with herself. "I knew her ass wasn't shit. Fuck her. Give me one more chance. I promise, I'll make you forget all about that bitch." She kissed him softly on the lips then eased her way down.

Shyhiem closed his eyes. He and Keesha hadn't been intimate on any level in over a year and a half. He swore he'd never take it there with her again. He tried to fix his mouth to tell her to stop. Shyhiem opened his eyes and looked down at her. Keesha smirked as she slowly unzipped his jeans and pulled his hard dick out. Shyhiem reasoned with himself that he needed to release the pent-up frustration he had bottled inside. It was the only way he could justify fucking Keesha.

He hated this side of him. At the heart of him, Shyhiem was a monster. He would always inflict pain on himself and everyone around him. He wasn't any good to anyone but himself. He only did what made him feel good in the moment. All he knew was savage behavior. When he hurt, he spiraled out of control.

Any logical thinking had gone out the door. The vicious beast in him had taken over. Messiah was a few floors above him sucking another man's cock. Why not have his sucked too? As Keesha wrapped her plump lips around his dick and swallowed him whole, he imagined that it was Messiah down on her knees sucking him off. Shyhiem envisioned her face while wrapping Keesha's hair around his fist tightly. All he wanted was Messiah.

When he didn't get what he wanted, Shyhiem acted out. The old, familiar, sting of anger seethed through his blood stream. He'd regret his actions in the morning; but right now, Keesha made him feel good. She fulfilled a deep craving in him that needed satisfying. And yes, he was

giving her a false sense of hope. He should've felt bad...
but he didn't.

Keesha was a monster too. Like him, she didn't
have a heart. He realized that once he was locked up. He
could never take her seriously or give her another chance.
What they had was dead and gone. Shyhiem's eyes went
dark as he lifted Keesha off the ground and slammed her up
against the wall. Her face was pressed against the wall
along with her breasts and hands. Shyhiem spread her legs
apart and pulled her thong to the side.

Never one to go without a condom, he swiftly
placed the one he had in his pocket on. Seconds later, he
was balls deep inside Keesha's wet pussy. She whimpered
as soon as the head of his penis hit her cervix. She'd never
get used to his size and girth. Shyhiem held her hips in
place and fucked her at a feverish pace. With each stroke,
visions of Messiah's face danced in his brain. Shyhiem let
out a primal growl and fucked Keesha faster.

"Shyhiem, slow down." She panted, as her head
bounced off the wall.

Shyhiem heard her cries but was in the zone. He
had to fuck Messiah out of his head. Sweat beads formed
on his forehead. The liquor and nut building in the tip of his
dick was making him feel sick. If he didn't cum soon, he
was going to pass out. He didn't want to be inside Keesha
too long anyway. Nothing had changed. He still didn't want
her. This was nothing but sex. He'd bust a nut and go back
to giving her the cold shoulder.

"Shyhiem, baby, slow down. I wanna feel you,"
Keesha begged, trying to hold on.

Her cries landed on deaf ears as Shyhiem pulled
out, snatched the condom off and squirted on her behind.

142

"Agggggggh!" He groaned, holding his head back.

Shyhiem came for what seemed like hours. Keesha's ass was covered in his semen. Out of breath and tired, he stuffed his dick back in his jeans and staggered down the hall to the master bath. Keesha carefully stood up straight. *Is that it,* she thought, catching her breath. She wanted more. Shyhiem's pipe game was too good to only get a small dose. Taking off her top and thong, she made her way to the bathroom, only to find the door locked.

"Open the door." She twisted the knob.

"Nah, I'm about to get in the shower."

"I wanna get in too."

"You can get in here when I get out." Shyhiem pulled the shower curtain back.

"Come on, Shy, let me in," Keesha whined. "I wanna suck yo' dick."

"I'm good."

"Pleaaaaaaaase," Keesha begged.

"No! Go sit yo' ass down somewhere!"

"I can't sit down! Yo' cum on my ass!" Keesha stood outside the door, cold and naked.

"Sound like a personal problem to me." Shyhiem undressed, ignoring her plea.

The moment was over, and once again, he wanted nothing to do with her. He'd got a solid nut and was ready to go to bed. If Keesha thought she was going to get anything else from him, other than an unemotional fuck, she was out of her mind.

"Really, Shyhiem? It's like that? I can't get a warm rag or nothin'?"

Shyhiem chuckled and turned on the water. Feeling stupid, Keesha kicked the door and screamed, "Fuck you, Shyhiem! Ooooh... I hate you! I hope yo' fuckin' dick fall off!"

"I'm not feeling like myself since the baby."
– Beyoncé feat. Drake, "Mine"

#13

Messiah

As Messiah expected, she and Bryson never made it to dinner that weekend. Instead, they spent the entire time laid up in bed with one another. Bryson couldn't keep his hands off her. If they weren't fucking, they were eating or sleeping. Messiah dreaded the moment he'd have to leave. Unfortunately, the day was there and it was time for him to go. She had to be at the diner for an eight-hour shift in two hours. Messiah didn't want to go but desperately needed the money if she was ever going to get her car out the shop.

Plus, the loan officers were on her ass. They'd upped the ante and started calling her a few times a day. Messiah didn't want to think about her unpaid debts or clunky, old car. The afternoon sun was peeking through the blinds, shining a soft glow on their naked bodies. No sounds could be heard throughout the apartment, except her moans. Bryson was on top of her, studying the features of her face as he stroked her slow. He'd never looked at her with so much intensity in the six years they'd been together. It was as if he was displaying his emotions with each grind of his hips.

This wasn't fucking. They were making love like it was their last day on earth. The friction between her thighs was blissful. She wanted to hold onto him forever. Bryson wasn't a perfect man, but he was hers and she loved him dearly. All the lonely nights, hard work, aching limbs, creditors and long-distance conversations would be worth having him in her life for an eternity. Whatever he needed, she'd willingly provide. Seeing the sincerity of her love in her eyes, Bryson cupped her chin and planted a tender kiss on her lips.

"I love you," he whispered, pressing the side of his face against hers.

"I love you too." Messiah wrapped her arms around his back.

Moments like this she'd cherish until the day she died. The way she loved him scared her sometimes. She couldn't imagine living one second without him. He was her family and the only male figure in her life. Bryson was her anchor. Without him, she'd surely float away into outer space, never to be seen again. Lovingly, she placed a small kiss on his cheek as his back arched. He was cumming and so was she. Their bodies were completely in sync.

In his arms is where she belonged. The thought of saying goodbye and him boarding a plane tugged at her heart. She didn't want him to leave. She needed him there with her. Each time they parted ways, a piece of her died. Messiah had to remind herself to be strong. Their long-distance romance was months away from being a thing of the past. Soon, she'd have him all to herself.

Inhaling and exhaling, she and Bryson came down from their orgasmic high. It took everything in him to pull out. Her pussy was the perfect home for his penis. Fucking her was paradise. He'd miss it implicitly. Spun, Bryson rolled over onto his back and looked up at the ceiling. Messiah sat up on her elbows and eyed his limp dick. She'd sucked the life out of him that weekend. She would be surprised if he had an ounce of cum left in him. Hopefully, all the sex they'd had would satisfy him till the next time he visited.

"What time is it?" Bryson asked, catching his breath.

Messiah checked her phone.

"1:10."

"Fuck, I gotta get up." He swung his long legs over the side of the bed. "My flight leaves at 3:45."

"I don't wanna get up either but I gotta get ready for work. These bills are killin' me." She kissed his shoulder blade, hoping he'd get the hint and offer some help.

"What time you get off?" Bryson went into the bathroom to wash his dick off.

"Eleven, then I gotta turn around and be at Charter at seven and back at the diner by six."

"Damn, babe, that's a lot. You gon' overwork yourself."

"Yeah, but if I don't work, I'll be in more debt than I already am. The last thing I need is to get sued by Sun Loan and Capital One." She slipped her t-shirt and panties back on.

"Nah, you don't want that." Bryson put on his pants.

Messiah thought he'd offer some assistance but that didn't seem to be something on his mind. She didn't want to outright ask him for the money to pay the light bill. Messiah hated asking people for money, but at this point, she had no choice. If she didn't ask, her lights would get cut off.

"Speaking of bills… I was wondering if you could—" Messiah stopped speaking mid-sentence.

As she was talking, she couldn't help but notice Bryson pick up her engagement ring and place it inside the pocket of his jeans.

148

"Why you taking my ring? I mean, I know it's a little dirty, but I can clean it myself."

"Messiah, we need to talk." He pulled his shirt on over his head.

Messiah stood on the opposite side of the bed on edge. Nothing good ever came behind "we need to talk".

"What is it?" She held her breath.

Bryson let out a regretful sigh and said, "I can't marry you."

"What?" She replied, confused.

"We can't get married."

"I heard that part. Why?" She panicked.

"'Cause I'm in love with someone else and I'm going to ask her to marry me."

Suddenly, Messiah's heart started to pound through her chest. She couldn't breathe. A piercing noise that only she could hear vibrated in her eardrums causing her to wince in pain. In agony, she placed her hands over her ears to block out the excruciating sound. She couldn't have heard him right. They'd just made love. Was she being Punk'd? This had to be a cruel joke. How could he love someone else? He promised to love her forever.

"Messiah!" Bryson called out her name.

He knew she'd take the news hard, but he didn't expect her to have a mental breakdown. She was standing there, holding her head, repeating the word 'no' over and over.

"Messiah!" He called her name once more, to no avail.

"No-no-no-no-no-no-no." She shook her head, pacing back and forth. "No, you didn't fuck me and break up with me. No, you didn't. You didn't. He didn't. He ain't do that, Jesus. He didn't. I know he didn't."

Messiah was losing it. She figured if she kept saying no it would make his words untrue. Worried for her mental health, Bryson rushed to her side and grabbed her by the arms.

"Messiah!" He shook her violently.

Snapping out of her trance, she looked up at him with tear-filled eyes, praying to God this was his version of a sick joke.

"Tell me you're lying," she begged.

"I wish I was, baby, but I'm not." Bryson answered, feeling like crap.

He never wanted to hurt her but he couldn't keep up a facade anymore.

"But you can't leave me. You can't. I love you. You love me. We were supposed to get married. Whatever I did wrong, I can fix it. I swear to God I will. Just don't leave me, please," Messiah sobbed in distress.

"I'm sorry, but I can't be with you no more," Bryson said, regrettably.

"No-no-no-no," Messiah wailed as her tears swallowed her whole. "Please don't. Bryson, please! Baby, please, whatever it is, we can fix it. Whatever you need, I'll give it to you." She stared at him, helplessly.

Bryson just stood there holding her arms, staring at her with nothing to say.

"You want me to beg? Is that it, 'cause I'll do it. I'll beg; just don't leave me." Messiah tried to wrap her arms around him.

"Messiah, stop!" He pushed her back. "You're making a fool out of yourself."

Before Messiah knew it, her legs gave out on her and she fell to her knees. The cold, concrete floor almost shattered her knee caps but she couldn't feel a thing. Her whole body was numb. Bryson tried to help her back up but her body had gone limp. In a matter of seconds, the confident, strong woman she normally was disappeared. Messiah sat on the floor in a heap of tears. She never saw this coming. She thought she and Bryson were set in stone. She thought their love would withstand the odds. She never thought she'd see the day where something so concrete could so easily be thrown away.

"You can't leave me. You can't. I love you." Her chest heaved up and down.

"Messiah, get up." Bryson tried to lift her to her feet.

Messiah couldn't stand if she wanted to. Her whole world had just evaporated into thin air.

"No. I'm gonna move to Philly. We're gonna get married and have a family. Nothing's gonna change." She rocked back and forth.

"Listen, Messiah, I'm tryin' to talk to you like an adult, but if you wanna sit there like a child and talk to yourself, then go 'head." Bryson spat, fed up with her sad display.

He didn't want to be a dick, but he had a flight to catch that couldn't be missed. Messiah watched as his feet rounded the corner of the bed and disappeared. A million questions swarmed her at once. She needed answers but didn't know if her poor soul could accept them. Staring blankly at the floor, she parted her dry lips. Snot trickled from her nose.

"Who is she?"

"Oh, you done actin' like a five-year-old?" He asked, mockingly.

"Who is she?" Messiah raised her voice.

"A girl I go to school with name Kenya." Bryson replied, gathering his things.

"How long have you been seeing her?"

"A year."

Messiah squeezed her eyes tight. Each omission was more unbearable than the last.

"So, you've been lying and cheating on me for a year?" She kept her eyes shut.

"If that's how you wanna put it, then, yeah."

"What the fuck you mean if that's how I wanna put it?" Messiah's eyes popped open.
"Ain't that what you've been doing?" She turned and looked at him.

"Look, I wish the circumstances were different, but this is my reality. I love you, Messiah, I do, but I can't make my feelings for her go away—"

"Your feelings for her?" Messiah yelled, finding some of the strength she'd just lost. "What about me? What about my feelings? Don't they count for anything? I've invested six years of my life in you. Now you done went out there and had a Philly cheesesteak and lost yo' fuckin' mind! If you don't get the fuck out my face with this bullshit!" She wiped the snot from her nose and rose to her feet, weak.

"It means everything to me. I can never say thank you enough for everything you've done for me. None of that will ever go unnoticed, but I love her more, and she's having my baby."

Messiah clutched her chest and inhaled so deeply she thought she was going to have a stroke. Everything was spinning out of control. The image of Bryson with another woman and baby almost killed her.

"I didn't mean for any of this to happen but she makes me feel good about myself. We have fun together, enjoy the same things, have the same goals, she's going to be a cardiologist, she comes from a good family and they like me. With her, it's easy. I don't have to talk about bills and loans and death and be sad all the time. I can just chill."

Messiah's entire body trembled. She couldn't believe the words that were coming out of his mouth. He was painting her out to be some depressed, broke bitch, who complained too much and didn't have shit going for herself. This wasn't the same man who'd just whispered I love you during the throes of passion. She had no idea who this imposter was, or maybe she'd neglected to see this was who he was the whole time.

"Listen, Messiah, I just wanna be happy and she gives me that. I tried to stick things out wit' you—"

"Now I'm a charity case? What you felt obligated to be with me?" She said with a sudden fierceness.

"No, but you and I both know this isn't going nowhere."

"How you gon' say this ain't going nowhere? What was this weekend about? Did you come here just to fuck me and break up with me? Is that it?" She furrowed her brows.

"I thought you deserved for me to tell you in person, rather than on the phone."

"Well, thank you! That's the most considerate thing you've ever done for me!" Messiah shot sarcastically. "I'm glad my feelings meant so fuckin' much to you!"

"Messiah, this relationship is at a dead end. I'm never coming back to St. Louis. My home is in Philly now."

"I was supposed to come with you," Messiah cried. "That's what we've been working towards."

"Come to Philly and do what? Go to school? If you wanted to go to school, you would've been gone."

"I haven't gone to school 'cause I've been too busy paying for yo' fuckin' ass!" She pointed her finger at him like a gun.

"And I'ma pay you back, but that won't take away the fact that we can't be together. You're a great woman, Messiah, you are." He walked over and brushed her hair to the side. "Any man would be lucky to have you; but I always knew, deep down inside, I would want kids and you can't—"

"Don't say it!" She cut him off. "Don't you dare fuckin' say it." Messiah threatened, on the verge of losing it.

"Messiah, no matter how much you try to wish it way, you can't fuckin' have kids!" Bryson snapped.

"How could you say that to me?" Messiah looked at him with disdain.

"I gave you everything I had and more. I put my dreams on hold for you. I robbed Peter to pay Paul to make sure you were straight, to make sure you got an education. I did all of that 'cause I loved you. And if you succeeded, I succeeded, our family succeeded. Maybe then, the death of our baby wouldn't have been for nothing!" Tears trickled down her face.

"But now you stand here and tell me I get nothin' but a dead baby and a broken heart?" She hyperventilated.

"This isn't about just you, Messiah. It's about us," Bryson reasoned.

"How you think I feel seeing you cry like this? That shit don't make me feel good. For six years, I knew I could never live up to this fairytale fantasy you wanted us to be. Life ain't perfect, Messiah. It's hard and it hurts. It's not easy for me to admit that I can't love you like you want me to. What we had was good and pure in the beginning, but after the accident, you changed. You gave up on life. I didn't. I don't wanna be sad and miserable all the time. Kenya makes me happy. She pushes me forward. Staying wit' you is taking 10 steps back. Kenya and our baby are my future." He said, unapologetically.

Messiah felt like she was in the twilight zone. Everything she thought was true in life was a complete and utter lie. Bryson had shot her in the head and left her for dead. It fucked her up to learn she'd been nothing but a burden to him this whole time.

155

"You didn't think I ever wanted more?" She said in a trembling voice. "I wanted to be happy, but you try having the memory of your baby being ripped from your stomach, and your parents lying dead in the middle of the street on repeat." Messiah sobbed.

"You tell me how you go on with life after that, since you know so much! I would love to have a good night's sleep without seeing their faces. You don't think I wanna be young and carefree? You think I like walking around feeling like I'm 57? I feel old as fuck! I get tired of feeling like I'm a single mom in a Wal-Mart commercial! You know, sometimes I look in the mirror and I don't even recognize myself! I wish I knew what it felt like to laugh and smile without feeling like I'm dying on the inside. When our son died, I buried myself in you and I held on tight 'cause you were all the good I had left in this world. I hate my life, but you made living worth it! I gave you my heart, my soul, my time, my body, my money, everything! And you turn around and give my love to some bitch name Kenya? Fuck you, Bryson!" She mushed him in the head repeatedly.

"Fuck you, that bitch and that baby! On my son, I hope you have to bury that one too!" Messiah hacked up as much spit as she could and spit in his face.

Bryson stood still. Spitting on someone was the worst thing a person could do. He knew if he acted off emotion he'd put his hands on her. He swore to God he'd never hit a woman. It took everything in him not to fuck Messiah up. He had to remember the circumstances in which they were in. She was trying to hurt him so he could know how she felt. Sure, she was in pain, but wishing death on his unborn child was unforgivable. Once he regained his composure, he wiped her spit from his face and packed up

156

the rest of his things, silently. He didn't have shit else to say to her.

"That's right, nigga, pack up yo' shit and get the fuck out my house!" Messiah screamed, following him to the door. "Yo' bitch-ass don't fuckin' deserve me!" She tried to convince herself, as he walked out.

As he boarded the elevator, she tried to act like she didn't care that he was leaving and she'd never see him again. But just as the elevator doors were about to close, Messiah couldn't let him leave without getting one more thing off her chest. Quickly, she ran and placed her hand in-between the doors causing the censor to stop it from closing all the way.

"C'mon now, what the fuck are you doing?" Bryson said exasperated.

"This." She reared her hand back and slapped him so hard his bottom lip began to bleed. "Now you can leave, muthafucka." She stepped back and placed her middle finger up.

"I stay in my room. No reason to leave. We had something good. Why'd you did that to me?" –OrlandoVaughn feat. Tayllor Kaye, "NoGood4Me"

#14

Messiah

Stevie Wonder's *Songs In The Key of Life* played softly. Messiah gazed at the window, barely audible. When she wasn't working, she lay in bed incoherent to the world around her. She didn't want to live anymore. Over and over she asked God to take her life, to bring her home and reunite her with her parents and child. The last few days had been hell. Her insides felt like mush. She was weak and her body was drained of all its energy. Sadly, she'd hoped that Bryson would call and say he was sorry and beg her forgiveness. That never happened.

She'd called him several times and each time her calls were forwarded to voicemail. He didn't care that he'd broken her heart or that he'd led her on to believe he'd satisfy her needs. He'd mistaken her love for fun. Messiah felt like a fool for trusting him and believing all the empty words he spit in her ear. She didn't want it to be her reality but it was over between them. When Bryson said he didn't wanna be with her anymore, he meant it.

Messiah was sick of being in pain. She hadn't had any respite since the accident. It'd been one fucked up situation after another. She was starting to wonder if there was a curse over her life. Nobody on the planet had as much bad luck as she did. She needed a break. She needed God to shine some light on her. She couldn't take anything else bad happening.

Her stomach felt hollow. She hadn't eaten a solid meal in days. Her appetite had completely vanished. Messiah didn't want to eat anyway. All she wanted to do was sleep her misery away. Messiah spent all her time in bed. If she could, she would stay there and wither and die. She didn't know how she'd missed all the signs. When she went on his Instagram page, she realized they had been there all along. Bryson had pics of Kenya all over his page.

She was always there, hiding in the background, or in a group selfie. She'd put smiley faces and heart emojis in his comment section. Messiah had never felt so dumb. He'd played her for a fool for the world to see and she'd willingly been his lapdog. Messiah had hoped that Kenya would be ugly so she could one-up her in the looks department. But nooooo...God couldn't let her have that win.

Kenya was so damn pretty, she almost turned Messiah gay. She understood perfectly well why Bryson had cheated on her. Hell, she would've cheated on her too. The bitch was beautiful. She had long, thick hair that reached the middle of her back, even, mocha brown skin, slanted eyes, full lips and a Coke bottle shape. Kenya came from an affluent Philadelphia family. Her father was a prominent judge. They lived like royalty in a mansion. Now she knew what Bryson meant when he said she came from a *good* family. They had money.

Bryson always yearned to have the finer things in life. Messiah never aspired to have millions, wear designer clothes or travel the world. She always wanted a simple life with a family she could call her own. Kenya now had what was rightfully hers. She'd reap the benefits of the man she'd groomed Bryson to be. Messiah stupidly made him the perfect man for another woman to come swoop up.

He and Kenya would be the real-life Barack and Michelle. They'd have stellar careers with a gorgeous home, four-car garage, kids and a dog. Messiah would become an afterthought. She'd just be an old girlfriend he left behind while they lived their best life. The reality that she'd been left for dead tore her up inside. Without Bryson, she had nothing. Her entire world revolved around him. She put all her faith in him and what they could be. The two of them not being together was never a possibility.

She never once thought about what she'd do if he wasn't around. She always figured she'd move to Philly, get married, go to school, major in something, graduate, start a family and live happily ever after. Messiah had worked her body to the bone just to survive. Her life consisted of grinding hard just to keep herself afloat. She never had stars in her eyes. She didn't aspire to be anything except a wife and a mother. The only thing she'd ever aspired to do was get her GED, which she'd already done.

Ballet was a thing of the past. She was too old to start a career in dance now. After the accident, she vowed never to slip on a pair of pointe shoes ever again. The memory of how she let her parents down by quitting was too much to bear. Ballet reminded her of what her life could've been if she'd never been young, dumb and in love. At the time, the teenage love affair she had with Bryson was invigorating and thrilling. She found life in his arms. But as she lay lifeless, a regretful tear slipped from Messiah's eye.

She could've avoided all of this. Her daddy warned her about men like him but she didn't listen. She was too wrapped up in delusions of grandeur to see the truth. He'd used her for his own personal gain. He played off her love and devotion for him. Messiah was easy prey. She let him manipulate her. Deep down, she always knew she was being used. She allowed it because she wanted to feel wanted and cared for.

She figured, if she had some resemblance of love and a relationship, life would be worth sticking out. She wouldn't feel so alone. It felt good knowing someone out there in the world loved her back. Even if she had to pretend that their engagement was more solid than it was.

Messiah turned on her back and eyed the ceiling. Hot tears trickled down the sides of her face, wetting the sheets. She didn't want to admit it, but she'd allowed herself to be used by Bryson because she felt unworthy of love. What other man would want a high school dropout, with no money, no family, who couldn't bear kids? No one. She was washed up. A big fat loser.

For the life of her, Messiah didn't know why God spared her life that fateful night. She didn't want to be here anymore. There was nothing left for her. Messiah wasn't lovable. She had nothing to offer anyone. Her entire existence was a curse. Anyone that came near her, darkness followed. It was apparent that God had it out for her. She didn't know what she'd done that made Him hate her so much but she was over it.

"Just kill me, why don't you?" She groaned, rolling her eyes.

Messiah lay wishing she'd take her last breath but minutes went by and nothing happened. God obviously wasn't done with her. He wanted her to suffer some more.

"Punk-ass," she hissed.

If God wouldn't take her life, she'd eventually have to do it herself. Messiah grabbed the covers and placed them over her head. Just as she was about to get comfortable, there was a knock at the door. She didn't feel like being bothered. She'd already told Bird that she wanted to be alone. Bird normally respected her wishes. No one else cared enough to come check on her.

Unwilling to get up, she lay there pretending not to be home. Whoever it was would eventually get the hint and leave. After a few knocks, the uninvited visitor left. Relieved that she could continue her pity party for one in peace, Messiah curled up in a ball and closed her eyes. As soon as she got comfortable again, the music went off. Immediately, her eyes popped open. Messiah sat up and looked around. The light on her cable box was off. Messiah snatched the covers off her and walked into the living/kitchen area. The clock on the stove was off too.

Suddenly, it dawned on her that the person at the door was someone from the electric company. With all the drama going on in her life, she'd completely forgotten about her unpaid light bill. Hurriedly, she ran to the door, snatching it open, to see if the worker was still there. To her displeasure, the hall was clear. There was a note stuck to her door saying she would have to pay the full balance of $450.62 to get the lights back on since she failed to pay the minimum balance due. Distraught, she slammed the door shut. She didn't know what she was going to do. She didn't get paid for another week and a half and that money had to go towards the rent.

"Fuck-fuck-fuck-fuck-fuck!" She kicked the side of her couch, repeatedly.

She couldn't live without power for a day, let alone a month. She would ask Bird for the money but she was just as broke as she was. Bryson obviously wasn't an option. Messiah had to swallow her pride and call the one person she vowed to never ask for help. Swallowing what little dignity she had left, she dialed Lake's number. A part of her hoped she wouldn't pick up. That would've been too much like right. Lake answered on the third ring.

"What you want, li'l girl? I hope you're calling to apologize for ruining my bridal gown appointment." Lake said in a mocking tone.

"Excuse you? You ruined your own appointment by being a bitch. I ain't have nothin' to do with it," Messiah clarified.

"Anyway, I'm getting all my girls together next week to go bridesmaid shopping."

"Let me know what day, 'cause nine times out of ten, I'll be working."

"It'll probably be Friday or Saturday. Ooh... and you'll have to have the deposit money for your dress to put down."

Messiah's head instantly began to hurt. She didn't have money for her light bill, let alone a damn bridesmaids dress.

"That's gon' have to wait." She massaged her temples, stressed out.

"What you mean that's gon' have to wait?" Lake screeched. "You been knew about this. Why haven't you saved up?"

"Lake! I know money problems are foreign to you, but I barely have enough money to eat this week! I don't have a rich, white man taking care of me. I have bills and rent to take care of!" Messiah snapped.

"Ummmm... simmer down, sweetheart. You choose to be over there struggling. You better put the good looks Mama and Daddy gave you to good use and stop bullshittin' around with Bryson broke, pathetic-ass."

"You'll be glad to know it's over between us."

"Girl, you almost made me drop this phone! Look at God! Won't He do it? What happened? Please tell me you broke up with him," Lake said energetically.

Messiah sighed heavily. She did not want to have this conversation with Lake. It would only lead to an argument.

"No, he broke up with me," she sighed heavily.

"Huuuuuh!" Lake frowned. "Why, 'cause he got a baby on the way with that pre-med bitch?"

Messiah's heart stopped beating. A cold sweat washed over her.

"How you know about that?" She asked, petrified.

"She's a Delta. I know all of my elite sorority sisters."

"You knew and didn't tell me?" Messiah shrieked, dumbfounded.

"Girl, I don't get involved in grown folk's business. You know you can't tell a chick shit about her kids or her man." Lake studied her gel-manicured nails.

Messiah felt like she'd been stabbed in the chest. Her own sister didn't even have her back. She couldn't trust anyone... Not even her damn sister.

"Plus, we're line sisters. We have a code that we live by to protect and be there for one another."

"You mean to tell me that your line sister means more to you than your fuckin' blood sister? So much for family, right?" Messiah spat. "I can't believe you."

"Don't be mad at me. Be mad at that nigga. I told you he wasn't shit. That's why I don't fuck with black men no more. They too damn trifling for me."

"Whatever, Lake. I don't give a fuck about your preference in men. You got $450 I can borrow until the 7th?" Messiah asked, ready to get off the phone.

"What you need $450 for, Messiah?" Lake said at once.

"My lights got cut off."

"Christ on a cracker, Messiah! How you let yo' lights get cut off? What the fuck are you over there doing with your money? You need to be more responsible. Instead of buying that outfit you bought last week, you should've paid yo' damn bill. Nah, I'm not giving it to you. I ain't got it," Lake fumed. "Well, I got it. I'm just not giving it to you. I ain't got money to be wasting."

"Bitch, you just spent $20,000 on a punk-ass wedding dress but you can't let me borrow $450 to get my lights cut back on? Really, Lake? That's how you gon' do me? I swear to God you bet not ever ask me for shit!" Messiah stated furiously, ending the call.

Pacing back and forth, she tried to comprehend the fact that her sister knew the whole time that Bryson had been cheating on her and hadn't said a word. She knew Lake was a bitch but this was taking it to a whole new level. She could never forgive her for this. Messiah never had to talk to or see her again. As far as she was concerned, she was an only child. She didn't have a sister. Messiah couldn't depend on Lake for shit. All she had was herself in this cold, sad world.

It was time to go into survival mode. It would be getting dark in a few hours and she'd need light. Thank

God, she had candles. Messiah searched her kitchen drawers for a lighter or matches. Thankfully, she found two lighters. As she tried to use them, she quickly realized neither of them worked.

"Goddammit!" She threw them across the room.

Messiah grabbed her phone and called Bird. She was her only saving grace. After five rings, her voicemail kicked in. Messiah hung up and text her to call her ASAP. She would've called Twan and asked for help but he talked too much. By the time, she made it to work the next day, everyone would know her business.

It sucked she didn't have very many friends. Aunt Mae would've been there for her in her time of need if she were still alive. Messiah stood silent and tried to think of her next plan. The little food she had would go bad in less than 24 hours if she didn't get it into someone's fridge. Her stove was electric, so she wouldn't be able to cook or warm up her food in the microwave. Her phone was at 35% and would die out soon. She was royally fucked!

Think, Messiah, think, she told herself. Then a thought popped in her head. It was a long shot but her only choice. Nervously, she found Shyhiem's number in her contact list. She hoped and prayed he didn't have her blocked. She wouldn't blame him if he did. She deserved it and much more. Her first instinct was to call him but Messiah was too much of a chicken to be that brave. Instead, she texted him.

Messiah: Hey, it's me, Messiah. I'm sorry to bother u but I need ur help.

Taking a much-needed deep breath, she pressed send and hoped for the best. Four floors down in his apartment, Shyhiem held his phone in his hand stunned. He hadn't expected to hear from Messiah at all after the way she'd played him. He was just starting to get to a place where he was over wanting to talk to her. Seeing her name come across his screen only brought back the feelings he'd been trying to hide.

Anger and longing panged his chest. She didn't merit a response from him after how she'd done him. Nope, he wasn't going to fall into her trap. As far as he was concerned, Messiah could kiss his ever-loving black ass.

Twenty minutes had gone by. Messiah sat nervously biting her nails. It was becoming clearer and clearer that Shyhiem wasn't going to respond. Messiah's heart sank down to the floor. She didn't know why she thought he would have mercy on her. She'd done him dirty after he'd been nothing but kind to her. Then, she had the audacity to turn around and ask him for help. How narcissistic was that? This was exactly what she got. Feeling like shit, she texted him again.

Messiah: I understand why u haven't responded. I was a total bitch to u. I'm so sorry for lying. I should've been honest and told u the truth but I didn't and I'm sorry for that.

Shyhiem read the message, unsure of how to feel. He was happy that she'd apologized but that still didn't stop him from being pissed. A part of him felt like she was only apologizing 'cause she wanted something. Curious to see what exactly it was she wanted, he replied:

Shyhiem: What u want?

Messiah's heart skipped a beat when she heard her phone beep. Maybe God was a little bit on her side.

Messiah: Can u meet me on the 3rd floor?

Shyhiem screwed up his face. Why did she want him to meet her on the third floor? That was a weird request.

Shyhiem: I'll be there in a min

Messiah let out a sigh of relief. She didn't want to meet up on the first floor, in case Keesha was home. The third floor was neutral territory. Normally, she would've tried to make sure she looked good but now wasn't the time to be trying to be cute. She didn't care that her curly hair was practically matted to her head or that she wore a stained, holey, oversized t-shirt and lint-ridden jogging pants. Shyhiem would have to take her how she was. Now wasn't the time to be putting on airs. Messiah grabbed her keys and boarded the elevator with her house slippers on.

Once she got to the third floor, her heart pounded through her ears. She prayed she didn't faint when she saw him. She didn't have to worry about that happening because Shyhiem was nowhere to be found. Messiah rolled her eyes, feeling stupid. He wasn't coming. He'd made her believe he was so he could get revenge. On the verge of tears, she sadly turned her back to board the elevator when he called out her name.

Swiftly, she spun around to face him. He'd taken the stairs. The sight of him standing at the top of the steps, looking like a chocolate dream, caused the air in her lungs to restrict. Like always, his hair was freshly cut. Shyhiem's beard was trimmed and lined with precision. He stood with his back pressed up against the rail, wearing a longline, white t-shirt, ripped, denim jeans and crisp, new, white Air Force Ones. Messiah couldn't help but notice that he was looking her up and down with an expression of disdain on his face. She knew she looked a mess but he didn't have to be so blatant about his distaste of her appearance.

"Hey." She spoke anxiously, playing with her hair.

"What's up?" Shyhiem avoided giving her direct eye contact.

He couldn't risk falling for her again.

"Umm… this might seem crazy, but do you have a lighter I can borrow?" She bounced from one foot to another.

Shyhiem wrinkled his brow and glared at her.

"Is that what you called me up here for?"

"Yeah, I didn't wanna come knock on your door 'cause I thought that would be disrespectful. I just really need a lighter." She continued to fidget with her hair.

"You basing?" He mean-mugged her.

"What?" Messiah said, caught off guard by his line of questioning. "No. Why would you ask me something like that?"

"Have you looked at yourself lately? You got dark circles around ya eyes. It look like you ain't slept or ate in days. You shaking and shit. What the fuck is wrong wit' you?"

"I haven't eaten or slept." Messiah hugged herself.

It felt like she was being attacked, for the second time that day.

"But that's neither here nor there. Do you have a lighter or not?" She quipped with an attitude.

"Who you gettin' an attitude wit?" Shyhiem drew his head back.

"You! I don't have time for a bunch of back and forth bullshit! Just answer the question! Do you have lighter or not?" She bobbed her head from left to right.

"Fuck outta here wit' that. You askin' me for help. Don't come at me wit' no fuckin' attitude. You got life fucked up. Go ask that nigga you fuckin' for a lighter." Shyhiem turned to walk away.

"You know what? Fuck you! I don't know why I called you anyway!" Messiah's voice cracked, as she pressed the up button on the elevator.

Shyhiem tried to act like he didn't hear the desperation in her voice but couldn't ignore the sound.

"You really gettin' ready to cry over a lighter? You must be smokin'." He said, taken aback by her actions.

"Forget I even asked you. Forget I even fuckin' called." Messiah pressed the button again.

If the elevator didn't come soon, she was sure to become a blubbering fool.

"Come on!" She pled as her eyes flooded with tears.

"Messiah, you need a lighter that bad?" Shyhiem eased towards her.

Messiah ignored him and continued to slam her fingertips into the button. When the elevator didn't come, she balled up her fist and banged on the door as hard as she could. She couldn't hold back her emotions any longer. She didn't care if Shyhiem or their neighbors saw her break down. If she didn't let out the galloons of tears that begged to fall, she'd choke.

Shyhiem watched as she clasped her hands to her face and cried. He wasn't good with female emotions. He

171

didn't know if it was just that time of the month or if she was truly going through something. Whatever the source of her pain was, he wanted to be there for her. Cautiously, he took her by the arms and turned her towards him. Messiah fell into his awaiting embrace.

With her head on his chest, she let out a bucket of tears. Shyhiem reluctantly wrapped her up in his arms. He didn't want to get sucked back in, but little did he know, he'd already fallen down the rabbit hole. As soon as he saw her somber face, she had him right back on a leash. Messiah had complete and utter control over him. Around her, he couldn't contain himself.

"Tell me what's wrong." He gently patted her hair.

The sensation soothed her worries some.

"My lights got cut off," she sobbed.

Damn, that's why she needed the lighter, he thought, feeling like a dick.

"When?"

"An hour ago," she tried to steady her breathing. "And before you ask, no I don't have the money to get them cut back on and my fiancé called off our engagement so I can't ask him either. He left me for another girl he got pregnant, and my sister knew the whole fuckin' time and didn't tell me. I'm crazy in debt, the li'l bit of food I have is gonna spoil and I have no one to help me!" Messiah pulled away from his hold and wiped the steady stream of tears away. "My life is so fucked up. I can't take it anymore."

Shyhiem knew it was in poor taste to smile at her misery, but he was happy as hell to hear she and her man had broken up. With ole boy out the way, maybe they'd have a chance after all.

"I'm glad you find it funny." Messiah shook her head.

"Nah, it ain't even like that… I'm just… I'm sorry all that happened to you," he replied seriously.

"Yeah, me too." Messiah sucked in her bottom lip.

She thought she'd feel embarrassed by telling him all her personal business but Shyhiem made opening up to him easy. He didn't judge her, which felt good. Shyhiem examined her angelic face. He wanted to kiss her pain away but now wasn't the time. He had to figure out another way to take some of her stress away.

"I got an idea." He took her by the hand. "Go get dressed and pack a bag."

"Huh?" She said confused. "Pack a bag for what? I gotta go to work in the morning."

"You coming wit' me tonight."

"I can't," she panicked.

"Yes, you can, and I'm not taking no for an answer. Meet me out front in an hour." Shyhiem gave her a quick peck on the cheek before disappearing down the steps.

"You gonna be a really hard egg to crack. The more you try to resist, the more I keep wantin' that." – Anthony David, "Let Me In"

#15

Shyhiem

Shyhiem grinned as Messiah strolled down the steps with a tan, leather book bag in her hand. She looked nervous, as usual. Shyhiem pondered if she feared him or herself around him. Either way, he had to make her comfortable with being in his presence. Telling her to get dressed must've done the trick 'cause she looked 10 times better than she had an hour before. There was some color back in her cheeks. She didn't look so sickly anymore.

Shyhiem still wanted to get some food in her system. Messiah looked like she'd fuck a crackhead for a chicken sandwich. Despite how famished she appeared, her beauty still shined through. Shyhiem hadn't seen her dolled up since the night they met at Blank Space. Since then, he'd only seen her in her work clothes. He'd almost forgotten how pretty she could be when dressed up.

Messiah looked like a supermodel. Her hair was parted down the middle and pulled back into a messy ponytail. Two pieces of hair framed the sides of her face. A pair of oversized, round-framed shades shielded her weary eyes. From what he could tell, she wore no makeup. Just a dab of nude, pink lip gloss to accentuate her voluptuous lips. She wore a sky blue, strapless, swing dress that tied into a bow on each arm, brown, suede, platform, strappy, open-toed heels and a brown, leather, fringed purse. The suede, strappy heels intertwined around her slim ankles and tied into a bow, emphasizing her bronzed legs. Shyhiem loved that she didn't have to do much to be sexy. Her style was simple and fly.

"I'm here. Now what?" She stood before him.

"Let me just take you in for a second." Shyhiem made love to her body with his eyes.

"Stop. You're making me nervous." Messiah fidgeted with a piece of her hair.

"Stop fidgeting." Shyhiem grabbed her hand and placed it down to her side. "You look beautiful." He assured, taking the bag from her hand.

"Thank you." Messiah allowed his compliment to sink in. "Where are we going?" She asked, as he escorted her to the passenger side of the car.

"To the movies first." Shyhiem placed his hand on the small of her back and helped her inside.

A tingle shot up Messiah's spine.

"Why do I need an overnight bag if we're going to the movies?" She questioned as he got in.

"'Cause you're spending the night with me." He said, as his phone started to ring.

It was Mayhem. Shyhiem sent the call to voicemail.

"Oh, hell naw." Messiah tried to open the door.

"Chill." Shyhiem stopped her from escaping. "I just want you to have a good night's sleep. That's it." He grabbed her seat belt and pulled it firmly over her chest.

Messiah inhaled deeply as the strap caressed her breasts.

"I'm not tryin' to fuck you." Shyhiem stared deep into her eyes, wishing the strap was his hand. "I mean, I am, but not yet. Not until you beg me to." He clicked the seat belt closed then winked his eye.

Completely turned on, Messiah tried to steady the heartbeat in her clit.

"At least you're honest," she blushed.

"You'll only get the truth from me." Shyhiem started the engine.

"I have a question though. How am I going to spend the night with you? What you gon' tell yo' baby mama to scoot over?" Messiah teased.

"Ha-ha-ha. You got jokes. Nah, I got this li'l spot I wanna take you to." Shyhiem pulled away from the curb.

I need to take my ass back in the house, Messiah thought, staring anxiously out the window. She had no business going anywhere with Shyhiem. There was no telling what might happen if she was around him unsupervised for too long. If he kept on looking at her like she was his last meal, they'd never make it to the theater. All Messiah could think about was herself... between his legs... on her knees. The fact that she was having thoughts like that was ridiculous.

She was still experiencing internal bleeding from the way Bryson ripped her heart out. Messiah didn't want to drag Shyhiem into her mess. Her head was all over the place. She didn't know what she wanted or what her next move was. The only thing she knew for sure was that liking Shyhiem wasn't an option. It didn't matter how fine he was or how much he made her feel like a queen; they could never be together.

Messiah glanced over at Shyhiem while he focused on the road. It was hard convincing herself that she wasn't as into him as she let on. The mere sight of him made her want to push her panties to the side and let him slide through.

"I can't even remember the last time I went to the movies. It used to be one of my favorite things to do," Messiah tried to get her mind off the friction between her thighs.

Shyhiem's cologne was driving her nuts. She wanted to straddle his lap and let him take her right then and there.

"That's all I do is go to the movies. I got my kids loving it too."

"What are their names?" Messiah asked curiously.

"Sonny and Shania."

"That's cute. They're twins, right?"

"Yeah. They bad as hell but they're the best things that's ever happened to me. They keep me grounded. Without them, I don't know where I'd be. I used to be a wild boy."

"I bet," Messiah grinned, slightly.

"I ain't gon' even lie. I was bad as fuck growing up."

"I kind of figured that when you broke my customer's nose."

"He was a shithead. He deserved it," Shyhiem scowled, gripping the steering wheel.

He'd forgotten all about the prick from the diner. If given the chance, he wouldn't do anything differently, except break his nose and blacken his eye.

"He deserved a lot of things, but not that. I believe in standing up for yourself, but violence only begets violence," Messiah reasoned.

"I guess," Shyhiem shrugged.

Being violent was how he survived and functioned. He didn't believe in doing a lot of talking. People mistook kindness for weakness. In the hood, you could never be looked at as weak. You had to stand firm, confident and tall. You couldn't go around letting people punk you. Maybe Keesha was right. Maybe he and Messiah were too different. She'd never accept his temper or street mentality.

But he was in too deep to give up now. He liked her a whole hell of a lot. Shyhiem finally had Messiah right where he wanted her. Which was with him. He hoped that once she got to know him, she'd understand why he was the way he was.

"So, what movie are we going to see?" Messiah asked as they pulled up to MX movie theater.

"I thought I'd let you pick but I really wanna see Suicide Squad."

"Shut up! Me too!" Messiah shrilled, shaking his arm. "I've been dying to see that movie. I'm a huge DCEU and MCU fan. I usually only get to see the movies on bootleg but I love comic book films," she smiled, gleefully.

Shyhiem looked at her in awe. He never thought a girl as elegant and poised as she was would be a comic book nerd. She didn't seem like the type to be into the genre. Still skeptical, he asked, "Who's your favorite superhero?"

"Well, it depends. If we're talking about the MCU, then I love Black Panther, Wolverine, Scarlet Witch, Iron Man, Black Widow and Bucky aka The Winter Soldier. Then from DCEU, I like Harley Quinn, of course, The Joker, Batman, Wonder Woman and Dead Shot."

"Damn, you ain't lying. You really are a fan." He said amazed.

This girl gotta be my soulmate, he thought.

"What? You thought I was lyin'?" Messiah nervously tucked her hair behind her ear.

"Man... you keep it up and I'ma fuck around and fall in love with you." He traced the corner of her lips with his thumb.

The touch of his hand caused Messiah's body to quake. His charm was wearing on her heart. If he kept it up, their friendship would turn into something more.

"We should go inside." She turned her head to avoid further contact.

Messiah liked Shyhiem a lot but she'd only been single a few days. She couldn't possibly jump into anything else so soon. Her heart still belonged to Bryson, no matter how dirty he'd done her.

Shyhiem peeped how quickly she jumped out of the car. He hated that she was so cautious with him. He wanted her to let down her guard and give herself to him freely, without hesitancy. He understood that her dude had just left her. He'd betrayed her trust. Her heart was on high-alert. She needed time to heal but Shyhiem wanted her all to himself. It was high time she learned what it felt like for a real man to love her.

"Have you ever been here before?" He asked, as they walked in.

"No, going to the movies is a luxury for me."

Shyhiem eyed her quizzically.

"Why, 'cause you work so much?"

"That's part of it, but the real reason is because I can't afford it," Messiah replied, truthfully.

It was best she lay everything on the line upfront. If Shyhiem didn't wanna be friends with her 'cause she was a broke-ass, it was best she knew now.

"I understand. Waitresses don't make that much money. Have you ever thought about doing something else for a living?"

"That's the thing, waitressing at the diner is my second job." Messiah said as they boarded the elevator. "I work at Charter doing the day."

"Damn, and you still broke?" Shyhiem blurted out.

As soon as he said it, he regretted the way it came out.

"My bad." He said, noticing her face drop. "I ain't mean it like that."

"It's ok. To be honest wit' you, I'm in a lot of debt. I took out a few loans and maxed out my credit cards to put my ex through school. He promised to pay me back, but now that we're broken up, I'm not going to see that money."

"That's fucked up." Shyhiem balled up his fist.

He wanted to find her so-called ex-fiancé and beat the shit out of him. Shyhiem mentally vowed that if he ever saw his wack-ass again he was going to fuck him up on sight.

"I'm a big girl. I'll be alright... eventually," Messiah responded unsure.

Shyhiem wanted to say something comforting but didn't know her well enough to know what would make her feel better. He didn't want to offend her any more than he already had, so he stayed quiet and followed her inside the theater. It was a Thursday afternoon so the place wasn't packed. There were only a few people there. The men in attendance couldn't take their eyes off Messiah. They eyed her like she was a piece of steak.

She was totally oblivious to all the male attention she received. Messiah was just happy to be there. She truly didn't know how effortlessly pretty she was. Shyhiem appreciated her good looks but didn't like all the dudes ogling her. Messiah was his and he'd fuck up every nigga in there to make them understand that. After standing in line for a few minutes, he ordered their tickets and then asked her what she wanted to eat.

"Nothing. I'm fine." She lied, as her stomach growled.

"Messiah, stop wit' the shy girl shit. Yo' stomach over there sounding like an African safari."

"I swear, I'm fine," she giggled. "You gettin' me out the house and paying for the tickets is enough for me."

"Look, I don't know what type of dudes you used to dealing with, but when you're around me, you can have whatever you want; so stop bullshittin' and let me take care of you."

Messiah gazed into his eyes, wondering if she could trust him. She wasn't used to relying on anyone but herself. People always had an ulterior motive. As far as she knew, Shyhiem could've just been being nice to her so he could get inside her pants.

"I'm not used to anybody doing anything for me. I've always had to take care of myself."

"Not anymore." Shyhiem slipped his hand into hers. "I'm here now."

"Forget your foolish pride." –Aaron Neville, "Tell It Like It Is"

#16

Messiah

For two hours and seventeen minutes, Shyhiem and Messiah sat inside the dark theater feasting on popcorn, quesadillas and soda. The David Ayer written and directed Suicide Squad movie had its flaws, but overall, they enjoyed the madcap array of zany characters. Messiah couldn't remember the last time she had so much fun. Getting out of the house and watching a movie was exactly what she needed.

She felt her age, for once. For two hours, the weight of the world was lifted off her shoulders. She had Shyhiem to thank for that. He kept her mind off her troubles for a while. However, when they exited the theater, the thought of returning home to no power and spoiled food flooded her mind. She couldn't act like the problem didn't exist forever; but for one night, she wanted to live without worry. Who knew when she'd get to have another night like this.

By the time, they made it back to the car, the sun had fallen. Messiah relished every second of the warm September air on her skin. She'd forgotten how alluring St. Louis could be at night. Soft, R&B music played as they rode down Washington Avenue. It wasn't long before they arrived at their destination. Messiah looked up at the extravagant, loft building.

The place looked like something out of a magazine. Shyhiem grabbed her bag and unlocked her door. With her hand in his, he led her into the building. The entrance on Washington Avenue was tree-lined and opened to a welcoming lobby with views of the courtyard. The courtyard had an indoor pool and a fitness center with plenty of floor space, machines, and equipment so the residents could stretch out. The building even had a children's playroom and a rooftop terrace.

Shyhiem checked in with the 24-hour front desk concierge before heading upstairs. Messiah's jaw dropped when they walked inside the lavish loft. Upon entry, she was introduced to a spacious kitchen/living room area. The kitchen was stunning. It was equipped with a gas cooktop, retractable, downdraft hood, and wine storage to keep vintage wines cool.

Floor-to-ceiling windows lined the entire living room with a perfect view of the downtown skyline. The loft had a soothing master bath. The Roman tub was made from Calacatta Paonazzo marble. There was even a second bathroom that was used as a powder room for guests. A gorgeous master bedroom with a balcony attached finished off the magnificent space. There was no way that a man that delivered packages for UPS could afford such an extravagant loft.

"This place is amazing." Messiah stood outside on the balcony, shoeless.

Millions of twinkling stars gleamed around the moon. Messiah held onto the railing like it was a ballet bar and flexed her toes. She had no idea that Shyhiem was standing in the doorway of the balcony filming her every move. He was blown away by the fact that she was standing on the tips of her toes as if it were nothing. The strength she had in her lower body was remarkable. Her toned legs were a work of art. Shyhiem zoomed the camera in as she flexed and arched her foot. Everything about Messiah was perfect. God made pure gold when he created her.

"Let me find out you sell dope." She looked around at the city view, astonished.

"Not anymore," Shyhiem confessed, still filming her.

Messiah did a pirouette around to face him causing the hem of her dress to fly up and slightly reveal the fabric of her underwear. Shyhiem was thankful he'd caught it all on camera.

"Is that how you could afford this place?"

"Nah, this one of my brother's cribs. He barely ever comes here so he let me use it whenever I want to get away."

"'I'ma let you know right now… I don't deal with no drug dealers or nothing like that."

"You good, shawty. That part of my life is over with."

"Good. I'm happy to hear that," Messiah smiled, and twirled her leg from side-to-side.

"How did you do that?" Shyhiem eyed her legs.

"Do what?" She looked down.

"That thing with your feet." He pointed.

"Oh, I took ballet for over 16 years." Messiah noticed that he was filming her on his iPhone. "Why are you filming me?" She immediately became self-conscious and stood flat on her feet.

"So, I can have memories of you when you're not around." He focused the camera on her face.

Messiah bit the inside of her lower lip and hid behind her hair. She didn't have time for Shyhiem to force his way into her heart. She wasn't ready to open herself up to him, or anyone else, for that matter. Shyhiem was nothing short of persistent. He was the kind of man that could fill up all the empty spaces she tip-toed around.

"What are you, an amateur filmmaker or something?" She twirled her hair around her finger.

"I used to wanna go to film school but now it's just some shit I do for fun. Stop hiding yourself." He demanded, wanting to see all of her.

"No." She shook her head.

"What are you afraid of?"

Messiah looked directly in the camera lens and said, "You."

Shyhiem drew his head back and promptly stopped recording.

"Why?" He died to know.

Messiah paused for a second. Shit was getting too real too fast.

"'Cause… I don't get it." She met his gaze then looked away quickly.

"Get what?"

"Why you like me so much. Look at me. I have nothing. My own fiancé doesn't even want me. And I have no electricity, in case you've forgotten."

"Your ex is a fuckin' idiot and I haven't forgot about your lights." Shyhiem placed his hands inside his pocket. "They're back on, by the way."

"How?" Messiah said taken aback.

"A friend of mine works at Ameren. I called before we left and had it taken care of for you."

"Why did you? How—" Messiah held her head confused.

Shyhiem walked over to her and tenderly placed a kiss on her forehead.

"Why did you do that?"

"'Cause I like you and I wanna make sure you're straight."

"But why? No one ever does anything for me. No one ever chooses me." She admitted, wrapping her arms around his waist.

Shyhiem cupped the back of her head and massaged her scalp.

"Messiah, before I met you, I didn't believe in love at first sight. I thought it was a bunch of bullshit and then I saw you. This shy, lonely girl who'd forgotten how beautiful she was, and I thought if I could wake up every morning to that face, I could get through anything."

"Really?" Messiah said in a daze.

"Really."

"Wow… I'm like, totally wet right now. That's like the sweetest thing I've ever heard."

Shyhiem took a step back and took out his phone.

"Take off your clothes." He pressed record.

"What?" The heartbeat in Messiah's clit started thumping.

"Take... off... your clothes." Shyhiem's eyes went dark.

Messiah was a good girl, but behind those pretty, little eyes of hers was a beast. She wanted to be daring. She just needed a reason to give into her dark desires.

"Umm, why on earth would I do that? I don't know you. Besides, what if somebody sees?" She looked around.

"Let 'em see if they wanna look." Shyhiem took a seat in one of the patio chairs.

"This is crazy." Messiah coiled into a ball on the inside.

She couldn't even look Shyhiem in the eye. If she did, her knees would weaken. The thought of revealing the most sacred parts of her body to him turned her on. It scared her that she wanted to get naked. What did she have to lose? She'd lost her dignity ages ago. Messiah was tired of being a good girl. She wanted to live life on the edge. After all she'd been through in the past week, it was time she left her inhibitions at the door.

Life was too short to be so tightly wound all the time. *Fuck it. You only live once,* she thought, untying the bows of her dress and letting it fall to the ground. Messiah tried to muster up the confidence she needed to be a sexpot but failed miserably. When she realized, she was standing butt ass naked in front of a man she'd known for five seconds, she almost passed out. She had completely forgotten about her stomach.

190

"Oh, my god. What the hell have I done?" She bent down to pick up her dress.

"Leave it there." Shyhiem spoke in a commanding tone.

Messiah didn't know why, but she listened and stood up straight. All day long he'd fantasized about ripping her clothes off and placing a trail of kisses from her tits to her clit. Shyhiem eyed her tear-drop-shaped breasts and small hips. There wasn't a blemish on her body except for a long, surgical scar going down the center of her stomach. Shyhiem wondered how she'd got it.

"Do you know how sexy you are?" He admired her golden frame.

"No." Messiah covered her breasts.

"Put your hands down. Let me see you."

Flushing in distress, she reluctantly did as she was told. Shyhiem stopped recording and got into her personal space.

"I'm gonna make love to you now." He said, as a statement and not a request.

"That's not what I want tonight." Messiah melted as he lifted her up into his arms.

"What is it that you want then?"

"You know," she replied sheepishly.

"Say it." Shyhiem's dick grew inside his pants.

Messiah paused for a second. She couldn't be afraid. It was time to be the grown woman she claimed to be.

"I want you to fuck me… hard."

Seconds later, her back met with the sheets. Messiah was dripping wet. A deep moan of pleasure escaped through her lips as Shyhiem stroked the outer part of her thigh. Oh, how she wished she could control her trembling lips. She couldn't. Shyhiem looked down at her body. He didn't know where to start.

"Praise be to the fool that let you go." He kissed the base of her foot.

Her ex couldn't possibly know how rare she was. He would bet a million dollars that the bitch he'd knocked up was half the woman Messiah was. Her ex was a loser. He probably told her life was black and white. Shyhiem would show her the truth. He'd add a little color to the canvas. With each kiss, a piece of Messiah's broken heart started to mend.

Shyhiem reached her stomach. Without hesitation, he caressed her abdomen and lovingly kissed her scar. Tears stung Messiah's eyes. She knew the feeling was only temporary but she'd take what she could get. She needed him to take her mind off the hole in her chest. Having sex with him was the perfect remedy, but before they went any further, there was something she had to confess.

"Wait!" She placed her hand on his chest.

"What's up?" Shyhiem panted, just getting started.

"Before we go any further, I have to tell you something."

"What is it?" Shyhiem kissed her hard nipple.

"I've only been with one person."

Shyhiem grinned slowly. The only thing that would've been better is if she said she was a virgin.

"No worries, love. That just means I'ma be your last." He enveloped her lips with a steamy kiss.

Messiah released a throaty moan. Shyhiem's hands were all over her body. His tongue tickled the base of her ear. Messiah wanted to taste him. Never in her life had she wanted to suck a man's dick more. Up on his knees, Shyhiem pulled his shirt over his head, revealing a stomach full of firm abs. His sweet, mocha skin shone under the night's sky. Messiah had to be dreaming. This was too good to be true. Shyhiem's body was carved out like an African god.

His arms reminded her of mountain peaks. The man looked like he worked out every day. He even had the Ken doll slits going down the sides of his waist. Messiah swallowed hard. She wasn't sure if she was ready for this. Things were moving way too fast. Yet, she still wanted him more than the air she breathed. With a deliberate gaze, Shyhiem unbuckled his belt. Messiah bit her bottom lip. There were no words to describe how fine he was. Shyhiem made her want to be bad. Maybe with him she could live out her fantasies and not be demeaned because of them. Ignoring her fear, she lifted her arms and surrendered her wrist to him.

Messiah didn't want to make love. She didn't love him. She was enthralled by him. She wanted him to fuck the sadness out of her. Shyhiem examined her face before making a move. He had to make sure this was what she really wanted, because once he went there, it was no turning back. There wasn't a hint of uncertainty in her eyes. She wanted to be controlled. Shyhiem was more than ready to give her exactly what she wanted. Taking each of her wrists, he pulled her up. *This is really happening,* Messiah thought, as he placed her hands behind her back and secured the belt around her wrists.

Hungry for more, she watched as he unzipped his jeans and pulled his long, thick instrument out. Shyhiem's dick was more than a mouthful. It was so big, she wasn't sure all of it would fit inside her pussy or her mouth. His dick was massive. It was beautiful, black and wide. Never the one to back down from a challenge, she licked her lips as Shyhiem stroked his shaft.

"I wanna taste." She said, gazing up into his eyes.

Shyhiem happily obliged her request and lined his swollen cock up to her mouth. To his surprise, she closed her eyes and greedily took her first lick. It was sinful. Shyhiem's dick reminded her of the finest chocolate known to man.

"Mmmmmmm." She moaned, sucking on the tip.

"Look at me." He commanded, grabbing the back of her head.

Messiah did as she was told and stared up at him through her long lashes. The expression on his face sent her into a tailspin. Shyhiem gave her a look of pure longing and desire. Hunger pulsated through her veins as she took more of him in her mouth. His dick was so large, it caused her to gag but Messiah liked it.

"It's so big." She whimpered as spit slid down her chin.

"You can handle it." Shyhiem assured, running his fingers through her curly hair.

Messiah wanted to sing his name, his dick tasted so good. His paralyzing gaze had her trapped. Shyhiem could do with her as he pleased. The belt wrapped around her wrists made her his for the taking. Messiah's overheated flesh tingled as his dick stretched her mouth wide. She could cum just like that. Messiah had never gotten off on sucking dick before, but with Shyhiem, her senses were on overload.

"Shyhiem." She moaned, sliding her tongue up and down his rigid shaft. "Oh, my god, you taste so good. Fuck my mouth." She urged, surprised at her own omission.

Messiah couldn't believe she was acting like this. She didn't even recognize herself. All her inhibitions had vanished. Shyhiem held his head back and tried not to explode. Messiah was already giving him the best head he'd ever received. If he fucked her mouth, he was guaranteed to cum. He tried to hold out but the sight of him fucking her tight, wet mouth was too good to pass up. Shyhiem gripped her long, black hair and slid his dick up and down her taste buds.

"Yessssss." Messiah groaned, loving every second.

The bed had become their king-sized wrestling mat; and so far, Shyhiem was getting the best of her. The head of his dick throbbed with distress, ready to shatter. Shyhiem wasn't ready to cum yet. He had to give Messiah the best of him. Swiftly, he pulled out of her slick mouth and nudged her back onto the bed. The restriction of laying on her back with her wrists tied heightened what would happen next. Shyhiem commanded that she part her legs for him. Wetting his fingers with her spit, he placed his hand

195

on the face of her pussy. Never taking his eyes off her, he circled her clit with his fingertips.

"Ahhhhhhh," Messiah breathed heavily.

She wanted desperately to stroke his shaft while he played with her pussy but she couldn't. The belt had her bound. Shyhiem had complete control of her.

"Ahhhhhhhhhhhhhhh!" She shrilled, unable to keep still as he placed two fingers inside her and kissed her lips.

"Fuck!" She squeezed her eyes shut.

Shyhiem was fingering her pussy like a pro. The sound of his fingers pumping in and out of her wanton pussy echoed throughout the bedroom. Messiah enjoyed the sensation and allowed herself to be deeply submerged in pleasure.

"Look at me." Shyhiem's deep voice urged.

Flushing in distress, Messiah's eyes popped open and glared into his. He had no idea what he was doing to her. Feeling his breath on her ear while he manipulated the folds of her pussy was torture of the best kind. She would never forget this night. Messiah moved her hips to the rhythm of his velvet touch. She was going to ride his fingers like a wave.

"Please, don't stop. Please… don't." She begged as the belt dug into her skin.

Shyhiem could tell she was only seconds away from cumming. Like the control freak he was, he quickly pulled his fingers out of her cave.

"No-no-no, please don't stop. I was just about to cum," Messiah whined.

Shyhiem ignored her plea for gratification. Messiah would climax when he let her. Plus, the longer he prolonged her orgasm, the more intense it would be. After placing on a condom, he lay behind her in the spooning position. His dick slipped into her hot, awaiting canal with ease. Shyhiem's eyes rolled to the back of his head as he gripped Messiah's throat.

"Mmmmm! Ahhhhhhhhhhh, Shyhiem!" Messiah's head bounced as he fucked her slow and hard.

"You like that, don't you?" He squeezed her throat tighter.

"Yes!" Messiah wailed, sounding like a little girl. "Don't stop fucking me."

Shyhiem pounded her pussy at a steady pace. Messiah's tight, little pussy could barely hold all of him.

"Oh, my god, Shyhiem!" She screamed as he flipped her over onto her back.

Face-to-face, Messiah wrapped her legs around his back as he ran his tongue up her neck.

Sitting on his knees, Shyhiem teasingly glided his wet dick up and down the lips of her pussy, as she looked on in agony.

"Please, Shyhiem, fuck me." Messiah wanted him back inside her in the worst way.

So much that she began to wind her hips until the tip of his dick slipped in.

"Oh, my god," she quivered.

Shyhiem gripped both of her thighs and fucked her pink pussy at a feverish pace. Messiah's breasts jiggled back and forth as she cried out in ecstasy. Shyhiem had begun toying with her clit while fucking her. It was too much. Messiah couldn't keep up. His dick was too big and filling. It felt like she was going to break. Shyhiem's dick was hitting her spine. Wanting all of him, she wound her hips some more. Shyhiem held onto her waist, as her clit rubbed against his pelvis.

"FUCK!" He groaned, unable to keep his composure anymore.

Messiah's melodic moans and her slick pussy was driving him insane. He wanted to fill her up with his hot cum. She was fucking him back and he loved it. He hated when a woman just lay there and did nothing. Messiah let it be known how bad she yearned for him. Shyhiem wanted to stay inside her forever. He wanted to wear the scent of her on his tongue until it naturally slipped away.

"Shyhiem, I'm finna cum!" She cried.

The build up to her orgasm was so intense, tears literally fell from her eyes.

"Cum for me, baby. I wanna see you cum." Shyhiem quickened his pace.

"Ah-ah-ah… mmm… ahhhhhhhhh!" Messiah arched her back, climaxing.

Shyhiem's lips never left hers as she came long and hard all over his dick. He couldn't contain his load as she continued to circle her hips. Shyhiem wanted to cum all over her lips, supple tits and taut nips.

"Fuuuuck." He closed his eyes as his body shuttered.

Shyhiem lay spun. He'd never experienced a nut so intense. It was magnificent. He had to have her again and again and again. There was no way he was done with her. Now that he'd gotten a taste, he was never letting her go.

"What we did last night, ooh it was amazing." – SiR feat. Masego, "Ooh Nah Nah"

#17

Messiah

Your heartbeat woke me up this morning. Still got the taste of you on the tip of my tongue. The lyrics to SiR's song *Ooh Nah Nah* came to mind as Shyhiem lay awake gazing at Messiah's innocent face. Her long spiral curls were sprawled over the pillowcase. Her bottom lip was poked out. Messiah looked so peaceful while she was asleep. He didn't wanna wake her but his dick was hard and he was ready for round four.

They'd gone at it three times the night before. Each time better than the last. The orgasms they experienced were mind-blowing. Fuck weed and liquor, Messiah had become his drug of choice. Her kisses were addictive. He hated that they had to get up for work in an hour. Shyhiem wanted nothing more than to stay balls deep inside her for the rest of the day.

"No." Messiah stirred in her sleep.

Shyhiem watched as her face tightened in despair. She was having a bad dream.

"No-no. I'm sorry. I didn't mean it." She tossed and turned. "Mama, I'm sorry. Please, don't leave. Come back!" She cried, jumping up out of her sleep.

Shyhiem watched as she sat up and tried to catch her breath. Her chest heaved up and down, frantically. Messiah ran her hand through her unruly hair and glanced around. For a minute, she couldn't remember where she was. Then, she looked over and spotted Shyhiem's worried face staring back at her. He must've thought she was crazy.

"You a'ight?" He asked, genuinely worried.

All the color had drained from her face.

"I'm fine." She flushed in distress.

Messiah wanted to curl up into a ball and die. It was way too soon for him to see the crazy side of her. Messiah didn't even know if she wanted him to see that side of her at all. What they'd done the night before was a mistake. She had too much shit on her plate to be adding fucking Shyhiem to the pile. Messiah had to pull it together - and quick. Lake was right. She couldn't continue to make one bad decision after another. When was she going to learn her lesson?

Spending time and having sex with Shyhiem was good for the moment, but after the moment faded, reality set in. She still loved Bryson. It was stupid but she did. Messiah couldn't erase the last six years of her life as if they didn't happen. And yes, he'd moved on to someone else, but that didn't stop her from hoping he'd realize he'd made a huge mistake.

She and Bryson belonged together. Deep down inside she knew he still loved her. They could work it out. It would be hard but she'd accept his child - eventually. She'd love it as if it were her own. Maybe him getting another girl pregnant was a blessing in disguise. Since she couldn't have kids of her own, this would solve their infertility problem. Messiah didn't want to lead Shyhiem on or break his heart but she couldn't possibly give him what he wanted. No matter the circumstances, she belonged to someone else.

"What was that about?" He studied her face.

"Nothing, I just had a bad dream. Listen, I gotta go. I gotta get home so I can get ready for work." She pulled the covers off her naked body.

"Hold on." Shyhiem stopped her. "You packed an overnight bag, remember?"

"Aww... yeah." Messiah recalled. "Well, let me get up so I can start getting dressed."

"You still got an hour before the alarm goes off."

"I move really slow. If I don't start getting dressed now, I'll be late," she lied.

She needed to be as far away from Shyhiem as possible.

"Why you keep running?"

"I'm not," Messiah lied again. "I just don't wanna be late."

"Lie to me again and see what happen." Shyhiem threatened, frustrated.

Messiah glared at him. She wasn't in the least bit afraid of him. She knew behind his menacing demeanor was a man whose feelings were hurt. Messiah hated that she was doing this to him. She wished she could be what he wanted her to be.

"I gotta go, Shyhiem. I shouldn't be here in the first place." She tried her best to keep it together.

It was too early in the morning for a breakdown.

"What are you talkin' about?" He asked confused.

"I shouldn't be here." Messiah's face grew hot.

"I get that, but why not? We had a good night. Don't ruin it by gettin' all in yo' head." He wrapped his arm around her waist.

"Shyhiem, please, just let me go." Messiah moved his arm from around her.

"Nah, I'm not lettin' you get away that easy." He pulled her into him and kissed her stomach.

Messiah stroked the top of his head, enveloped by his touch. This shit was crazy. Every time he touched her, she spiraled out of control. She hated that her body betrayed her mind each time they came in contact. She needed to get out of there but her body was paralyzed. All she could do was lay still and relish in his erotic kisses.

"How did this happen?" He traced her scar with his finger.

"I don't wanna talk about it." She tried to push him away again.

Talking about the accident wasn't an option. She had to get out of there but Shyhiem was too heavy for her to move. Instead of letting her get out of bed, he made her straddle his lap. Messiah closed her eyes and inhaled deeply. As soon as she sat down, Shyhiem gripped her ass cheeks and slipped deep inside her honey-coated walls. He wasn't playing fair. He knew she could never say no to his dick. She hadn't been able to the three times before.

Messiah would do anything for the high. His hand was creeping up her neck. Messiah placed her head down causing her hair to fall over her hooded eyes. Shyhiem hated when she tried to hide herself from him. He wanted to see all of her. Watching her facial expressions as he fucked her wet hole gave him ultimate pleasure. Shyhiem pushed her hair back and made her look at him. Messiah locked eyes with his and groaned. She should've been on her way home, not riding his dick like it was breakfast, lunch and dinner.

She had to find a way to break the spell he'd cast on her. His voodoo was black magic. If she allowed herself to succumb to his love, she'd fall so deep she'd never be able to come up for air. Messiah couldn't allow that to happen. *But my God does he taste good,* she thought, gliding her tongue across his lips. He had her wide open. It didn't even matter that he hadn't used a condom. She was sprung. At that moment, whatever he wanted of her he could have.

"God, help me." She panted, about to cum.

Messiah had been bullshitting about getting to work late, but after what was supposed to be a five-minute quickie ended up being an hour and a half long fuck session. She'd rode Shyhiem's cock until her thighs burned and he'd fucked her bent over in the shower till the water turned cold. Messiah had never cum so much in her life. She didn't know if she could take anymore. She needed time to think, to get her head on straight.

Normally, when she rode the MetroLink home, she'd decipher her thoughts. Shyhiem insisted that he'd pick her up from work though. He said there was no way in hell she was taking public transportation as long as he was around. Messiah appreciated his generosity but it was all too much. He was rushing her into something she wasn't ready for. He acted like she wasn't engaged to marry someone else just a few days before. The way she was fucking him, she was acting like she hadn't been either. She had no right to be upset with him when she was constantly sending him mixed signals.

205

"Well looky-looky. Here come Cookie." Twan raised his brow as she walked in.

Messiah glared at him and stifled a laugh.

"Meeting in the ladies' room. Now!" Bird insisted, getting her attention.

Messiah rolled her eyes and followed her and Twan inside the restroom. If she didn't get to her cubicle soon and log into the system, she'd get written up. Her pay would already be docked for being late.

"Umm... excuse me," Colleen snapped. "You aren't supposed to be in here." She looked Twan up and down.

"And you ain't supposed to wear white after Labor Day but you did anyway." He curled his upper lip, disgusted by her all-white getup.

"I'm telling Tom." Colleen stormed out of the restroom.

"Fuck off, Colleen!" He yelled after her.

"Girl, where in the hell have you been?" Bird questioned, worried sick. "I got your message. I have been tryin' to call you all night. Are you alright?"

"I'm fine. I'm sorry. I forgot to call you back. I had a very *busy* night," Messiah smirked, smoothing back her hair.

"Stop, rinse and repeat." Twan sniffed her neck. "You got some dick."

"I thought it was something different about her." Bird eyed her quizzically. "Please don't tell me you fucked Bryson again."

"No." Messiah waved her off. "He's not even in town."

"Good."

"Well, who you give the drawz to, girl?" Twan died to know.

"Remember that guy I met that night at Blank Space?" Messiah asked Bird.

"No." She shook her head.

"He was the one I bumped into outside," Messiah probed.

"Ohhhhhhhhh… ok, now I remember. Li'l sexy daddy. He could get it."

"He got it last night." Messiah raised her hand for a five.

"Get the fuck outta here." Bird said surprised.

"Didn't you just play him about a week ago?" Twan inquired.

"Yeah, y'all was supposed to go out, then Bryson punk-ass came into town and fucked everything up," Bird snarled.

"We worked everything out. He even got my lights cut back on for me," Messiah announced.

"Ok; sexual chocolate gotta coin."

"Messiah, your lights were cut off and you ain't tell me? Girl, I would've helped you." Twan pushed her arm.

"I love you dearly but you got a big mouth. I wasn't telling you shit," she laughed.

"Rude." Twan scoffed, appalled.

"Ain't she," Bird agreed. "Shyhiem sound like a winner, girl. This nigga up here paying light bills and shit. You betta keep him. He sounds like a good man."

"No, he's not," Messiah disagreed. "He's perfect," she sighed.

"And what's wrong with that? You act like that's a bad thing." Bird challenged, seeing the expression on her face.

"The problem is, I can't see myself being in anybody's arms but Bryson's," she replied, honestly.

"Girl, ain't you tired of being a fool?" Twan quipped. "This nigga is about to have a whole baby with someone else."

"Right," Bird agreed. "I went on that heffa Instagram page. They just found out the sex of the baby. She posted the ultrasound."

"Didn't that baby look a mess?" Twan clutched a set of invisible pearls. "I'm like, 'y'all can't put no filter on yo' baby ultrasound?'. That li'l muthafucka needed a Valencia, Hefe or something."

"You're ridiculous," Messiah cracked up laughing. "I'm sure the ultrasound looked fine. What are they having?" Her heart rate slowed down.

"You sure you wanna know?" Bird asked wearily.

"Yeah." Messiah tried to appear strong. "I can handle it," she lied.

"A boy."

Messiah bit her bottom lip. The whole world had stopped. She wanted to spit in God's face. His beef with her was apparent. It couldn't be hidden anymore. He hated her. There was no other explanation for all the hell He allowed to happen to her. God let the devil have his way with her and didn't bother to stop her misery once.

"That's good." Her voice cracked. "Really, it's good," she sniffed.

"Oh, friend." Bird hugged her tightly.

"I swear to God we gon' fuck him up." Twan punched his own hand, ready to fight.

"I know you're hurting right now, but holding on to this fantasy that you and Bryson are gonna get back together is unrealistic. He's moved on. It's harsh, but he doesn't want you."

Bird hated that she had to be the one to crush her friend's dreams but somebody had to tell her.

"Fuck that!" Twan rolled his neck.

"Fuck him not wanting you. You shouldn't want his ass. Look at what he did to you. You don't deserve that shit. You deserve a man that's gon' worship the ground you walk on. Not somebody that's gon' sell you a whole dream for six years then dip out on you like you ain't shit for another bitch. This nigga lied to you for a whole year, girl!" He stressed. "If I ever hear you say you wanna be back wit' him, I'ma punch you in the face."

"And I'm gon' come right in behind him wit' a two piece to the dome," Bird pursed her lips.

"I know I sound crazy. It's just hard getting over everything," Messiah cried. "I did everything for that man and he acts like none of that matters. He's just gone and being so cold. He won't answer any of my calls. I can't be around him. It's like I don't even know who he is anymore.

I love him. What am I supposed to do? How do I let my feelings go?"

"By loving yourself more." Bird wiped the tears from her eyes.

"But what if I don't know how?"

"You got that ADT on your heart. Ya keep stoppin' before we start." – Anthony David, "Let Me In"

#18

Shyhiem

Just as promised, Shyhiem was parked right out front waiting for Messiah to come outside. After getting off work, he had just enough time to go home, get the kids situated and change clothes before picking her up. While he did all that, Keesha lay in the bed asleep. The only thing she did was take them to the bus stop and answer the door when they came home. Shyhiem was getting real sick and tired of her lazy mothering. If it weren't for him, the twins would be fucked. There had to be a way for him to gain custody without taking Mayhem up on his offer.

With Shyhiem's criminal past, it didn't seem likely he'd ever gain full custody. Doing one, quick job wouldn't hurt anything. It would better him and his kids' living situation. He'd be able to get far away from Keesha and live out his dreams. Keesha would take money over being a mother, for sure; but if he did the job with Mayhem, there was the risk of getting caught. But if the job went off as planned, then he could move.

The thought of leaving Messiah behind caused his heart to contract. They hadn't been messing around long enough for him to ask her to go with him. Getting out of St. Louis and starting over would be best for her. As far as he knew, there was nothing holding her there.

If they moved away to the country side of L.A., life for each of them would be far more peaceful. He wondered if he brought up the notion of moving away to her how she would react. When the time was right, he'd broach the conversation. First, he had to get into her head and see where her mind was at. Messiah seemed like she had a pretty good head on her shoulders, but there was a lot of sadness behind her eyes. She often doubted herself and didn't come across confident or self-assured.

Shyhiem wished she could see how wonderful she was. Maybe her lack of self-esteem came from her mother dying or her shitty-ass boyfriend. No matter where it came from, Shyhiem was going to help her fix it. It was detrimental to her well-being and their budding relationship that she saw herself as he saw her in his eyes.

For the first time since she'd worked at Charter, Messiah's eight-hour shift went by faster than anticipated. For once, she wanted the day to drag on. The longer she was at work, the longer she'd have time to herself to think. Shyhiem being the upstanding man he was, was right on time. Messiah tried not to smile but he looked so fucking fine leaned back in the driver's seat of his car. The windows were down. The sound of Drake's *Child's Play* bumped causing Bird to bend over and twerk.

"Aye! Aye! Aye!" She bounced her ass up and down.

"If you don't stop," Messiah hissed, mortified.

"I rode that dick like a solider!" Twan sang, joining in.

"I do not know y'all." Messiah swiftly walked towards the car.

"Uh ah! Introduce us to your friend." Bird ran behind her.

Messiah took a deep breath and rolled her eyes to the sky. Shyhiem saw her coming and hopped out the car. Messiah pretended to be indifferent to his handsomely good looks, but on the inside, she was a quivering mess.

Shyhiem got finer each time she saw him. There was a slight breeze in the air so he donned an olive-green bomber jacket, white, crew-neck t-shirt, charcoal, ripped, skinny jeans and grey, suede, Nike athletic sneakers. He made streetwear attire look so expensive, edgy and cool.

"Hi." He kissed her tenderly on the cheek.

"Hi," Messiah blushed as his phone began to ring.

Shyhiem checked the screen and saw that it was his father calling. Screwing up his face, he sent his call to voicemail. He had no idea what his father could possibly want and wasn't in the mood to find out. They didn't fuck with each other and he was more than pleased to keep it that way.

"Hello, young sir." Bird curtsied. "I'm Bird. Messiah's best friend."

"Nice to meet you. I'm Shyhiem," he chuckled, opening Messiah's door.

"Mmm hmm…Bird, you was right. He can get it." Twan licked his lips in approval. "Hi, how you doing? I'm Twan." He stuck out his hand for a shake.

"What's up wit' you?" Shyhiem shook his hand, unenthusiastically.

He wasn't used to being around flamboyant, openly gay men.

"Ooh… and he gotta firm grip. Shiver me timber," Twan shuddered. "Oh, me so horny. Me love you long time."

Shyhiem immediately withdrew his hand from his. He didn't want to disrespect Messiah's friend, but if homeboy kept it up, he'd have to check him.

"I'll talk to y'all later." She said, getting inside the car.

"Don't get nothin' on ya," Bird quoted a line from their favorite movie - What's Love Got To Do With It.

"Bye." Messiah waved.

Shyhiem got in and placed his key in the ignition.

"I'm sorry about that. My friends are idiots," she apologized.

"Yeah, yo' homeboy was trippin'. I don't do all that gay shit."

Messiah sat speechless for a second.

"He's a little extra but he's harmless. You don't have anything against gay people, do you?" She asked as they pulled off.

"They cool, I guess." Shyhiem tried to block thoughts of his son from his head. "They don't fuck with me. I don't fuck with them."

"Oh." Messiah dropped the subject.

She didn't feel like checking Shyhiem on his ignorance. It didn't take a rocket scientist to see he wasn't comfortable being around gay people. Most men weren't comfortable being around gay men. For some odd reason, they thought that all gay men wanted them just because they liked dick. Straight men also liked to think that being friends with a gay man would stigmatize them as being gay too. It was sad that in 2016, people still thought that being gay, lesbian or transgender was a sin or just outright wrong. Messiah didn't like the idea that Shyhiem could be homophobic. She liked him a lot but she wouldn't tolerate any gay-bashing whatsoever.

"Welcome to mi casa." Messiah held open the door.

Shyhiem entered her apartment, expecting to see a typical living room set up. Most people had either a black or brown leather couch with a coffee table and television in their living area. There was nothing traditional about Messiah's decorating style. He'd never seen anything like it but it suited her well. Her decorating choices were an exact extension of her style aesthetic. The living room had a hippie vibe to it.

Her home automatically made you feel warm and welcome. There wasn't anything dull about it. The walls were painted royal blue. Tons of photos, a yamaka and a pair of ballet slippers hung above a dark grey couch. Covering the couch was a yellow, pink, black, purple and blue Native American, printed quilt and graphic throw pillows. On each side of the couch was an end table with a white, porcelain lamp. Off to the side was a tan, sixties-inspired chair with a white, fur throw draped causally over it.

Instead of a typical glass coffee table, there was an old, wooden chest that had been restored with chalkboard paint. Hearts, numbers and words like: love and hope were written on it. On top of the chest was old books she bought from the thrift store. Under the chalkboard chest was a tribal print rug.

"It's a lot, I know." She downplayed her home.

"I love it." He stroked her cheek.

A sense of relief swept over her body. She didn't know why, but she'd secretly been awaiting his approval. Messiah didn't like fitting into a box. She liked creating her own lane. No one could ever say she tried to be like anyone else. She got off on finding buried treasures at thrift stores and garage sales.

"Make yourself at home. I'll be right back." She said, disappearing into her bedroom.

Alone, Shyhiem took the time to do a little bit of snooping. Messiah was so private. He barely knew anything about her, besides her birthday, her fiancé leaving her and the fact that her mother was dead. She'd yet to reveal what caused her mom's death or the scar down the center of her stomach. Shyhiem was going to get answers, if he had to pry them out of her. In front of the couch, he leaned over and looked at her pics.

In one of the frames was a picture of Messiah when she was like one or two years old with her mother. A yellow visor shielded her mom's eyes as she held Messiah cheek to cheek. Shyhiem couldn't get over how much she and her mom looked alike. Messiah was the splitting image of her mother, except her mom had dark, ebony-colored skin.

In another frame was a pic of Messiah as a baby, her mom and a man who looked to be her father. The man was white. He was tall with olive-colored skin, fine, black hair and a dimpled chin. Messiah possessed his deep brown eyes. Shyhiem had no idea Messiah was mixed. He thought she was a lighter skin black girl with big, curly hair. Shocked, he continued to investigate.

Most of the photos where of her when she was a toddler or child. There was only one picture of her when she was a teenager. It was an outdoors family photo of herself, her parents and an older girl who she resembled. Shyhiem put two and two together and concluded the girl was her sister. Everyone was smiling and seemed so happy. They looked like the picture-perfect family.

Shyhiem's heart warmed when he spotted a picture of Messiah doing ballet. In the pic, she wore a white, lace leotard with ivory-colored, satin, pointe shoes. She stood on the tip of her left foot while her right leg arched high in the sky behind her. Shyhiem thought that pic was dope until he saw one that blew his mind away.

Messiah was crouched down low with her arm folded across her knees, while standing on the tips of her toes. Her hair was wild like a lion's mane. She wore a black, long sleeve, cashmere top, tight-fitting jeans rolled up and a pair of ballet toe shoes. The picture screamed black power. She looked so poised and graceful. There was a fire in her eyes. He hadn't seen her look that confident since they'd met. He had to make her feel that way again.

"You couldn't tell me nothin' when I took that photo." She said out of nowhere.

Shyhiem was so into her photo gallery that he didn't even notice she'd returned.

"You looked like you were an amazing dancer."

"I was a'ight." She downplayed her abilities, once again.

At one point, she was considered one of the top 10 up-and-coming ballerinas in the country.

"You look just like your mom."

"Everyone says that. I think I look more like my dad." Messiah ran her fingertips over her father's black yamaka.

"You know, this whole time, I thought you were just black."

"No," she giggled. "I'm black, Native American and Jewish. My father was a practicing Jew but my mother was Christian. She refused to convert. Somehow they made it work."

"Wow, that's crazy," Shyhiem looked at the wall of photos in awe. "I know your mother is no longer here, but why you ain't got no new photos of your father and your sister? What, y'all don't get along?"

"You want something to drink?" Messiah quickly changed the subject.

It wasn't time for him to learn her deep, dark secret. She didn't trust him enough to reveal such a tragic part of her life.

"You can't run forever, Messiah." He followed her into the kitchen.

"I don't know what you're talking about. I walked in here," she joked.

"I'm being serious right now."

"I am too. That's why I wanted to let you know I'm going to pay you back for getting my lights cut back on. I'ma have to set up a payment plan with you, but unlike your friend Tricky, I'm actually gonna pay you back."

"You done?" Shyhiem yawned, unimpressed by her affirmation.

"Yeah."

"You out yo' mind if you think I'm taking a dime from you," he clarified.

"Shyhiem, I'm not taking no for an answer. I don't care what you say. I'm paying you back," Messiah challenged.

"Since you wanna be a strong, black woman," Shyhiem made air quotes with his hands. "...And pay me back so bad. Pay me back by tellin' me something about yourself. For us to get closer, you're gonna have to open up to me. If not, this ain't gon' work."

"What do you wanna know?" Messiah folded her arms across her chest.

Shyhiem glared at her. Whenever she folded her arms, that meant her guard was all the way up.

"I wanna know everything about you." He leaned against the kitchen island.

"Ok; I'm 22, I'm a Virgo, I don't watch much TV, I love comic books, wrestling and Stevie Wonder. I hate raw onions, I think milk is the cow's piss—"

"How did you get the scar on your stomach?" Shyhiem cut her off.

He didn't wanna know a bunch of surface bullshit. He wanted to know what kept her up at night, her fears and what she loved more than anything in life.

"I'm not talkin' about that." Messiah bent over and opened the refrigerator. "What you want to drink? I got some bottled waters, Canada Dry and juice."

"Fuck the juice." He slammed the refrigerator door closed and gripped her tiny waist.

It seemed like the only time he could get her to cooperate was when he had his dick so far up her canal she couldn't breathe. It was the only time she succumbed to his will. It infuriated him that she wouldn't give herself to him when he was willing to lay everything on the line for her. Messiah held on to the fridge as his hands roamed up her thighs. The white, rayon, bell-sleeve shirt and pinstripe,

220

bibbed, mini dress she wore had been calling his name the entire day. The dress was so short, it barely covered her ass. Since Messiah didn't want to act right, he would fuck the truth out of her.

Shyhiem slipped his hands under the hem of her dress and ripped her panties off. Messiah gasped for air. Her legs had already started to tremble in anticipation of receiving all 10 inches of him. Messiah's bare ass and shaven pussy were a sight to see. Shyhiem's dick was rock solid. He'd imagined fucking the shit out of her the entire time he was at work. Taking her into his arms, he lay her down onto the kitchen island. Messiah's legs were parted and awaiting him. Shyhiem quickly undid his jeans and planted his face between her thighs.

"Mmmmmmmm," Messiah whimpered upon his first lick.

"You like that?" He gripped her thighs tightly.

"Yessssss."

Messiah's pink pussy glided against his tongue with ease. Shyhiem stroked his massive cock while burying his tongue between the folds of her slit.

"Shyhiem," she purred, contracting her pelvis. "Oh, my god. Your tongue feels so good."

If he kept on licking her pussy the way he was, she'd be cumming in a matter of seconds.

"I wanna fuck your mouth." He whispered into the lips of her pussy.

"I want you to fuck my mouth," Messiah wailed, cumming all over his lips.

Shyhiem happily lapped up every bit of her sweet nectar.

Stroking his shaft, he placed his 10-inch cock so deep inside her pussy, all she could do was shudder and moan.

"You love this dick, don't you?"

"Yes," Messiah's eyes rolled to the back of her head.

"You want me to stop?"

"NO!"

"I'ma stop fuckin' you if you don't tell me something you've never told anyone else before," he threatened.

"What?" Messiah shot him a look of annoyance.

"You heard me." He stopped stroking her middle.

"What are you doing? Don't stop fuckin' me." Messiah rocked her hips back and forth.

"Not until you let me in." He hungrily placed a wet kiss on her thigh then hit her with the death stroke.

A jolt of electricity shot up Messiah's stomach.

"Fuck, Shyhiem," she moaned, falling down the rabbit hole.

"I'ma stop again. You betta tell me something," he advised.

"Ok-ok-ok," Messiah panted heavily.

What she was about to tell him was beyond embarrassing. Shyhiem wanted to know more about her, so she was going to strip away a layer of armor.

"Sometimes, I think I'm unlovable." She confessed, as he hit her spot.

Shyhiem watched her climax in disbelief. He couldn't fathom why she would feel that way.

"You happy now?" She shot, coming down from her orgasmic high.

"No." Shyhiem pushed her dress up over her breasts and toyed with her nipples. "Play wit' yo' pussy for me," he demanded.

Messiah did as she was told and rotated her fingers across her eager clit. Seeing her fingers go around and 'round over her pink, swollen clit while his cock eased in and out of her hot cave drove Shyhiem insane.

"Mmmm… yeah! Ahhhhh… fuck!" Messiah rotated her fingers faster. "Oooooooh, yeah. You love when I play with my pussy. Don't you?"

"Yes." He held her head in place. "I love everything about you." Shyhiem planted a deep, sensual kiss on her lips.

Messiah swallowed hard. She assumed from the way he treated her that his feelings for her ran deep.

"Fuck, Messiah," he groaned. "Can't you see I love the fuck outta you? I've loved you from the day we met."

Messiah wasn't a liar, so saying she loved him back wasn't an option. She loved the way he made her feel. She loved how he took care of her and made her smile, but to say she was in love with him would be a lie. The feelings she had for Shyhiem scared her more than anything. She never knew that being with someone could be so blissful. Shyhiem gave her a natural high that she didn't want to come down from. He was perfect; so perfect he seemed unreal. There had to be something wrong with him. Then, Messiah remembered his ghetto baby mama, his bad temper and his case of homophobia. She couldn't open her heart to him and risk getting hurt all over again. The wound from Bryson was still freshly open.

"Fuck, I'ma cum." He fucked her savagely.

"I want you to cum, Shyhiem. I want you to cum in my pussy. Cum for me. I want that cum. Give it to me," Messiah shrilled, trying to ignore his confession.

She hoped the nastier she talked, he'd forget she hadn't said she loved him back.

"Give it to me, Shyhiem. I want all of it."

"Yes, baby. I'm gonna cum in you, real fuckin' deep. Real fuckin' slow and deep." He gave her slow, even strokes.

Messiah looked between her legs at his rock-hard abs and dick. It was dark and erect, just how she liked it.

"I want your cum, Shyhiem! Give it to me." She rotated her hips, matching his rhythm.

Shyhiem moved her hand and began to thumb her clit himself.

"God, I love this pussy." He quickened his pace.

"Ooooooooooh… yes! Fuck my pussy, Shyhiem! I want that cum!" Messiah reached her peak.

"Fuuuuuuuuuuuuuck!" Shyhiem squeezed his eyes shut.

He had every intention in the world to pull out but Messiah's pussy had him trapped. He couldn't pull out if he wanted to. Before he knew it, he'd cum in her so much that it spilled out the sides of her pussy and slid down her asshole.

"Ahhhhhhhhhhhhhh!" He rested his face in her bosom.

"That's it, baby, cum for me." Messiah rubbed his back as both of their bodies quacked.

Out of breath, Shyhiem continued to pound her pussy. He thought he was done, but another nut had built in the tip of his dick.

"Oh fuck! Aww shit!" He pounded his cock into her pelvis. "I'm gonna cum again. I'm gonna cum! Here I come. You ready, baby?" He pulled her hair.

"Yes!" Messiah moaned. "I can feel it." She screamed, cumming again too.

Shyhiem lay on top of her in silence. He was fully aware that she hadn't said she loved him back. His feelings were slightly hurt but he kinda figured she needed more time. He wasn't delusional enough to believe that she'd completely gotten over her ex so quickly. He and Messiah just needed time. He was willing to be patient while she healed from another man's betrayal. He loved her enough to walk her through the pain her ex left behind. He was willing to do all of that because once it was all said and done, Messiah would love him so much that her ex would become a vague memory.

"I bought some VVS's then she caught the chain flu." – Future, "Rent Money"

#19

Shyhiem

Rance John Styles & Barbering shop was always busy on Thursday afternoons. People in St. Louis gave it five stars and ranked it as one of the best barber shops in the Midwest. The owner, Rance John, and his crew were known for their creative, precision haircuts, male grooming, friendly and professional customer service. It was the only place Shyhiem went to get his hair cut. Rance had been his barber for years, and now he cut Sonny's hair as well.

The day was October 6th, 2016. The weather was slowly starting to change. The leaves on the trees were turning from green to yellow and orange. Some days, you'd need a jacket, then on other days, it was over 75 degrees. Fall was always Shyhiem's favorite time of the year. Particularly, now that he had kids. All the things he couldn't do as child, he got to experience with his children. Growing up, his mom couldn't afford fancy Halloween costumes, big Thanksgiving meals or extravagant Christmas presents.

Every Halloween, Shyhiem had to be a ghost. It was the most cost efficient. All he had to do was get an old, white sheet and cut two holes in it for the eyes, and voila, he was a ghost. Kids in the neighborhood used to clown him for being the same thing every damn year. The jokes got worse when he was caught using his mother's EBT card to buy groceries. Shyhiem hated being made fun of. It made him feel like he wasn't good enough. He and his mom didn't have much but it wasn't their fault.

She was a young mom whose parents kicked her out for being pregnant at 16. With nowhere to go, she stayed on friends' couches and in her car until she could afford to get a small efficiency apartment. They lived in the cramped space until Shyhiem was five. After that, they moved into a two-bedroom house in Pine Lawn. His mom worked her fingers to the bone to make sure they had a roof over their heads. Shyhiem often thought back on when they had to count change just so they could have money to eat.

When the gas would get cut off, they'd have to boil water on the stove just to take a hot bath. The older he got, the more Shyhiem hated not having money. He was tired of wearing dingy, hand-me-down clothes and old, worn out tennis shoes. He was done with hearing his mom cry herself to sleep at night. Since his father rarely ever came around and helped, there was only one way to better their living situation. Shyhiem started hustling. He didn't want to hit the block, but at the age of 13, he couldn't get a job. There was no way around it. He had to do what he had to do.

His extracurricular activities didn't go unnoticed. His mom quickly saw that the refrigerator stayed stocked and that Shyhiem started to dress better. When she came home from work, he'd leave money on her dresser to help her pay the bills. She confronted him on what kept him out so late during the week. At first, Shyhiem denied what he was doing, but after a while, he didn't care about hiding his street dealings. Selling dope afforded them a better life than the one they had before he started hitting the block.

He wasn't ashamed. He'd stepped up to the plate and did what his father refused to do. If his mother didn't agree with his career choice, then so be it. She never said no to his drug money. She took it with a disapproving look on her face and warned him that the streets would swallow him whole. Shyhiem didn't listen. His head was in the clouds. Money was coming in hand over fist. Hoes stayed on his dick and the guys that used to clown him now clamored to be his friend.

In Shyhiem's mind, he was untouchable. Until one night, he got pulled over for driving with a suspended license. Shyhiem never went around with drugs on him, but he always kept a burner by his side. The police demanded that he get out of the car, and when they patted him down, his gun was found. The gun came back unregistered. Shyhiem had already been booked for minor offenses, so the judge hit him with the book when he showed up in court again.

When he got locked up, Mayhem took over his territory. Shyhiem had every intention of getting back into the game until he realized that living the fast life wasn't all it was cracked up to be. He didn't want to be an absentee father to his kids. He never wanted them to visit him behind bars or bury him six feet deep. He wanted to be a present and constant figure in their lives. He was determined to give them the love and devotion his father never gave him.

Once Rance was done cutting Sonny's hair, Shyhiem hopped in the chair. Sonny sat across from him in the waiting area watching YouTube videos on his iPad. It wouldn't take Shyhiem long to get finish. He was getting the usual, low-cut fade with a part and his beard groomed. As Rance worked his magic, the shops door opened and in walked Mayhem. Shyhiem hadn't seen or talked to him in weeks. Between work, the twins and Messiah, he didn't have time for anything else.

When Mayhem walked through the door his presence was known. People revered and feared him. His demeanor was dark and intimidating. He was larger than life. His muscles made it through the door before he did. It stunned Shyhiem how muscular his brother had gotten over the years. He still remembered when he was only a hundred pounds soaking wet. Now he was as big as 50 Cent.

Mayhem spoke to Rance and the other barbers, then gave his brother a quick head nod and a pound. His attention was on Sonny. He was a miniature version of himself. They had the same dark skin and piercing, almond-shaped eyes. Every time he got to see him and Shania, his heart flatlined. They were a constant reminder of the selfish, poor decisions he made at the age of 20. At the time, when Keesha learned she was pregnant, they both thought it was best Shyhiem take on the role as father. His brother was levelheaded, responsible and up for the challenge of raising kids.

Mayhem didn't want to be tied down. Plus, his father would kick his ass if he found out he'd gotten a low rent girl like Keesha pregnant. They'd raised him better than that. Neither he nor Keesha cared that they were ruining an innocent man's life. They both got what they wanted. She got the man of her dreams and he got his freedom.

The older the twins got, the more Mayhem began to regret his decision. He wanted the kids to know he was their father. He wanted to be the one to take Sonny to get his hair cut. If he was in the picture, Sonny wouldn't be so goddamn fruity. Shyhiem let him get away with doing too much feminine shit. Mayhem wouldn't have none of that, but there was nothing he could do about it.

On the surface, he was nothing but the fun-loving uncle that spoiled them rotten. He didn't have any say so about how the twins were raised. He never gave Shyhiem a reason to think that he could be anything more. For the most part, he kept his distance. Shyhiem had no idea that a week after he fucked Keesha in the backseat of his car,

Mayhem fucked her too. After she'd dissed him, he had to prove that he could pull her as well. He hated when girls played him to the left for his brother.

He was the one that had the world at his fingertips. Shyhiem was nothing but a good-looking guy with a little bit of street money, so when he saw Keesha at a mutual friend's house, he got on her. It didn't take long before he had her bent over the bathroom sink. Neither he nor his brother used a condom with her. The only difference was, Shyhiem smashed her once, whereas Mayhem knocked her down raw several times in a row.

There was no question that the twins were his. Since their first encounter, he and Keesha had been fucking around off and on for years. While his brother was in prison, he was the one she used all his stash money on. Mayhem felt terrible about all the things he'd done but he was in far too deep to turn back now.

"What up, nephew?" He lifted his son in the air and kissed his forehead.

"Hi, Uncle Mayhem," Sonny giggled. "Can I have a dollar so I can buy some candy?"

"You can have more than a dollar." Mayhem reached inside his pocket and pulled out a fifty-dollar bill. "Here you go, li'l man."

"Look, Daddy!" Sonny hopped out of his uncle's arms and ran over to Shyhiem. "Uncle Mayhem gave me 50 whole dollars!"

"That's what's up. You say thank you?"

"No." Sonny faced Mayhem. "Thank you, Uncle Mayhem."

"You welcome, mini me." He sat down and made himself comfortable. "What you been up to? Me and Pop been tryin' to call you." He turned his attention to Shyhiem.

"I've been busy." Shyhiem said evenly.

"Busy, doing what?" Mayhem looked at his brother like he was full of shit.

"I got my hands full."

"Got yo' hands full doing what?" Mayhem cocked his head to the side. "Pop really need to speak to you. You need to hit him back. It's important."

"What he need to talk to me about?" Shyhiem screwed up his face. "I ain't talked to that nigga in years, and I'd honestly like to keep it that way."

"Just call him," Mayhem urged.

"Whatever." Shyhiem replied, knowing damn well he wasn't going to.

"I ain't seen you around lately. Where you been?" Mayhem fished for information.

"You know that girl I was tellin' you about?" Shyhiem couldn't help but smile at the thought of Messiah.

"Yeah."

"We've been kickin' it."

"Is that right?" Mayhem massaged his jaw.

"Yeah, li'l mama might be the one."

"Wow… I ain't never heard you talk like that. Keesha know about her?"

"She's knows of her, but that's about it."

"How you think she gon' react when she finds out that you're serious about her?" Mayhem quizzed.

"I don't know and I frankly don't give a damn," Shyhiem shrugged. "Keesha do what she do and I don't ask her no questions. She knows we not together. I can see whoever I want. If she got a problem with that, then that's on her."

"I feel you." Mayhem nodded, apprehensively. "Have you thought about what we discussed?"

"Yeah, I'm good. I'm strictly focused on my kids and shorty right now."

Mayhem's face turned to stone. This wasn't what he wanted to hear. He needed his brother by his side. He had so much coke coming in that there was no way he could handle it all by himself. He didn't need some bitch coming around and fuckin' up his plan. Whoever this chick was his brother was fuckin' had his nose wide open. Shyhiem didn't need any distractions in his life. If Mayhem could get rid of this mystery girl, his brother would be all in.

"I would give my soul, just to make you feel good, baby. Never leave you left alone." – Ro James, "Holy Water"

#20

Shyhiem

It was a little after 8pm when Shyhiem and Sonny made it home. After getting their haircuts, Shyhiem took Sonny to the mall. While there, he copped him some new clothes and a pair of sneakers. Then they grabbed something to eat at the food court. It had been a while since they had a father/son day together. For Shyhiem, it was detrimental that they had one-on-one, quality time. He wanted to show him and his sister that they were individuals and that he loved them both for different reasons, outside of being twins.

Sonny laughed and smiled the whole afternoon. He acted like he didn't want their time alone to end. Shyhiem had a great time as well. It was his duty to make his son happy. Sonny was a good kid. He was obedient, loving and kind. It always pleased Shyhiem when strangers complimented him on how polite and well-mannered Sonny was. Shyhiem appreciated the feedback that he was raising him right. He loved Sonny more than words could express. He and his sister were the apples of his eye and his greatest creation. Shyhiem didn't know what he'd do without them. Thank God, he'd never have to find out.

In front of the building, he parked his car and texted Messiah. He hadn't seen or heard from her all day. She was getting her hair braided, which was an all-day process, so he didn't want to bother her. Despite their lack of communication, he'd thought about her every second of the day. There wasn't a time she escaped his mind. Now that the sun had fallen, he couldn't go a second longer without talking to her. He missed her like crazy and hoped to God she missed him even more.

Shyhiem: What u doing, big head?

Future Wife: Still gettin' my hair braided. We almost done tho'. What u doing?

Shyhiem: Just gettin' home. U miss me?

Future Wife: Of course I do... lol. The question is: do u miss me?

Shyhiem: You'll find out when I put this dick in u

Future Wife: ☐ ☐ ☐ U so nasty

Shyhiem: U like it. Finish up... I'll swing through later tonight.

Future Wife: Ok

Grinning from ear to ear, Shyhiem grabbed the shopping bags from the back seat of the car then hopped out. When he and Sonny walked inside the apartment, he found Keesha sitting on the couch Indian-style, smoking a blunt. The house smelled like weed and chili cheese Fritos. Shyhiem's mood went from blissful to heated in a matter of seconds. Keesha knew damn well he didn't like her smoking in the house, let alone, around the kids.

Shyhiem scowled and closed the door behind him. He hated when he had to be there. He tried to avoid being around Keesha as much as possible. She was fucking disgusting. Shit was everywhere. The girl hadn't swept, mopped or dusted. She had rolling papers, soda cans, used paper plates and an empty Imo's pizza box on the floor. She didn't care that her house looked like a dumpster had exploded in it. All that mattered to her was that she looked good. Her hair was filled with brand new bundles of weave. Her nails and toe nails were freshly painted, and she'd even gone to get lash extensions.

"Well, look who decided to come home." She spat, sarcastically.

"Hi, Mama." Sonny spoke cheerfully.

"Hi." Keesha responded, dryly.

"Look at what Daddy bought me." He raced over to the couch with his bags.

"I'll look at it later." She shooed him off.

Keesha hated looking at his face. Sonny was a constant reminder of her dirty, little secret. It was uncanny how much he looked like Mayhem. She couldn't stand it. Sonny glared at his mother, sadly. His heart had dropped. All he wanted was his mother's approval, love and affection. Shyhiem peeped her dismissal of him and grew angrier.

"Go get ready to take a bath, li'l man, and tell yo' sister to get ready too." He patted Sonny on the back.

"Ok, Pop." He ran down the hall.

Once he was out of ear shot, Shyhiem focused his attention back on Keesha.

"Put that shit out," he demanded.

"Last time I checked, I ain't gotta do shit. This my damn house." She snarled, taking another pull off the blunt.

"What the fuck is yo' problem? You know I don't like you smoking around my kids." Shyhiem took the blunt from her mouth and put it out.

"You ain't been home in weeks. Now you wanna act like a concerned father? Nigga, please. Get the fuck outta here with that. I ain't that bitch upstairs. You can't fool me."

"Oh, so that's why you mad?" Shyhiem chuckled, flabbergasted. "You in yo' feelings 'cause I'm wit' somebody else."

"I don't give a fuck about you or that funny-lookin' bitch."

"You know, you're really boring me with your jealousy. It's not a good look on you."

"Boy, please, you want me to care but I know the real. That shit between you and her ain't gon' last. Once she sees who you really are, she's gon' leave yo' ass high and dry. Watch what I tell you."

Shyhiem glared at her. Once again, Keesha had struck a nerve. His biggest fear was that Messiah would see him for the monster he really was and cut all ties between them.

"When it happens, don't come running back to me."

"Keesha, I'd rather raw dog a beehive than be back with you." Shyhiem shot, repulsed by her presence. "So, say what you wanna say, but what you not gon' do is bad mouth me in front of my kids," he cautioned.

"What, you don't want them to know the truth? You don't want them to know you chose a bitch you barely know over them?"

"What are you talkin' about? I'm here every day when they get out of school. I'm the one that help them with their homework and make sure they have something to eat. I put them to bed every night, while you sit yo' fat, lazy-ass on yo' behind! You don't do shit around here but bitch and complain!"

"I ain't fat! I'm thick!" Keesha rolled her neck.

"Like I said, don't get it twisted. Just 'cause I don't fuck wit' you don't mean I'm not a good father."

"Where you been every night, Shyhiem?" Keesha squinted her eyes. "You back selling?"

"It ain't none of yo' fuckin' business where I'm at." He started to clean up the mess she'd created in the living room.

He didn't want his kids living in filth.

"I know you been upstairs wit' that bitch. If you think, for one second, I'm puttin' up with that shit, you got another muthafuckin' thing coming."

"What I tell you? Watch your fuckin' mouth," Shyhiem warned.

"No! You must've forgot. I'm yo' family, nigga. I'm the mother of yo' kids. You disrespect me, you disrespect them. So, if you disrespect me, then you won't get to see them."

"That don't even fuckin' make sense." Shyhiem's blood boiled. "You just mad 'cause I'm happy, for once in my life. So, since I'm with someone that makes me happy, you ain't gon' let me see my kids?"

"Ding-ding-ding-ding-ding! Ten points for you!" Keesha mocked him. "If I'm gon' be miserable, then you gon' be miserable too. That's how this whole scenario goes."

Shyhiem clenched his jaw. He wanted to wrap his strong hands around her delicate neck and squeeze so tight her face turned blue. He hated Keesha with every fiber of his being. She was the fuckin' devil.

"How you think Miss Neo Soul gon' feel when I tell her you just fucked me a few weeks ago?" She grinned devilishly.

Shyhiem's nostrils flared. He wasn't the type of nigga to take well to threats. If he didn't leave out the room fast, he was liable to go back to jail for murder.

"Yeah, that's right. Walk yo' goofy-lookin' ass away like you always do." Keesha rolled her eyes as he left the room.

She knew she was pushing her luck but didn't care. She hated the thought of someone else having what she thought was rightfully hers. Shyhiem was her meal ticket. She wasn't letting him go without a fight. Crouched over the tub, Shyhiem tried to seem unfazed by Keesha's threats, as he gave the kids their nightly bath. He didn't want them to see how enraged he was. That night, he let the kids stay in the bath longer than usual. He needed the extra time to calm his nerves. Plus, he knew there would be another battle on his hands as soon as he dotted the door to leave.

Shyhiem didn't know how much more of Keesha's antics he could take. It was like she was punking him. Shyhiem wasn't no pussy-ass nigga. She could only push him so far until he burst. There had to be a way to get from underneath Keesha's thumb without jeopardizing his freedom or his relationship with his kids. He had to figure something out because this would be the last night he tolerated her bullshit. She couldn't continue to test his gangsta.

The twins smelled like two, newborn babies after they got out of the tub and he placed lotion on them. When that was done, he told them to go put on their PJ's and get ready for story time. Thirsty, he headed back to the kitchen and opened the fridge. Shyhiem pulled out a chilled bottle of water and gulped it down. He wanted a beer but knew if he had one he'd have to have another. He wanted to have a clear frame of mind when he saw Messiah. Outside of his children, she was the only beacon of light in his fucked-up life.

As he disposed of the bottle, he could feel Keesha's beady, little eyes bore into him. He thought about chucking the bottle at her bowling ball-shaped head but decided against it. Her punk-ass would only call the police. No, he'd keep his hands to himself. Once he read the kids their bedtime story, he would be the fuck outta there.

"Look, Mama!" Shania gleamed. "Me and Brother dressed alike." She held Sonny's hand as he twirled from side-to-side.

Shyhiem's eyes damn near popped out of their sockets. Sonny and Shania were dressed in matching nightgowns. Shania had on a Little Mermaid one and Sonny, Malibu Barbie. Seeing his six-year-old son smile in delight because he was in a gown made Shyhiem want to vomit. His night was going from bad to worse. Before he even had the opportunity to say anything, Keesha lost her shit.

"Have you lost your fuckin' mind? Why do you have on your sister's nightgown?" She yanked Sonny by his frail arm.

"I don't know," he lied, fearing for his life.

He knew why he'd put the gown on. He wanted to make his mother happy by looking like her. To him, Keesha was the prettiest woman on the planet. Sonny wanted to look and feel just like her. He didn't know why, he preferred girl's clothes to the boy stuff his mom and dad

241

bought him. He also didn't understand why he thought other little boys were cute. Sonny wanted to appease his mother and father by liking sports and other masculine things, but he'd much rather play dolls and dress up with his sister.

"What have I told you about doing this gay shit?!" Keesha shook him hard. "You are not a fuckin' girl! You are a little boy! You have a penis! Not a fuckin' vagina! Act like it!" She hit him on the butt with her hand.

"I'm sorry, Mama. I won't do it again," Sonny cried, looking at his father for help.

"You are not gay! And if you are, I'ma beat it out of you! You do not dress like a girl! It's wrong! Do you hear me? It's wrong!" Keesha continued to swat his behind.

Unable to take her hits, Sonny tried to block her hand with his, which only infuriated her more.

"Oh, yo' li'l faggot-ass think you grown!" She forcefully bent him over and pulled up the gown to spank his bare bottom with an extension cord.

The whip of the extension cord against Sonny's bare skin felt like thunder. Welts immediately popped up on his behind. The blows to his butt hurt so bad, Sonny could hardly catch his breath. The blows were too much for a six-year-old little boy to handle.

"Daddy! Make Mommy stop! He didn't mean it!" Shania pled, tugging on her father's arm.

Paralyzed from the shock of what he'd seen, Shyhiem snapped back to reality. He didn't necessarily agree with Sonny's behavior, but he also didn't think he deserved to be beat because of it. He was still his son and he'd protect him from harm at all cost.

"Keesha, chill!" He jumped in and tried to push her off him.

"No! This my damn son! It's your damn fault he acts like this in the first place!" She pushed him back.

"What?" Shyhiem shielded Sonny from his mother.

"You heard me!" Keesha jumped in his face. "If you were home to show him what a real man is supposed to look like, he wouldn't be on this gay shit!"

"He's a fuckin' li'l boy! He don't know what he's doing!"

"Stop making excuses for him! You act like the shit is ok! I don't know about you, but I'll be damned if my son grow up to be a fuckin' faggot! Only muthafucka up in here that's gon' be suckin' dick is me!"

"On my mama, Keesha, I swear to God, get the fuck out my face." Shyhiem ice-grilled her.

"And if I don't, what the fuck you gon' do?" Keesha placed her hands on her hips and looked him up and down.

Shyhiem stood silent, trying to keep calm.

"Exactly; nothin'. Now I see where he gets the shit from. I guess the saying, like father, like son is true. It takes one pussy to know another." Keesha spat with venom.

Shyhiem didn't even realize he'd blacked out and slapped her till he saw her torpedo across the living room floor. In shock, Keesha held the side of her face.

"Did you really just put yo' hands on me?" She yelled, bewildered.

"That's what you wanted me to do! You wanted me to put my fuckin' hands on you!" Shyhiem shouted, disappointed with himself.

"Get the fuck out!"

"I ain't going nowhere! I ain't leaving my kids here wit' yo' crazy-ass!"

"Leave or I'ma call the police!" Keesha grabbed her phone.

Shyhiem shook his head. He needed to be the one threatening to call the police, not her. Fed up with her nonsense, he looked over at the twins. Their little faces were drenched with tears. Sonny was on the floor curled up in the fetal position, hyperventilating. Shania tried her best to console her brother, but she was a nervous wreck herself. Shyhiem went over and picked Sonny up off the floor. He hated to see him cry. The sight of his snotty nose and bruised legs tore him up inside.

"It's ok, li'l man." He rocked him gently in his arms. "Daddy's here."

Sonny held onto to his father's neck for dear life. He never wanted to let him go. In his arms was the only place he felt safe.

"I just wanted to be pretty, Daddy."

"Shhhh… I know." Shyhiem placed a loving kiss on his forehead as a tear slipped from his eye.

He'd never felt so helpless in his life.

"I'm not gon' tell you again, Shyhiem! Get the fuck out 'for I call the police!" Keesha pressed the number 9 on her phone.

"Daddy gotta go but I love you, ok?"

"Please, Daddy, no, don't leave!" Sonny refused to let his father go.

"I have to, li'l man. I'll be back tho'. Just go in your room and go to bed." He placed Sonny down onto his feet.

"No, Pop! You can't leave me! She's gonna kill me if you leave!" Sonny kicked and screamed while holding onto his neck.

Shyhiem's eyes welled with tears. Pure panic was written all over Sonny's face. There wasn't a feeling worse than not being able to shield your child from pain. He wanted to take away Sonny's fears but Keesha was the big, bad wolf he couldn't kill. He already had two strikes against him. He was black and on probation. If he stayed, she'd call the police and tell them he'd hit her. If he was in jail, Sonny really wouldn't have any protection.

Shyhiem didn't want to leave but it was best for the kids that he did. Giving the twins one last kiss, he grabbed his keys and headed towards the door. Sonny screamed for him to come back, but with each scream, Shyhiem kept walking. It was the longest and hardest walk he'd ever taken in his life. The weight of the world was on his shoulders. He needed some holy water to ease the ache in his soul. Closing the door on his son's desperate cries for help took away a piece of Shyhiem's manhood. For the first time in his life, he wondered if there was truly a God. The God he served wouldn't allow this to happen to him or his kids. Maybe Messiah was right. Maybe there wasn't a God.

"Do you want it raw? Do you want it real?
I'ma give it to you real honest." – Ro James,
"Burn Slow"

#21

Messiah

Messiah lay in bed tired as hell. Sitting on her butt for nine hours straight while getting her hair braided wore her out. She couldn't wait to go to bed. Now that she was there, her mind wouldn't stop racing. At night was when she thought of Bryson the most. It had been a month since they'd broken up, but she still thought of him every day. She'd tried calling him but he never picked up. Each time she reached out and he didn't answer cut her deep. It was really fucked up how he was acting.

She'd given him her time, her money, her love and her soul, and he couldn't even talk to her. Messiah didn't exactly know what she wanted to speak to him about. It was more about hearing his voice and feeling close to him. She knew she was being a fool for holding onto what they used to be, but she couldn't let go. Maybe she was addicted to the pain. He was the last bit of family she had left. Letting him go meant she had no one. Messiah didn't want to be alone in this cold, cruel world.

And yes, she should've been focusing on her future with Shyhiem instead of the past, but her past made her who she was. It consumed her thoughts and actions. The joy Shyhiem brought her was intriguing but his intensity scared the hell out of her. She wasn't used to anyone showing her so much love. She wasn't ready to give her heart to someone new. If she allowed herself to fully give into him and he ended up breaking her heart, she'd literally die. Messiah couldn't take another L.

There was still a lot about Shyhiem she didn't know. The things she did know were all red flags. Shyhiem

couldn't be her man. He could only be a casual fuck...
Someone to help her pass the time. He was great in bed and
allowed her to be the nasty freak she'd always wanted to
be. He was sweet, affectionate, caring and supportive. He
was everything she wanted Bryson to be but he never was.
Bryson was home. He was her safe place.

She hated that Shyhiem loved her, 'cause even if
she wanted to love him back, she couldn't. Messiah was
obviously unlovable. Everyone she loved either died or
went away. No one in her life ever stayed. She couldn't risk
caring for Shyhiem and him one day leaving too. No, she'd
continue to enjoy his company until things got too heavy.
When that time came, she'd dip. Messiah had concluded
that she wasn't wifey material. Loving her was the
equivalent to loving a black cloud.

There in the dark, she looked at her phone and
wondered where Shyhiem was. It was midnight and he
hadn't stopped by yet. A pang of jealousy shot through her
lower stomach as she envisioned him laid up with Keesha.
She wasn't naïve enough to think they still didn't have
dealings with each other. They lived in the same house, for
God sake. They probably even slept in the same bed. There
was no way on God's green earth he could lay beside her
and not touch her. He could barely keep his hands-off
Messiah, and Keesha had a way better body than she did.

Her physique was insane. If Messiah was a man,
she wouldn't be able to keep her hands off her either. The
thought of Shyhiem still fucking his baby mama made her
sick to her stomach. She'd be devastated if she found out he
was. Messiah didn't want to be his girlfriend, but she also
didn't want to share him with anyone else. Besides that, if
he put her life in jeopardy by fucking them both at the same
time, she'd kill him.

Feeling lonely, she went to her text messages and read her and Bryson's old text thread. She missed when he'd text her out the blue just to say I love you. A cold sweat washed over her, as she thought about texting him. Every time she hit him up, she became anxious. She hated making a fool out of herself. When it came to matters of the heart, she would willingly place her pride to the side... Even if it meant she'd end up hurt. No amount of pain was going to stop her from trying to win him back.

Messiah: Hey

Messiah held the screen up to her face, hoping he'd give her conformation that he still cared. For once, God had her back. A text bubble popped up letting her know he was replying. Messiah lay with baited breath. The palms of her hands began to sweat as she waited for the text to come through. Then, just as quickly as the text bubble appeared, it went away. Once again, he'd built her up to let her down.

Messiah wanted to cry. This was pathetic. She needed to find a way to stop loving him. If she didn't, he'd destroy what little self-esteem she had left. The fact that he was about to respond gave her some hope though. Messiah would take what she could get. If she continued to be patient, she and Bryson would be back together. Just as Messiah was about to accept the fact that she'd be sleeping alone that night, her phone beeped. Quickly, she looked at the screen, praying it was Bryson. It wasn't. It was Shyhiem.

Shyhiem: U up

Messiah: Yeah

Shyhiem: Come open the door

Messiah threw her phone down and hopped out of bed. The concrete floor was cold against her bare feet. It wasn't until she unlocked the door that she realized just how much she missed him. Messiah's emotions were all over the place. She had feelings for two men; but at that moment, everything was about Shyhiem. He stood on the opposite side of the threshold. A look of sadness and yearning burned in his irises. Immediately, she knew something was wrong. He was hella high. She'd never seen him in such a state. A potent mixture of weed smoke and cologne bounced off his skin.

Shyhiem leaned against the doorframe and stared at her. The light from the hallway illuminated Messiah's curvaceous frame. The braids in her hair gave her a whole new vibe. She looked primal, like an African huntress. He didn't think she could get any prettier but she proved him wrong. Long, black, box braids touched her ass cheeks. She wore a simple, nude-colored, stretch-knit, seamless slip with a plunging neckline, cami straps, and a crisscross back. The body-hugging night attire showcased her hardened nipples and round hips.

Shyhiem didn't utter a word, as he grabbed the back of her neck and passionately kissed her soft lips. Messiah kissed him back with reckless abandon. Now that she was in his arms, there was no other place she wanted to be. Bryson never made her feel this good. She had to be careful not to let Shyhiem slip away. Nothing compared to the way he loved her. Messiah gasped as he lifted her off the ground and carried her to the bedroom.

Following his lead, she wrapped her legs around his well-developed back. As their tongues found their way to one another, Messiah helped Shyhiem undress. Unlike all the other times they'd had sex, there wasn't a sense of urgency to his movements. Shyhiem didn't want to fuck. He wanted to slow things down and make love. Normally,

Messiah wouldn't have been down with that, but that night, she needed to feel loved too.

Since they'd met, Shyhiem had done his best to give her the world. She never had to want for a thing. It was time she returned the favor. Underneath the light of the moon, she decided to make love to him the way someone should've made love to her. She was going to do the one thing that scared her the most: give him her all. Naked, she gazed into his eyes, reassuring him there was no other place she'd rather be than underneath him.

Enamored by her beauty, Shyhiem wrapped her braids around his hand, pulled her head back and ran his tongue up her long neck. The pain from the tug on her hair hurt but Messiah was too swept up in the moment to care. Shyhiem's hard-on magnified as he watched her quiver from his touch. Messiah closed her eyes as his hand traveled down her scarred stomach and landed on her wet pussy. Shyhiem could play in her wetness all night long. Her silent cries and carnal, brown eyes revealed the darkness she tried to hide deep inside.

Messiah needed him just as much as he needed her. The moonlight shined down upon her face as he entered the most tender part of her being. Captive to his savage thrust, Messiah submitted her body to him. He had complete access to all her feminine portals. Her figure was his personal playground. Lovemaking never felt so good. Now that she'd gotten a taste of it, she wanted more. Each push, pull, stroke and moan showcased his desire for her. It was like he needed her to breathe.

He did. Shyhiem was drowning in sorrow and regret. The day's events had him frozen in time. Messiah was the only person that could release him from his mental prison. He found comfort in her bosom. He wanted to get lost in her. She was so wonderful; sometimes, she seemed unreal. Somewhere between dreams and nightmares they existed. Things between them were so confusing. Shyhiem knew she wasn't ready for a nigga like him, but he loved her anyway. Messiah made him want to be a better man; and with all the chaos going on in his life, he needed her more than ever.

Messiah dug her nails into Shyhiem's back and arched her spine. The beast from his cage was erupting, overflowing down her thigh. She was climaxing too. With a glazed-over look, she stared into his solemn eyes. Shyhiem kissed the tip of her nose and rolled off her. Messiah caught her breath and pulled the sheets over her body. It unnerved her that Shyhiem wasn't paying her any attention. Usually, after sex, he'd hold her close. Instead, he lay on his back, looking aimlessly at the moon.

"What's wrong?" She rested her chin on his peck and rubbed his chest.

"Nothing. When is your next day off?" He quickly changed the subject.

"Sunday."

"Cool, don't plan nothin'. I got a surprise for you."

"Shyhiem, you do not have to do anything else for me. You have done enough."

"Just be ready Sunday around one, ok?"

"Alright." Messiah shook her head.

The last thing she wanted to do was fight.

"Now, are you going to tell me what's wrong with you?"

"I told you, I'm good."

"Shyhiem, you look like somebody stole your bike. Let me be there for you. Tell me what's bothering you," she urged.

"I don't even know if I have the energy to talk about it," he sighed.

"I got time."

Shyhiem lay silent. Opening up to Messiah about Sonny was a big deal. He'd never talked to anyone about the challenges he faced. The whole situation was maddening. For the longest time, Shyhiem pretended like he didn't see the signs, but he couldn't ignore what Sonny was anymore.

"It's my son."

Worried, Messiah raised her head.

"He's ok, right?"

"Yeah, he's fine. We just had a little incident tonight." Shyhiem pulled her close.

"What happened?"

Shyhiem took a much-needed breath.

"I don't know. I think he might be—" He stopped himself before finishing his sentence.

Shyhiem couldn't even say the word. The weight of its significance burned his tongue. If he said it. It would make it true.

"Might be what?" Messiah died to know.

Shyhiem furrowed his brows.

"Gay." He let the word escape from his mouth.

"Oh." Messiah replied, surprised. "How do you feel about that?" She asked carefully.

"To be honest wit' you, I don't know how I feel. I don't understand it. I don't get it. I didn't grow up like that."

"Well, you didn't grow up like that 'cause you're not gay. Sonny was born that way. It's not something he chooses to be. I'm pretty sure he doesn't even understand what's going on."

"I get that. I know he doesn't. He's only six years old. I just don't know what to do about it. Keesha acts like she hates him because of it. She beat the shit out of him tonight 'cause he put on his sister's nightgown to go to bed."

"Wow." Messiah said speechless.

"Yeah. Me and her ended up gettin' into it. It got real ugly."

"I'm sorry to hear that. How do you even know he's gay?"

"He's always playin' wit' dolls and dressing up in his sister's clothes. He even asked me one time if he can kiss a boy."

"Oh wow."

"I can't let my son walk around in dresses and shit; kissin' li'l boys. That shit is crazy. It's weird," Shyhiem stressed, upset.

"Are you homophobic?" Messiah questioned, unwilling to beat around the bush anymore.

"I don't know," Shyhiem shrugged. "No... yeah... I... Listen, I don't know what I am. All I know is that I

254

don't hate my son. I love him to death; but… I don't know if I can accept him being gay either. I just want him to be normal, like me."

"But he is," Messiah rebutted. "There is nothing wrong with him; and as his father, it's your duty to make him understand that. There are people in this world who are going to tell him that because he's gay, he's not a child of God, he's weird, he's sick, he's the devil. But none of that is true. He's perfect. He's just like everybody else."

"I just don't want kids to fuck with him because of something he can't control. I know how that feels to have kids tease you." Shyhiem reminisced on his own childhood. "Kids can be cruel. They will fuck yo' head up if you let 'em. I don't want that for him."

"Kids are gonna fuck with you whether you're gay or straight 'cause they're assholes," Messiah laughed.

"You're right about that," Shyhiem chuckled. "I don't even know how to act around gay people. I don't have gay friends. I grew up in the hood. We don't get down like that. Being gay is considered being feminine and soft."

"Just because a man is gay doesn't mean that he's any less of a man than you are. You think it makes you a man 'cause you can beat up someone, pick up a gun or fuck a lot of bitches? Being gay just means you are a person who is attracted to someone of the same sex; that's it. It doesn't mean that you're a bad person. It doesn't mean you're soft. Look at it this way." Messiah sat up.

"What if being straight was considered a sin and we were considered out of the norm?"

"Damn," Shyhiem massaged his jaw. "I never thought about it that way."

"You have to," Messiah urged. "I know, being the type of man you are, this is hard for you. No one expects it to be an easy pill to swallow. We all have dreams of what our children will be. But all we are, are vessels for them to come through. What they do with their time in this world has already been written. You have no control over who he's going to be."

"You right," Shyhiem agreed.

"And look, your questions and fears aren't going to be answered or fixed in a day, but it must be drilled into your head that Sonny is not an alien. He's no different than you or me. Christians say it is a sin to be gay and hide behind Bible quotes to support their claims, but anybody that thinks being gay is wrong is nothing but a hypocrite and bigot. We're all sinners." She spoke with conviction.

"Now, I have my problems with God. Me and him ain't on good terms right now. Haven't been in a long while, but I believe he loves all his children. We weren't created to be the same. I didn't ask to be born black but people will still hate me because of the color of my skin or the fact that I'm Jewish. Your son doesn't have any control over being gay. He can't pray it away, he can't wish it away; dating a woman won't change it. It's who he is, and at the end of the day, you must remember he's still your son." Messiah stared off into space.

Tears were rising in her throat. Visions of her baby lying dead in the street flashed before her eyes. She'd give anything to be able to have a son, and here Shyhiem and Keesha were complaining about the one they had. They didn't even realize how blessed they were.

"You have to love him through this journey, Shyhiem. He's going to need you. More than he'll ever know." Tears scorched the brim of Messiah's eyes.

Shyhiem held her hand, astounded by her tears. The grief in her eyes exposed that her words weren't just about Sonny anymore. The words she spoke told a story of her own personal hell. He wanted to ask her why she felt so much sorrow. What was the source of her pain? Why was there so much grief in her eyes? If he knew, maybe he could help her heal, but it wasn't the time to ask such intimate questions. Messiah had some shit to get off her chest and he was going to allow her to get each and every word out.

"His journey in this world is going to be rough, harsh and scary. There are going to be many nights where he feels lonely and misunderstood. He's going to need your strength and your vigor to carry him through. Don't sit back and watch him come undone. Every child needs their parents' love and support. When you don't have it, a hole starts to erode in your chest and you lose your will to live. He needs to know that you're gonna be there, that you won't let any harm come to him. He's going to need his father 'cause you're his real-life, superhero." Messiah looked Shyhiem square in the eye.

"You're the only one who can save him."

"Fuck that new girl that you like so bad. She's not crazy like me. I bet you like that."
– JoJo, "Marvin's Room (Can't Do It Better)"

#22

Keesha

"Suck on my balls, pause. I've had enough. I ain't thinkin' 'bout you," Keesha bobbed her head up and down and sang along to Beyoncé's *Sorry*.

It was her anthem of the day. She wasn't sorry for shit that had gone down between her, Sonny and Shyhiem. She felt damn good about her actions. She would've been less of a woman, and a mother, if she didn't discipline her son for what he did. Keesha wasn't in the business of raising no punk. She'd be damned if Sonny grew up to be gay. And no, she wasn't like these other millennials that felt being gay was acceptable and normal. The way she was raised, it was a sin.

It was demonic and ungodly. She never wanted Sonny to think wearing girls' clothing or liking other boys was appropriate. In her eyes, it wasn't. If she had to beat his butt day in and day out for him to understand that, she would. It was obvious, Shyhiem wasn't going to step up to the plate and straighten his ass out. He was too busy running behind Miss Mulatto to raise their son.

Keesha wasn't that hands-on with Sonny. Most of the time, she hated the sight of his face. Sometimes, the weight of her secret was too much to bear. Keesha justified her decision by telling herself the past couldn't be undone. She'd already lived the lie way too long to turn back now. The kids would be devastated if they found out the truth, and she would no longer have Shyhiem there to take care of her. She'd grown comfortable in her lifestyle of leisure. She could be pretty, keep her appearance up, go to the club, have her bills paid, fuck Mayhem and whoever else she wanted. Without Shyhiem, everything would change.

She couldn't have that. The one thing she knew for sure was that she couldn't sit back and watch her son dive head first into homosexual behavior. She would disown his little-ass if he kept it up. It was cute to watch Rupaul's Drag Race or have a gay hairstylist and friends, but she didn't approve of the lifestyle. Being gay was a sick and nasty choice that men made. They didn't have to be that way, if they didn't want to be.

What real man would want another man's dick up his ass? The thought made her want to vomit. Men weren't supposed to be with other men. To be gay and wear women's clothes was even worse. Men like that were having an all-out identity crisis. She wanted no parts of it.

Keesha parked down the street from her apartment. There were no parking spaces in front of the building. That was the only downfall of living on the Southside. On the weekends, it was always packed in her neighborhood. She lived right by South Grand where numerous restaurants were.

Keesha took her keys out of the ignition and grabbed her purse. She was just about to run in the house when she spotted Shyhiem's mutt come out of the building. A brown, wide brim hat rested on top of her head, as her braids swung behind her. She wore a black, faux fur jacket, lace-up bodysuit, denim, cutoff shorts and knockoff, black, Chelsea boots. Keesha's upper lip curled on sight. She hated her ass with a passion. The bitch thought she was cute because she was light skin and had pretty hair. Keesha wanted to hop out the car and smack her.

The thought almost became reality, until she noticed Shyhiem walking behind her. He was dressed up too. He

260

had on a black, fitted cap turned to the back, a white hoodie that zipped on each side, dirty wash, grey, fitted jeans and six-inch wheat Tims. A gold chain with a Jesus piece hung from his neck. He looked fucking hot - which pissed Keesha off.

"His ass ain't been home in two days but got time to take this bitch out," she frowned.

Seeing the two of them together, so happy, made Keesha's skin crawl.

"I should run they ass over." She watched, as he helped her inside the car.

Fuming, she dug inside her Louis Vuitton purse and located her phone. There was only one person who would understand her plight and talk her off the ledge of insanity.

"What?" Mayhem answered the phone, sleepily.

It was going on one o'clock in the afternoon and he still wasn't up. Mayhem stayed out all night and slept all day. His life was so unpredictable. Keesha could hardly keep up.

"Wake yo' punk-ass up," she joked.

"Don't play wit' me. What you want?"

"To talk to you, nigga." Keesha smacked her gum in his ear. "What, yo' bitch at home?"

"Keesha, what the fuck you want," He groaned, not in the mood.

"What are we gon' do about your brother? This new bitch he fuckin' wit' got him acting crazy. Did he tell you we got into it the other night?"

"No." Mayhem rolled over onto his back, puzzled.

261

He was surprised that Shyhiem hadn't confided in him. He usually kept him abreast on all things Keesha.

"What happened?" He rubbed the cold from his eyes.

"Your son decided to put on his sister's nightgown and I whooped him. Shyhiem freaked out like a li'l bitch and put his hands on me."

"That can't be the whole story. Shy ain't gon' put his hands on you for nothing. I'm pretty sure you did something to make him go there."

"I don't give a fuck what I did! A man should never put his hands on a woman."

"You ain't no woman," Mayhem laughed.

"Whatever, asshole. Has he told you anything about this girl?" Keesha rolled her eyes.

"I've heard a few things." Mayhem kept it vague.

He didn't want to risk telling Keesha too much info and she end up repeating it to Shyhiem in the heat of the moment.

"The bitch gotta go. She's ruining everything. He's changed since he's got with her. He's all on this happiness kick. It's fuckin' disgusting. He's always with her. He ain't been home since we got into it, but I just saw them leave together. He got me fucked up if he thinks he gon' parade this bitch around like I'm not the mother of his kids."

"You're not," Mayhem reminded her.

Keesha had told the lie so many times, she'd started to believe it.

"You know what I mean." She waved him off. "What if he decides to leave me for good? What am I gon' do then?"

"Shyhiem ain't going nowhere," Mayhem yawned.

"You betta hope not, 'cause if he does, yo' ass gon' have to step up," she warned.

"I ain't got no problem with that. I wanna be there. You're the one that don't wanna tell them the truth."

"Shyhiem's the only father they know, Michael. It'll fuck they heads up if he goes from being their father to their uncle. They too little. They can't understand that. Plus, I love Shyhiem. We can make things right again."

"Stop lying to yo'self. You don't love that nigga. You love me."

"And you love Charisse funky-ass. That's why you're marrying her."

"Stop with the bullshit and tell that man the truth. It's high time he knows what's up," Mayhem urged, tired of living a lie.

"I'm not tellin' him shit! Shyhiem being the kids' daddy is what's best for them. Yo' ass is too fuckin' unstable. Shyhiem loves them and he teaches them stuff. You too busy out here fuckin' bitches, slanging dope and killin' folks to be somebody's daddy."

"I don't know what you talkin' about." Mayhem denied her accusations over the phone.

For all he knew, his line could be tapped. When he saw her in person, he'd get in her ass for saying that shit over the phone.

263

"I just got a fear that if he keeps on seeing this broad he gon' leave me."   .

"Leave you?' Mayhem repeated. "He been left yo' ass. The only reason he there is for the kids."

"Whatever! I can't allow that to happen. He can't leave me, Mayhem. He just can't." Keesha's voice cracked with fear.

"You'll be a'ight. Get off yo' lazy-ass and get a job."

"Umm, excuse you, rudeness. Pretty bitches like me don't do manual labor." She admired her yellow, stiletto nails.

"That's your problem, now. You're fuckin' delusional."

"Anyway, are you gon' help me or not?"

"What you want me to do?" Mayhem yawned.

"Talk to him," Keesha whined. "Get his head back on straight. Talk to him about doing that job with you. You know you need him. We can't have this bitch fuckin' this up for us. 'Cause if things get serious between them, it's gone be trouble for me and you."

"Funny you're the broken one but I'm the only one who needed saving." – Rihanna feat. Mikky Ekko, "Stay"

#23

Messiah

A black blindfold shielded Messiah's eyes so she couldn't see. Nervously, she sat beside Shyhiem in the passenger seat of his car. She had no idea where they were headed. He only told her it was a surprise. Messiah didn't want to sour the mood for him but she hated surprises. Not being in control of her whereabouts was something she detested. Messiah liked being hands-on with everything. To relinquish control, and let Shyhiem take the lead outside of the bedroom, was huge for her.

Not being able to see was something she wasn't comfortable with either. She needed to see what was going on around her - always. Especially, when she was in a car. She never had to depend on her other senses so much. All she could hear was the low hum of the engine, as they rode down the highway. A slight breeze came in from the sunroof. The sweet sound of STL native, OrlandoVaughn, put her in a good mood.

His song, *NoGood4Me,* featuring Tayllor Kaye, set the mood perfectly. It matched the laid-back vibe of the day. Messiah could zone out and listen to the song on repeat and never tire of it. Shyhiem held her hand the entire car ride, which gave her comfort. His thumb gently massaged the outer part of her hand and eased her anxiety. Anytime she was with him, she felt at ease. Life was good. Messiah sat back and relished the rare moment in time. If she stopped being her own worst enemy, she could get used to being at peace.

After what seemed like an hour-long drive, they finally reached their destination. Messiah was overjoyed.

She was ready to get rid of the blindfold and see what Shyhiem had in store for her. Being the gentleman he was, he helped her out the car.

"Don't let me fall." She reached out for his hand, unable to see.

"I got you." Shyhiem took her hand in his and guided her towards the door.

"This is so scary." Messiah took baby steps.

Shyhiem laughed at her walking like an old lady. She had no idea that he was recording her every move. He hoped she liked what he had in store for her. Once inside the building, he stood her in the center of the room.

"You ready?" He asked, standing behind her.

"Yes." Messiah smiled, unable to wait a second longer.

Shyhiem untied the blindfold and stuffed it inside his pocket.

"Open your eyes."

Messiah lifted her lids and found that she was inside an empty, white room. Sunlight shined through the windows, giving the space life. Messiah had no idea where she was, until she looked around. To the left of her was a mirror that stretched across the wall and a ballet barre. It quickly became crystal clear that they were at a ballet studio.

"Surprise!" Shyhiem gleamed with pride.

Messiah was speechless. She couldn't form the words to express how she felt. She was far too overwhelmed with grief.

"You excited?" Shyhiem studied her face.

He couldn't tell if she was happy or sad. After a brief pause, he put down his phone and ran over to the bench.

"Look, I got you these too." He handed her a black, camisole leotard, tights and a brand-new pair of ballet slippers.

Messiah looked down at the items in his hand, willing herself not to cry, but was unable to contain her tears. She could barely see, she was so upset.

"Why did you bring me here?" She gazed around the room in distress.

"What you mean? I thought you would like it." Shyhiem answered, confused by her reaction.

Ballet was something she obviously used to love. He figured she'd stopped dancing because she couldn't afford the lessons anymore. Shyhiem took it upon himself to rent out the studio for two hours, just so she could have the place to herself. He had to go into his stash to pay for it, but for her, it was worth it. He'd thought of the idea from the second he saw her old ballet photos. After the way, she helped him with his son, he was even more determined to do something special for her.

She'd schooled him on his bigotry and gave him a new perspective on homosexuality. He still had a long way to go, but he was on his way to accepting his son for who he was. Shyhiem looked at her reddened face. He thought she would've been delighted by his gesture but Messiah glared at him like she hated his guts.

"You shouldn't have brought me here." She doubled over in agony.

Her lungs had deflated. She felt like her chest was caving in, and at any minute, she would pass out. She hadn't been in a ballet studio since she was 16. She never had any intentions on ever setting foot inside one again. She initially stopped dancing because she fell in love with Bryson. She was so caught up in him that she didn't have time for it anymore. When the accident happened, ballet became a constant reminder of how she'd let her parents down by quitting.

They had such high hopes in her career as a world-renowned dancer, they'd given their blood, sweat, tears, time and money to make sure she succeeded, and she gave them her ass to kiss. Messiah was ashamed of herself. She hated herself for how she treated them and the choices she made. Being back in the one place that made her think of her parents the most caused her to lose it.

"I gotta get out of here. I can't breathe." She twirled around in a panic.

She needed to find the door, but she was so dazed, she couldn't concentrate.

"Messiah, calm down." Shyhiem rubbed her back. "What's wrong? Talk to me."

"Get your hands off me!" She swatted his hand away.

"You had no right to bring me here! You crossed the line!" She pointed her finger in his face. "I didn't ask for this!"

"What the fuck are you talkin' about? I thought you would be happy!" He said, shocked by her unpredictable behavior.

"Well, I'm not! I'm far from it! I'm pissed off!"

269

"What the fuck did I do wrong?"

"It doesn't even matter! Ju-just take me home! I want to get out of here!" She tried to walk away.

"No!" He pulled her back. "Not until you tell me what the fuck is wrong with you!"

"I don't have to tell you shit!" Messiah pushed him with all her might.

"You owe me a fuckin' explanation!" Shyhiem held her by the arms. "What the fuck is wrong with you? Why are you flipping out on me like this?"

"This is crazy. I barely even fuckin' know you." Messiah pushed him away again and paced the floor, holding her head. "Why am I even arguing with you?"

"'Cause you love me; admit it!" Shyhiem yelled, fed up.

He was sick of her ducking and dodging her feelings for him.

"What?" Messiah looked at him like he was crazy. "This has nothin' to do with love! Shyhiem, just take me home. I'm begging you. Please." She clasped her hands together in the praying position. "Thank you for this, but I can't be here."

"Why? Did I do something wrong?"

"Stop repeating yourself and shut up!" Messiah stomped her foot repeatedly. "Please! Just shut up!"

She was behaving like a child but she couldn't help it. Her eyes were bloodshot red. This was the side of herself she'd been trying to hide. She'd completely gone over the edge. Memories of when she used to do warm-ups and her mom would watch from the door plagued her mind, making her feel worse. Shyhiem would never understand that since the accident, she'd mentally been 16 ever since. Being at a ballet studio was forcing her to face her demons. Messiah wasn't physically or mentally ready for that.

"This isn't about you, Shyhiem! Stop treating me like I'm something that's broken! You can't fix me! How 'bout you fix yourself! Work on you! This is who I am! I know you think that I'm this *angel* but I'm not! I'm fucked up! You need to accept that I'm not the person you want me to be! I can't love you like you want me to!"

"You are the person I want you to be, except—"

"Except, what!" Messiah cut him off, throwing her hands up in the air.

"Except, you deserve more." Shyhiem said simply.

"No, I don't. I break people. That's what I do. That's why I avoided you for so long, 'cause I didn't want to break you. But this right here…" She pointed back and forth between them. "…Is so perfect that it scares the living daylights out of me. I can't handle it. I can't handle you."

"Why?"

"I told you! I'm unlovable!" Messiah felt her stomach contract with humiliation.

"That's not true."

"I can't deal with this right now. Just take me home."

"Nah, fuck that. You ain't runnin' today! We gon' lay everything out on the line." Shyhiem took his hat off. "You can act like a crazy person all you want. That shit

271

don't faze me. You ain't gettin' out of here until you let me know what's up."

"Maybe I am crazy! Have you ever thought about that? Have you ever considered that you're in love with a murderer?" She cried so hard her eyes burned.

"What?" Shyhiem screwed up his face.

"You heard me! I'm a murderer, Shyhiem! I'm a murderer!" Messiah's chest heaved up and down, as she fell to the floor.

She couldn't stand the weight of her own legs anymore. Shyhiem watched as she sat sobbing uncontrollably.

"You gotta explain to me what you talkin' about, babe." He sat down before her.

Messiah hung her head back, exasperated. Tears slid down the sides of her face and landed in her ears. She tried everything to avoid having this conversation with him. Now, it was inevitable. She had to tell him the horrendous truth.

"I killed my parents and my baby. That's how I got this scar on my stomach." She finally confessed.

"What you mean you killed your parents and your baby?" He eyed her skeptically.

"When I was 16, I was pregnant by my ex. My parents wanted me to give the baby up for adoption, so they drove me to Alabama to stay with my aunt until the baby was born. I was having a little boy," Messiah gazed off into space. "I refused to give my baby up. The whole ride there, it rained and snowed. I was being a bitchy, little brat. My father got fed up and tried to pop me while he was driving. I saw the tanker truck coming. I tried to warn my dad but it was too late. The car started to skid and flipped over several times. We were all ejected from the car. Everyone died on impact but me."

Messiah looked up into Shyhiem's solemn, brown eyes.

"And if all that wasn't fucked up enough, the doctors told me I'd never be able to have kids again. Now, do you see why I can't love you? The accident was all my fault. I killed them."

"Messiah, it wasn't your fault." Shyhiem dried her eyes.

"Yes, it was. If I would've listened and not been a bitch, they'd all still be alive. Shyhiem, I miss my parents so much. I think about them every day." She bit her bottom lip.

"Baby, come here." Shyhiem pulled her into his embrace.

Messiah rested her face on his chest and closed her eyes. Shyhiem rocked her in his arms. The sound of his heartbeat echoed in her ear. Minutes passed by where they sat in silence. Sometimes, it was best not to talk. Shyhiem let the sound of his heartbeat do all the talking. Messiah lay limp in his strong arms. Crying had taken the wind out of her sails. She hadn't talked about the accident in years. Revisiting it did a number on her.

She truly thought Shyhiem would hightail it out the door, when she told him her dark secret. To her amazement, he was still there, holding her down. No one, besides Bryson, had ever loved her enough to stick around. Even he ended up leaving her after a while. It would only be a matter of time before Shyhiem dipped on her too. Until

273

that day came, she'd hold on tight and cherish the precious time they had together.

Shyhiem kissed the top of Messiah's head. He never knew she carried around so much pain. If he could take an ounce of it away he would. Now, he understood why she'd built the wall she had up. She used it to shield herself from letting go and shedding tears. The lack of not having a father and mother, and losing her baby, made her not want to expose herself. Messiah didn't want to feel the pain of ever losing anyone again. All she had was herself.

He had to make her see that now that he was around, she had someone she could lean on. Her confession didn't scare him away. It made him love her more. She was human and humans made mistakes. He didn't care that she couldn't bear children. Loving her was enough. If anything, he yearned to know more about her. Any woman that could go through all of that, and still carry herself with self-respect and pride, was a winner in his book. He could barely make it after his mother died. There was no way he could keep it together if he lost his children too.

"I'm sorry," Messiah whispered.

"It's ok." Shyhiem held her close. "I ain't going nowhere. You ain't gettin' rid of me that easy."

Messiah laughed.

"You're just as crazy as I am."

"Trust me, I'm crazier," Shyhiem chuckled.

"I won't argue with that." Messiah wiped her nose with the back of her hand.

"I'm just happy that you finally opened up to me."

"I'm sorry it took so long. I just have a hard time talking about my past."

"I understand, but your past is your past for a reason. You gotta look towards the future and make that shit bright. Holding on to shit you have no control over will kill you."

"Maybe you can help me with that." Messiah gazed up at him.

Asking for help wasn't something she was used to but she felt safe with Shyhiem.

"You ain't even gotta ask. I'd do anything for you." Shyhiem spoke sincerely.

For the first time since the accident, Messiah didn't feel so weighed down. She felt a sense of relief. Shyhiem was right; it was time to let go of her past. God had given her more time on earth for a reason. It was time she figured out why.

"I love you, Messiah." Shyhiem leaned down and placed a soft kiss on her plump lips.

Messiah closed her eyes and became lost in his kisses. There, standing side-by-side, were her mother and father. Her son lay in her mother's arms. An amber glow shined down from up above. They all looked happy and at peace. Usually, Messiah would want to run towards them and join them in heaven. This time, she raised her hand slowly and waved goodbye. She hated to part ways but it was time. In order to live, she had to let them go. Her parents waved back at her and turned to walk in the direction of the sun. Messiah watched until they disappeared into the light. Content with her decision, she opened her eyes and rubbed the side of Shyhiem's face.

"I love you too."

"Waking up to you in the morning is better than sunrise. So, we can keep the curtains close." – Ro James, "Burn Slow"

#24

Shyhiem

October 17th, 2016, Shyhiem lay with his head resting on Messiah's belly. Droplets of rain pelted the window. The sun was hiding its face. Nothing but clouds filled the afternoon sky. The sound of the rain serenaded their ears. The smell of moist rain and sex filled the room. Neither of them wanted to get up. He and Messiah felt comfort in each other's hold, as they lay tousled in the sheets. They'd made love three times since they woke up that morning. He'd filmed them each time.

Shyhiem wasn't ready to let her go. Her caramel-toned legs had him hypnotized. Shyhiem lit a blunt and stroked her thigh. The three, gold chains around his neck twinkled underneath the muted light of the grey sky. He wore nothing but his chains, a pair of jogging pants and a gold watch. Shyhiem was a sexy sight to see. Messiah couldn't keep her hands off him. His thugged-out, cocky demeanor was a major turn on. Shyhiem passed her the blunt and let her take a puff.

Messiah didn't normally smoke, but Shyhiem had her doing things she'd never imagined doing. She could catch any type of vibe with him. He made her feel completely safe. Since the night, they met at Blank Space, they were finally on an even playing field. There were no more secrets to hide. Both their souls were on display for the world to see. Messiah no longer blocked him from entering her heart.

She'd been nothing but affectionate. The day at the ballet studio changed their relationship for the better. After her breakdown, Shyhiem held her in his arms for what seemed like hours. Messiah was content with sitting in silence. She never wanted to leave his embrace. His strength washed over her.

It took some coaxing, but Shyhiem was able to talk her into dancing. When Messiah came back into the room dressed in her ballet uniform, his eyes lit up. He'd never seen her look so beautiful. Her braids were pulled up into a bun and she'd wiped her face clean of any makeup. Shyhiem could tell she was a little nervous, when she first came out. Messiah hadn't danced in six years. Before she went into a full routine, she warmed up on the ballet barre. Shyhiem sat on the bench and watched her with wonder in his eyes.

Once she started warming up, Messiah switched into an entirely different person. She didn't crack a smile. She was fully focused. It was as if there was no one in the room but her. Her hips were aligned with her shoulders, as she turned her feet out.

Her posture was impeccable. She was tall and confident. Shyhiem learned that day there were five principle positions in ballet. In all five basic positions, the leg is rotated from the hip. She did each step with expert precision and flexibility. Once she was relaxed and her body got all the kinks out, Messiah played Stevie Wonder's *Never Dreamed You'd Leave In Summer* and started to dance a gloriously daunting solo.

"I never dreamed you'd leave in summer.

I thought you would go then come back home.

I thought the cold would leave by summer.

But my quiet nights will be spent alone."

279

As the song built, Messiah floated across the room like a butterfly, digging into the floor. Mesmerized by her skilled moves, Shyhiem captured the experience of seeing her dance on his phone. Every arch and point of her feet showcased courage and suffering. Stevie Wonder's lyrics matched the quietly commanding performance to a T. It was almost saddening to watch. Even after six years of not dancing, Messiah could out dance ballerina's half her age. If she'd never stopped studying the craft, there was no doubt that she could've been a principal dancer at some big-name dance company.

The brilliance of her moves was fueled by both abandon and vehemence. It was like she never missed a beat. She pounced breezily through the rapid-fire steps, devouring space elsewhere with boldness. By the time she was done dancing, tears of sorrow and joy erupted from her eyes. Messiah didn't realize how much she missed ballet. It was a missing part of her life that she urgently wanted back. She couldn't thank Shyhiem enough for pushing her back into it. Shyhiem was just thankful he could be of service. Seeing her happy made him happy. That afternoon at the ballet studio was one he'd never forget.

"I wish we could stay like this forever." Messiah rubbed the top of his head.

His smooth hair prickled her fingertips.

"We can." Shyhiem rolled over onto his back and pulled her onto his face.

"Baby, stop. You know I gotta go to work." Messiah tightened her sugar walls.

"No, you don't. Stay at home with me." Shyhiem kissed the lips of her pussy.

"I can't." Messiah held onto the wall, as his tongue worked its magic over her exposed clit.

"Yes, you can. Say you sick so I can stay inside you all day." He flicked his tongue across her clit with lightning speed.

Shyhiem never felt closer to her than when his face was planted between her thighs and she came on his greedy tongue.

"Shyhiem," she moaned, curving her back.

She couldn't take another orgasm. The way he gripped her ass cheeks as she rode his fervent tongue like it was a cock made her want to combust. An intense orgasm was budding in her lower abdomen. The sheen of perspiration rested on her breasts. The room was starting to spin. With each stroke of his tongue, she fell further down the rabbit hole. Now that she'd given herself to him, she prayed God never tore them apart. Messiah could feel herself about to climax. The fuse had been lit. Just as she was about to cum, Shyhiem's cellphone started to ring.

"Fuck," he groaned. "Get up, babe. I gotta answer it." He mumbled into the lips of her pussy.

"No-no-no, please don't stop. I was just about to cum," she whined.

"I have to. It might be the kids."

Messiah sighed and scooted down off his face. She now straddled his lap. Shyhiem picked up the phone and checked the caller ID. He and Messiah could've kept going. It wasn't the kids calling; it was Mayhem.

"I'll holla at that nigga later." He sent his brother's call to voicemail and tried to pick up where they left off.

He couldn't though. Mayhem called right back.

"You might as well answer it. I ain't even in the mood no more," Messiah lied.

"Yeah, right. You love when I suck yo' pussy," Shyhiem grinned, as the phone rang. "This better be fuckin' important." He said to his brother.

"Where you at?"

"At Messiah crib. Why? What's up?"

"I'm downstairs. Come take a ride wit' me."

From the sound of Mayhem's voice, Shyhiem could tell it was important that he go with him.

"A'ight, come upstairs. I gotta throw on some clothes."

"What's her apartment number?" Mayhem pressed the up button on the elevator.

"2E." Shyhiem said before ending the call. "I invited my brother, Mayhem, up here. I hope you don't mind." He sat up.

"If I did, it doesn't matter now." Messiah replied, unable to take her eyes off his rock-hard abs.

"My bad, babe. I should've asked first." He pushed her braids back off her face.

"It's ok. Just don't make it a habit. I'm excited about meeting him tho'. I haven't met any of your people yet, besides Keesha. Lord knows, I don't wanna run into her ass again."

"You ain't tell me you talked to her before."

"It was at the mailbox one day. She was coming up from the laundry room with the twins. She practically cussed me out 'cause I pointed out that Sonny was having a hard time carrying the laundry ba—" Messiah stopped herself mid-sentence.

It was at that moment she remembered the conversation she overheard Keesha having. *Girl, Mayhem ass ain't shit but that dick... ooooooh.*

"Oh, my god." She blurted out loud.

"What is it?" Shyhiem asked concerned.

"Nothing." She lied in a bewildered tone. "I just remembered I left my charger at work."

"Your charger's right there." Shyhiem pointed at the wall.

"Oh, there it is," Messiah laughed, nervously.

Keesha was fucking Shyhiem's brother and he had no idea what was going on. Messiah gazed up at Shyhiem's handsome face. Everything in her screamed *tell him* but the words were caged in her throat. How could she tell the man she loved that his brother and baby mama were boning each other on the low? They'd only known each other a month and a half. He could flip the script on her and say she was lying.

Plus, Shyhiem didn't need any more stress in his life. He'd just learned about her big, dark secret and he was still dealing with Sonny being gay. Any more bad news would probably send him over the edge. They'd just gotten over one hurdle. They didn't need any more drama. It seemed like they could never have a peaceful moment together. It was always one thing after another. Now wasn't the right time to tell him, but eventually, she would have to.

"Speaking of the kids... When are you going to go see them?" Messiah probed.

"Soon; I'm just giving it a little more time."

Shyhiem missed the kids like crazy. It had been a week since he last saw them. He'd talked to them every day but it was nothing like seeing their cute, little faces. The next time he went to the apartment, he wanted to be sure he and Keesha were on cordial enough terms that they wouldn't kill each other. Until then, he was enjoying spending time with Messiah. Being around her took his mind off the chaos in his life.

"I'm about to jump in the shower. I gotta be at the diner in 40 minutes." Messiah grabbed a bra and a pair of panties from the drawer.

"I wish I could get in there wit' you." Shyhiem lustfully stared at her blackberry nipples.

"I wish you could too." Messiah stroked his penis through his jogging pants and kissed his tantalizing lips.

The sweet taste of her pussy landed on her tongue.

"Mmm... I taste good," she smirked.

"We gon' pick up where we left off later." Shyhiem promised, playfully tapping her on the ass.

The doorbell rang and Messiah disappeared into the bathroom. Shyhiem answered the door and let his brother in. Mayhem walked through the door and immediately the energy in the room changed. Mayhem was an intense person. It was a ton of shit on his mind. The concerns that Keesha raised prompted him to pull up on his brother. He had to see where his head was at and hip him to some very important news.

Mayhem inspected Messiah's place. It looked like the Salvation Army threw up in there. Her decorating style was a hodgepodge of inexpensive bullshit. The place was clean and livable but that's where his compliments ended. He couldn't believe this was where his brother had been staying. He could've been at the loft, instead of in that dump.

"Have a seat." Shyhiem pointed towards the couch.

"Nah, I'm good." Mayhem tried to hide his displeasure.

Messiah's furniture looked like it had a thrift store smell to it. He didn't want the stench to get into his clothes.

"What's so urgent that you had to pull up on me?" Shyhiem grilled.
"Just go put on some clothes and wash yo' ass. It smells like hot ass in here." Mayhem covered his nose.

"Fuck you, nigga. No, it don't," Shyhiem chuckled. "Have a seat, muthafucka. I'll be right back."

Messiah was out of the shower. She was dressed and ready to go. All she had to do was put on her shoes and she was out the door. Shyhiem gave her a quick peck on the lips. His dick was hard again. Seeing her in her tight, fitted jeans reminded him of the snug fit of her pussy when he dove in.

"You feel that?" He whispered, pressing his cock into her stomach.

"Mmm hmm." Messiah flushed in distress.

She had to be at work in less than 20 minutes. She'd gladly risk being late for another taste of him.

"Let me stop fuckin' wit' you." He laughed, pulling away.

"Aww, man," she pouted. "Since you ain't talkin' about nothin', I'm about to head out." She gathered her things.

"Nah, hold up. You ain't walkin' to work in the rain. Give me a sec and I'll have my brother drop you off when we leave out."

"Shy, I can walk. I'm not gon' die if I get a little rain on me. It's not that serious."

"What I say?" Shyhiem gave her a stern look.

Messiah rolled her eyes.

"Huuuuuh… ok," she sighed.

She liked that he was so overprotective of her, but sometimes it could be a bit much.

"Now, go say hi while I get in the shower." Shyhiem closed the bathroom door behind him.

Messiah took her things into the living room. Now that she knew the truth about his brother, she didn't want to go anywhere near him. It was awkward enough meeting someone she barely knew, let alone her boo thang's slimy brother. When she entered the living room, his back was facing her. She was stunned to see how massive of a man he was. He wasn't fat by any means but he was muscular as fuck.

She could see his muscles through his jacket. An eerie feeling panged her stomach. Nothing but dark energy surrounded him. He was almost scary to look at, but Messiah swallowed her fear and spoke anyway.

"Hi." She stuck out her hand for a shake.

Mayhem turned to look at her. He'd been dying to see the girl who had his brother wide open. Instantly, he understood why Messiah had him so captivated. The girl was of a different breed of beauty. He'd risk it all and wife her up too. It genuinely fucked him up how Shyhiem always pulled the finest bitches. All this time, he thought Keesha was a winner, but Messiah had her beat by a long shot. She was bad. Mayhem had to shoot his shot and see just how loyal she was to his brother.

"How you doin'?" He gently took her hand into his and held on longer than he should have.

"I'm fine, and you?" Messiah tried to be as upbeat as possible.

Mayhem made her skin crawl. She was surprised to find that he and Shyhiem looked so much alike, except Shyhiem was way cuter. The scar on Mayhem's face was most certainly a turnoff. He didn't even try to hide the look of lust in his eyes, as he stared at her. His gawking made Messiah feel super uncomfortable. If he thought he was going to fuck her too, he had another thing coming. Messiah wasn't no pass around bitch. She hated that Shyhiem was in the shower. She didn't want to spend another second alone with him.

"It's really coming down out there, isn't it?" She asked, wondering when he was going to let her hand go.

"It is." Mayhem replied in a deep, sensual tone.

His eyes roamed every inch of her body. He didn't have any shame in his desire for her. Messiah nervously cleared her throat and pulled her hand from his hold. With his eyes glued to her, she sat in the chair and bent over to place on her shoes.

"You and my li'l brother getting serious, huh?" Mayhem admired her petite frame.

"I thought y'all were the same age?" Messiah quizzed.

"We are but I was born first." Pornographic thoughts of her riding his dick danced in Mayhem's mind. "But back to what I was saying. You feelin' my brother?"

"I care about your brother a lot."

"You care about him?" He repeated.

"Yeah."

"Interesting." Mayhem massaged his jaw. "I noticed you didn't say you loved him."

"I do." Messiah glared at him. "Very much so. We're just tryin' to take things slow, that's all."

"Is, that right?" Mayhem laughed.

He called bullshit. Messiah wasn't as into his brother as she claimed. He could tell by her choice of words. There was something holding her back. Maybe it was another nigga. If it was, maybe he had a bigger shot at getting at her than he initially thought.

"Let me find out you fuckin' the wrong brother."

"What?" Messiah said shocked, as Shyhiem walked into the room.

"You ready?" He asked her.

"Yeah." She replied, still thrown off by Mayhem's comment.

I can't believe this nigga tried to come onto me, she thought. Shyhiem noticed the puzzled expression on her face and quickly went into protective mode.

"You a'ight?" He asked, helping her into her jacket.

"Yeah, I'm fine." Messiah pulled it together.

"I was just tellin' her I got my eye on her." Mayhem chimed in. "Can't have her going around breakin' my brother's heart."

"We good. Worry about you and the situation you got going on with Charisse." Shyhiem checked him.

"Hey." Mayhem raised his hands in the surrender position. "I'm just being a concerned brother. Ain't nothing wrong with that. Is it, Messiah?" He ice-grilled her.

"No. Not at all."

"So I'ma put it out there and let the chips fall where they may." – Dawn Richard, "Vines (Interlude)"

.

#25

Shyhiem

"I'm finalizing that deal. You in or you out?"
Mayhem gripped the steering wheel of his 2017 Range
Rover.

"It sounds good but I ain't fuckin' wit' it, bro.
Things for me are finally coming together. Messiah and I
are doing good. They talkin' about promoting me down at
the job. All I gotta do is get this Keesha shit straightened
out and I'm good," Shyhiem explained.

"You know how much money you passing up? This
the type of dough you can retire from."

"I know, but Messiah has made me see what kind of
man I wanna be. I ain't tryin' to be out here in the streets.
I'm tryin' to set a good example for my kids."

My kids, Mayhem thought.

"I love Messiah and she ain't down with that type of
lifestyle—"

"Who the fuck is she? You act like that bitch is
Gandhi. She ain't gotta know yo' business." Mayhem cut
him off. "For all you know, this bitch could be a fraud."

"She a good girl, man. She gon' cut me loose if she
even think I'm in the game."

"All I keep hearing you say is Messiah this and
Messiah that. That bitch got you pussy whipped. Fuck her.
What you wanna do, nigga? You act like she yo' fuckin'
P.O."

"You don't get it. Until you meet a chick that make you see a new outlook on life, you'll never understand where I'm coming from. I just wanna chill wit' my girl and my kids. That's it. I ain't tryin' to fuck that up for nobody." Shyhiem put his foot down.

"I wanna build a family with this girl. She can't have kids, so getting her around the twins is important to me. For that to happen, I gotta make Keesha comfortable with the fact that she's gonna be around."

"I don't even know who you are right now, my G. This bitch got you gassed up. Where my brother at? Fuck all this kumbaya shit you talkin'. This girl gon' have you walking around wearing dashikis and crochet hats in a minute. What she got that Erykah Badu-type pussy or something?"

"She ain't gon' be too many more bitches," Shyhiem warned.

"I'm just sayin', you can't let a bi—"

Shyhiem glared at him.

"A chick..." Mayhem corrected himself. "...dictate yo' life. I need you. I can't do this without you. It's too much for me to handle alone and you're the only person I can trust. After all the shit, I've done for you. You gotta do this for me." He guilt-tripped his brother.

"You know I always got yo' back but I gotta sit this one out."

Mayhem's nostrils flared. He wanted to punch a wall. This wasn't the answer he wanted to hear. Now, he saw what Keesha was talking about. Messiah was all Shyhiem could talk about. She dictated every aspect of his life. It was obvious, she was the only person that had his

292

ear. Even he couldn't get to him now. That was a major problem. Mayhem wasn't willing to take no for an answer. He didn't give a fuck how bad Messiah was. No bitch was going to come between him and his paper.

He'd promised his connect that he could get rid of a large shipment of cocaine. It was 132 kilos. Mayhem had a loyal street team but he needed more manpower and muscle to distribute all of it. His brother had the connects to both. With Shyhiem by his side, he was unstoppable. He could take over the dope game in the Midwest with this new shipment. Without Shyhiem, there was no way he could pull it off. He had to figure out a way to get him on board and Messiah out the way. It was cool when she was just a nuisance to Keesha. He actually found her jealousy quite funny; but now that Messiah was fuckin' with his livelihood, the bitch had to go.

Shyhiem looked out the window wondering where they were at. Every time he linked up with his brother he was taking him to unknown places. They were all the way out in no man's land. Mayhem had driven into an upscale, gated community. He'd never been in that area before. None of the homes looked familiar. The only thing he could guess was that Mayhem had bought another crib, but even his money wasn't long enough to afford a spot in this neighborhood. Million-dollar mansions lined the streets.

"Who stay out here?" He finally asked.

"Pop."

Shyhiem cocked his head to the side.

At that instant, he knew exactly how Messiah felt when he took her to the ballet studio. Being at his father's crib was the last place he wanted to be. He hadn't seen or talked to him in over 10 years. Shyhiem wanted nothing to do with him.

"What the fuck you bring me out here for?"

"Y'all need to talk." Mayhem parked his car in the circular driveway.

"We don't need to talk about shit. Turn the fuckin' car around and take me back to the crib."

"Man, just get the fuck out the car."

"Nah, you know I don't fuck wit' that nigga." Shyhiem barked, furiously.

"I wouldn't have brought you out here if it wasn't important. Just get out the car and hear what he got to say." Mayhem opened the door.

Shyhiem stared at the huge house. He always knew his father had money but he didn't know he was living so lavishly. The house he grew up in with his mom could fit inside that home several times over. The realization that his father lived a life of riches, while he and his mom slummed it in the city, infuriated him. It only made him hate him more. In Shyhiem's eyes, his father was strictly a sperm donor. Nothing more, nothing less.

Shyhiem didn't give a fuck about him. As far as he was concerned, his father died the same day his mother took her last breath. If he wanted to talk, Shyhiem would indulge his request, and then give him a piece of his mind. Unwillingly, he got out of the car. He hadn't even set foot inside the house and already he felt like an outsider. He didn't belong there.

Mayhem walked into the foyer and took off his jacket and shoes. His parents had a shoeless home. Shyhiem looked at him like he was crazy. There was no way he was taking his shoes off. He didn't want to be there in the first place.

"C'mon, man, just take 'em off. It ain't gon' kill you."

Shyhiem scowled. Mayhem was really testing his patience. Annoyed, he kicked off his Tims and left them by the door. He wouldn't be there long, so he'd be back in them in no time. Shyhiem tried not to trip off the home, but it was hard not to be in awe of the $17 million, 15,000-square foot, limestone-clad mansion. It was expertly decorated. Twelve foot ceilings, marble floors and a view of the lake was the home's selling point.

"Mommy! Where you at?" Mayhem called out.

"Mommy?" Shyhiem screwed up his face. "Who are you Leave It to Beaver?"

"Shut the fuck up," Mayhem hissed.

"Bunny, is that you?" His mother came from the kitchen.

"Bunny, my nigga?" Shyhiem cracked up laughing. "I'm officially takin' yo' hood pass away."

"Look at my baby." Carol, Mayhem's mother, held out her arms for a hug.

"Hey, Mom." Mayhem hugged her back.

"Have you eaten? Faye just finished cooking dinner."

"Faye?" Shyhiem quizzed.

"She's our chef," Carol replied.

"Wow," Shyhiem shook his head in disbelief.

This deadbeat can afford a chef but didn't want to pay my mom child support? Pussy-ass nigga, he thought.

"Mommy, you remember Shyhiem." Mayhem stepped to the side.

"Of course, I do." Carol said coldly. "Shyhiem."

"Carol." Shyhiem replied, equally as cooly.

It was well-known that Carol didn't like him and he didn't like her. The few times he'd come around as a child, she was always standoffish towards him. She acted like he was gutter trash.

"How have you been?" She asked.

"Good. Look, I don't know why I'm here, but can we get this over with?" Shyhiem said, over the fake-ass pleasantries.

"I see much hasn't changed." Carol pursed her lips. "I'll be in the kitchen. Your father is upstairs in his room." She shot Shyhiem a look of disgust and disappeared around the corner.

"C'mon." Mayhem led Shyhiem up the steps.

Quietly, they walked down a long hallway until they approached a closed door. Mayhem tapped lightly.

"Pop, you up?"

"Yeah, come in."

Mayhem pushed the door open. Shyhiem didn't know what to expect when they went inside. What he saw almost knocked him off his feet. The last time he saw his father, he was a solid 190 pounds. The man lying before him was a shell of the man he used to be. He was skin and bones. Death surrounded him. His once supple, chocolate skin was ash gray. He was so feeble that he couldn't even make it to the bathroom on his own. A portable potty was next to his bed. Numerous medications filled his nightstand.

"Shyhiem." His father said breathlessly. "You came," he coughed.

Shyhiem watched as his father coughed into his hand uncontrollably. With each cough, it looked like he would take his last breath.

"What's wrong wit' him?" Shyhiem looked to his brother for answers.

"He has stage four lung cancer. He's dying."

Shyhiem felt like an asshole for thinking that's what his ass get. He didn't care when his mom died from the nasty disease. He didn't even bother going to the funeral, while he was locked up in jail.

"Is that what you brought me here for?" He shot. "You could've told me this shit over the phone."

"Son—"

"Nah, fam. Let's not even go there. I'm not your son!"

"Shyhiem," Ricky began again. "I asked your brother to bring you here 'cause there's so much I need to say to you."

"You had 27 years to say whatever you wanted to say to me. Anything you gotta say now can be kept." Shyhiem boiled with rage.

He knew he was being cold. The man was on his death bed but the anger and bitterness inside him outweighed his father's circumstance. Being in his presence brought back too many painful memories. Memories he

297

thought he'd buried. He was finally moving forward. He couldn't let the devil pull him back into darkness.

"Please, I know you're upset with me. You have every right to be, but just let me explain. I don't know how much time I have left."

"That sound like a personal problem to me. Ay yo, I don't appreciate you bringing me out here and springing this shit on me like this." He said to Mayhem. "This shit ain't cool, man. You know I don't fuck wit' him. You know better than that."

"You needed to know," Mayhem clarified. "At the end of the day, no matter how pissed off you are, he's still your father."

"That nigga ain't shit to me! He ain't never been my father!" Shyhiem shouted. "He never loved me! He loved you! I was nothin' but a burden to him! He barely acted like I was alive! So, save that 'he's your father' crap! I only had one parent and she died three years ago! Maybe you can apologize to her for the pain you caused when you see her in heaven!" He stormed out of the room.

If Shyhiem didn't remove himself from the toxic situation, he'd breakdown. Losing his sanity in front of the man he despised wasn't an option. There was no way that he was going to let his father see how upset he was over seeing him in such a delicate state. He'd secretly always looked up to him. Ricky was a good-looking man with a bald head and gray beard. He wore the finest suits money could buy and drove the finest cars.

People in St. Louis respected him for his shrewd business savvy. When Shyhiem was a little boy, he thought his father was a superhero. He wanted to be just like him. Deep down, in a sacred part of his heart, he always wished they'd be able to have the father/son relationship he always wished for. The closer he got to 30, the notion seemed unattainable. Now that his father was dying, the reality that he'd never have the father he yearned for scared him to the core.

"Never thought the circumstances would've changed you." – PartyNextDoor feat. Drake, "Come And See Me"

#26

Messiah

Three days had gone by since Messiah last saw or heard from Shyhiem. She'd been calling him nonstop to see what was going on but he wouldn't pick up. Messiah wracked her brain to figure out what she'd done wrong but couldn't think of anything. The last time she saw him, everything was good. They left off on good terms. He'd walked her to the diner door and kissed her lovingly on the forehead. He promised he'd call when it was time for her to get off so he could pick her up.

When he didn't call, Messiah called him. She knew how much he hated when she walked home at night, so she sat around and waited for him for 20 minutes before leaving. It wasn't like him not to call her or pick up her calls. He was very diligent with keeping in contact. Messiah lay in bed the entire night worried sick about him. By day three, she was overwhelmed with worry.

She didn't know if he was in trouble, hurt or dead. She'd thought about calling several hospitals to see if he'd checked in. She even thought about going down and knocking on Keesha's door. Something had to be wrong for him to ghost her. She couldn't blame him if he decided he wanted nothing to do with her. Messiah had a shit ton of baggage. Maybe the way she freaked out at the ballet studio was too much for him to handle after all. Better yet, maybe her omission that she'd killed her parents and child turned him off.

She prayed that wasn't the case. It would be really fucked up if he backed out now. She'd just begun to confide in him. Plus, she'd used her last paycheck to get

301

him a gift she knew he would love. If they didn't talk soon, she'd have to return it and·get her money back. Messiah didn't have money to be wasting.

Shyhiem promised never to hurt her. She was a fool to ever believe his words. She hadn't felt this type of anxiety since Bryson unexpectedly left her. Shyhiem's sudden disappearance kept her up at night. She hadn't been able to sleep or eat. She couldn't wait until she found out what was going on with him.

What she wasn't going to do was keep calling or texting him. She wasn't going to keep tellin' him how him not responding made her feel. Messiah wasn't going to try to read his mind or make assumptions for his behavior. She for damn sure wasn't going to force him to act right. She'd been there and done that. No, what she was going to do was save her energy and fall back and let him do him. If there was one thing she learned from Bryson, it was that she couldn't make a man love her. If he didn't want her anymore, then so be it. She'd been through worse.

Tired, she returned home from a long day at work. Charter had kicked her ass. By the time, she got home from the diner that night, she'd be comatose. In a zombie like state, Messiah entered the building and found the twins sitting outside their door. Their cute, little book bags hung off their backs. Shania was in a heap of tears. Messiah thought about walking past and pretending like she didn't see them. With her and Shyhiem not speaking and Keesha being the psycho bitch she was, it wouldn't be good for her to butt in. However, Messiah's motherly instincts kicked in. She had to lend a helping hand.

"Hi, sweetie. Are you ok?" She eased in their direction, cautiously.

She didn't want to scare them. They already looked deathly afraid.

"My daddy told us not to talk to strangers." Sonny scooted away from her.

"Your daddy told you right." Messiah crouched down to meet them at their level. "But I'm your daddy's friend, Messiah."

Sonny knew she wasn't lying because he'd heard her name float around the house several times.

"Hi." Sonny said apprehensively.

"Is everything ok? Did somebody hurt you?" Messiah asked Shania.

"No, I peed on myself and my mama gon' whoop me," she wept.

Messiah looked at her legs and spotted a puddle of pee under her. She felt terrible.

"Nobody's home?"

"No, my mama not answering the door." Shania wiped her eyes.

"How long have you been sitting out here?" Messiah stood up and knocked on the door.

"I don't know," Sonny shrugged.

When Messiah didn't get an answer either, she decided to hit up Shyhiem. It made her stomach turn to have to pick up the phone and call him but it was for the sake of his children. Five rings later, his voicemail picked up. Messiah didn't even bother leaving a message. Instead, she decided to take matters into her own hands.

"Ok, give me your hand." She held out hers.

Shania looked at her brother for approval. Sonny gave her a look, telling her it was ok. Shania placed her tiny, pink-painted nails inside of Messiah's hand and rose to her feet. Sonny followed suit.

"Until your parents get home, you're gonna come upstairs with me. First, let's leave them a note so they can know where you're at." Messiah retrieved a pen and a piece of paper from her purse.

Quickly, she scribbled a note saying: *The kids were locked out the house so I took them upstairs with me. Messiah 2E.* The note was short, sweet and straight to the point. There was no need to try to be polite when Keesha and Shyhiem had their kids sitting outside like hobos. If Shania sat in her piss too long, she could get a staph infection.

Messiah and the twins boarded the elevator and got off on her floor. She had to get Shania out the pissy clothes. She was starting to smell. Inside her apartment, Messiah went to her room and grabbed the smallest t-shirt she could find.

"Let's get you cleaned up." She said to Shania. "You know how to wash yourself up?"

"Yes." Shania nodded her head innocently.

"Ok," Messiah smiled. "What I want you to do is go into the bathroom and take off your clothes so I can wash them. You can put this on until your clothes dry. That sound ok to you?"

"Yeah, as long as you stay out there and don't try to touch my lady parts."

"Pinky swear, I won't." Messiah held out her pinky.

Shania linked pinkies with her and grinned. Messiah showed her to the bathroom and filled the tub with warm water.

"Here." She gave Shania a washcloth and soap. "Wash up really good, ok?"

"Yes, ma'am." Shania held the items close to her chest.

"When you're done, just come on out." Messiah held the doorknob.

"Messiah?"

"Yes, sweetie."

"You ain't a stank bitch like my mama said you was."

Messiah covered her mouth and tried not to laugh. What Shania said wasn't funny, because it let her know that Keesha did have ill will towards her, but hearing such a tiny, little thing say such foul words tickled Messiah's soul.

"I'm glad you don't think so," she giggled. "Your brother and I are right outside if you need anything."

"Ok."

Messiah closed the door behind her and rejoined Sonny in the dining room. He sat at the table silent, watching his surroundings. He was very much Shyhiem's son. Even though he was six, Sonny wasn't going to let anything get pass him.

"Are you hungry? Would you like something to eat?" Messiah opened the refrigerator.

"My daddy told me not to accept food from strangers."

"Right. Good boy." Messiah closed the refrigerator door shut.

"I will take some of those Cheez-Its you got tho'." Sonny pointed at the top of the fridge.

Messiah cracked a smile and grabbed the box. Shyhiem's kids were a mess. They kept her on her toes. Messiah placed a paper towel down before Sonny and poured some Cheez-Its on it.

"I think we should leave some out for your sister too." She left a paper towel full of crackers on the table for Shania.

Messiah sat next to Sonny while he ate his snack.

"Who normally gets you after school?" She fished for information.

Sonny eyed her apprehensively and said, "My mama, but she go back to sleep as soon as we get in the house. My dad helps us wit' our homework and feeds us, but he ain't been home lately."

Messiah's heart dropped. The fact that Shyhiem hadn't been at Keesha's house either put her on high-alert. *Where is this nigga at*, she wondered?

"Why hasn't your dad been home?"

"He and my mama got into it. He hit her in the face," Sonny replied, simply.

Messiah's eyes bulged. She wasn't expecting to hear that. Shyhiem had conveniently left that part out of the conversation.

"He hit her?" She repeated, shocked.

"Yeah, but he was just stickin' up for me."

"Oh," Messiah took his information in. "Have you talked to your dad?"

"Yesterday."

Messiah's heart dropped. Shyhiem hadn't disappeared off the face of the earth. He just wasn't talking to her.

"Can I have some more Cheez-Its?" Sonny rubbed his crusty nose.

"Sure." Messiah picked up the box.

She was pleased to know that Shyhiem had protected his son, but she didn't like that he'd hit the mother of his kids in the process. She never took Shyhiem as being abusive, but she'd only known him a short while. She'd seen him spazz out before. It wasn't farfetched that he'd flip out on a woman. *Bam, Bam, Bam!* Messiah jumped. Someone was pounding on the door. Messiah got up from the table. She knew fully well by the knock that it was Keesha. On ready, she opened the door calmly.

"Where the fuck are my kids?" Keesha spat with her hand on her hip.

Unfazed by her theatrics, Messiah took all of her in. Keesha's hair was laid to the gods. It was parted down the middle. Twenty-two-inch, Malaysian, body wave hair cascaded down her back. Her face was beat to capacity. She wore bold, glittery, red lipstick. A pair of black aviator shades covered her eyes. The woman had on every diamond she owned. Diamond hoop earrings dangled from her ears. A diamond necklace with a cross pendent hung from her neck. Even her wrist and hands were flooded with ice.

Meanwhile, her kids were walking around pissy with crusty noses. She wore a see-through, long sleeve, catsuit that strategically covered her breasts and ass. A pair of black Louboutin booties rounded out her ghetto girl outfit.

"Hi, Keesha. I'm Messiah." She tried to be cordial.

"Bitch, don't speak to me. You kidnapped my kids. You betta be happy I haven't called the police on you."

"Umm… your kids were locked out of the house. If it wasn't for me, your daughter would still be sitting in a puddle of piss," Messiah checked her. "I wasn't going to just let them sit in the hall unchaperoned. Anything could've happened. So, instead of having an attitude, you need to be saying thank you."

"Girl, who are you talkin' to? You had no business bringing my kids up here, Punky Brewster. I was on my way home. They was alright!"

"You really are as ignorant as Shyhiem said you were," Messiah scoffed.

Flabbergasted that Shyhiem had talked shit about her, Keesha stood speechless.

"Say thank you." Messiah said with an attitude.

"You need to take it down to a level one, India Arie, before I get on 10. Trust me, you don't want it wit' me." Keesha got in her face, invading her personal space.

"Please, get out of my face," Messiah demanded.

"What yo' punk-ass gon' do if I don't?" Keesha pointed her finger at her.

"Keesha, I'm not about to fight you. But you are going to get your hand out of my face," Messiah said, unwilling to back down.

Keesha was bigger than her and had more experience fighting, but Messiah wasn't going to let her punk her.

"Like I said, what you gon' do?"

"I will defend myself if I have to. I would hate for your kids to see you get popped."

"Mommy!" Shania ran out of the bathroom with her clothes in her hands.

Keesha looked past Messiah and saw that Shania was dressed in an adult-sized t-shirt.

"Oh, hell naw! Did you give my baby a bath?" She started to take her earrings off. "No, you did not put your nasty, pedophile hands on my daughter! Bitch, you gon' die today!"

"She bathed herself," Messiah clarified.

"I don't give a fuck if Jesus bathed her! You had no right! Bitch, you oversteppin' yo' boundaries. Let me tell you something. You may be fuckin' they daddy, but you ain't they mama. I am." Keesha pounded her chest. "Just 'cause yo' infertile-ass can't have kids don't mean you gon' try to take mine."

If Messiah hadn't been holding onto the doorframe, she would've lost her balance. *How in the hell does she know I can't have kids,* she thought. She could've only gotten that information from Shyhiem. She couldn't believe he'd betrayed her trust and told Keesha, of all people, something so intimate.

"Yeah, that's right, bitch. I know all about yo' sterile-ass pussy." Keesha shot her a mock-glare and grinned.

She enjoyed every second of knocking Messiah down a peg or two.

"You thought you was doing something, didn't you? You thought you and Shyhiem had something special? You thought he loved you?" Keesha spat sarcastically.

"That nigga don't love you. He loves his family. Me and his kids. You are a non-muthafuckin' factor, bitch. Shyhiem ain't gon' stay wit' you. You ain't nothin' but a slide. Once he gets bored wit' you, he'll be right back home with me. So, enjoy the dick while it lasts." Keesha said with a pleased expression on her face.

She'd crucified Messiah.

"Now get the fuck out my face. Polyester hurts my eyes." She waved her off. "C'mon, kids! It's time to go."

"Thanks, Messiah." Sonny placed on his book bag.

"You're welcome, honey. *Anytime.*" Messiah said with a deliberate emphasis on the word anytime.

She had to let Keesha know that she wouldn't be easily scared off, even though at that point, she wanted nothing else to do with Shyhiem ever again.

"What a wicked way to treat the girl that loves you." – Beyoncé, "Hold Up"

#27

Messiah

Positive vibes only. Positive vibes, Messiah repeated over and over in her mind. Keesha's little truth bomb wasn't going to rattle her. She'd gone for the knockout punch but Messiah wasn't down for the count. She'd promised herself, since the day at the studio, that she wouldn't continue to live in grief over things she could not control. Shyhiem was right. The accident happened, people she loved lost their lives but it wasn't Messiah's fault. If she continued to stay stuck in that fateful night, she'd never grow and prosper.

There was a whole world she'd yet to explore. She wanted to dance again. Thoughts of opening her own ballet studio motivated her to get her shit together. Her feelings were gravely bruised and battered by Shyhiem's dismissal of her, but Messiah was over forcing relationships that obviously weren't meant to be. The fact that as soon as she opened herself up to him he dipped said a lot. He was never serious about loving her. It was all a game. She'd played along and lost. It was ok. He'd regret playing her in the end. She was done being used by the men she gave her heart to.

Messiah wiped down a table, hoping service would pick up. Because of the rain, the diner was practically empty. Only five people had been in and she was halfway through her shift. Messiah low-key was happy it wasn't that packed. She didn't have to work as hard. After working all day at Charter and dealing with Keesha and the kids, she needed a minute to tend to her physical and emotional wounds.

Processing the info that Shyhiem was in contact with his children and not her, and that he'd told Keesha her personal business, was a hard pill to swallow. She needed a release. Messiah didn't want to think anymore. She didn't wanna stay cemented in misery. Finished wiping down the table, she asked Mr. Johnson if she could take a 15-minute break. He said yes, of course. Ever since Shyhiem came to the diner and showed out, he'd treated her like a princess. He didn't want to risk her going back to Shyhiem with any complaints. Messiah sat in the break room by herself and put her feet up in a chair.

"Aww… that feels good." She relaxed her weary body.

Her body ached from working nonstop. Pulling out her phone, she noticed she had several missed calls from Shyhiem. Messiah instantly froze. She hadn't seen his name grace her screen in days. Everything in her wanted to rush and call him back, but after the way he'd done her, there was no way she was gonna make herself readily available for him. Messiah was a lot of things but she wasn't a thirsty bitch. She'd talk to him when it behooved her. Shyhiem could kiss her ass. Whatever he had to say wasn't important enough for her to listen to. Instead of hitting him back, she called her bestie, Bird. She'd been so wrapped up in all things Shyhiem that she hadn't made any time for her.

"Whaaaat? Is this Messiah? I can't believe you callin' li'l old me," Bird teased. "Shit, I thought you forgot my number."

"Shut the hell up. I talk to you every day at work."

"Oh, a bitch gettin' dicked down on a regular so all I get is a work conversation. See how hoes do," Bird grinned.

"You done making me feel like a horrible friend?" Messiah laughed.

"Yeah, what yo' fake-ass want?"

"I called to see what you doing Saturday?"

"Fuckin' somebody's husband," Bird cracked up laughing.

"I'm tryin' to get on yo' level. Let's go out."

"Uh ah, this can't be Messiah." Bird took the phone away from her ear and looked at the cracked screen. "The Messiah I know hates going to the club."

"I do, but, girl, if you knew about the last few days I've had, you'd understand why I wanna turn up. Do people still say turn up?"

"No." Bird laughed at her friend. "You the one that like to keep yo' feelings bottled up. I don't know how you keep all that shit inside without going postal. You can't tell me you ain't a serial killer on the low."

"Only on the weekends." Messiah played along.

"You sure yo' man gon' let you out?"

"First of all, he's not my man."

"Girl, bye; you sholl fuckin' him without a condom like he is. Admit it, you love that nigga."

"I do," Messiah couldn't deny.

"See, I knew it," Bird popped her lips. "I'm happy you're happy, friend."

"Me too. He trippin' right now but it feels good to know that someone genuinely loves me."

"That's good. I'm down to go out tho'. You know I stay in the club."

"Bet, I'm ready." Messiah replied as the line clicked on her end.

It was Shyhiem. Messiah rolled her eyes to the sky. She wanted to be strong and not answer, but she was in too deep to completely shut him out.

"Let me call you right back. This him right now." She announced abruptly.

"Ok, girl. Handle yo' scandal." Bird hung up.

"What?" Messiah clicked over with an attitude.

"Fuck you mean what? I know you seen me call you," Shyhiem barked.

"Uhhhh… who you think you talkin' to?"

"You. Why you ain't answer the phone?"

"Same reason you ain't answer when I called you," Messiah shot back.

It amused her that he had the nerve to be mad at her.

"I was at work when you called earlier," he explained.

"Ok, but what about all the other times?"

"Man, fuck all that. What happened between you and Keesha today? Why she come callin' me sayin' you kidnapped the kids? What the hell did you do?"

Messiah burst out laughing.

"What the fuck is so funny?" Shyhiem died to know.

The fact that she took his kids wasn't a laughing matter to him.

"If you really believe that I just took your kids, then you're just as dumb as yo' ghetto-ass baby mama."

"Watch yo' mouth, Messiah," Shyhiem cautioned.

"No, fuck you. I haven't heard from you in three days and you have the nerve to call me with this bullshit."

"I had some shit I needed to deal with, but that's beside the point. What was you thinkin' taking my kids up to your apartment? You don't think that's kind of weird? You had to know nothin' good was gon' come from that. What was you tryin' to get back at me for not callin' you?"

"Wow," Messiah scoffed, sitting up straight. "You are one narcissistic dickhead. You and Keesha belong together 'cause both y'all niggas crazy." She hung up in his ear.

Not through with the conversation, Shyhiem called right back. A glutton for punishment, Messiah picked up.

"Stop callin' my phone, Shyhiem."

"Why the fuck you hang up on me?" He yelled.

"'Cause I ain't got shit to say to you."

"You need to check yo' attitude. This ain't even you."

"How the hell you gon' tell me who I am?" Messiah rolled her neck, as if he could see her. "You barely even know me."

"Here you go. Now we back to that shit. Whatever, Messiah. You're right. I don't know you. I don't know shit about you. What I do know is that you're wrong as fuck.

You should've never took my kids up to your place without my permission. Hell, you shouldn't even look their way without my say so. We cool, and I love you, but just because I talked to you about Sonny's situation don't mean you get to be around my kids."

"You know what?" Messiah said fed up. "Instead of tryin' to check me, you need to be checkin' yo' unfit-ass baby mama. She's the one that left them stranded outside. That bitch shouldn't be allowed to raise a dog, let alone some kids! As far as I'm concerned, you, Keesha and them pissy-ass kids can kiss my ass." She ended the conversation once and for all.

This time, she placed his number on the call block list so he wouldn't be able to call back. Shyhiem had her fucked up. He wasn't going to talk to her crazy and think the shit was ok. Messiah never thought in a million years that he'd take her good deed as something negative and spiteful. He didn't even bother to hear her out or ask for her side of the story. He immediately went on attack mode. Messiah didn't know what was up with him but she was good. If this was the real Shyhiem, then she wanted no parts of him or his stank-ass attitude.

Messiah was so upset, she was shaking. The last man to disrespect her this bad was Bryson. *Why do the men I love hurt me,* she wondered, making her way back into the dining area. She wasn't even back on the floor a good minute before Mr. Johnson called her name.

"Yes, sir?" She tried to hide her fury.

"Get your things. I'm letting you go home early tonight."

"Why? I still have a few more hours to go."
"I know, but it's slow tonight." Mr. Johnson fiddled with his hands, nervously.

"I don't mind staying. I really need the money."

"You'll still get paid for a full six hours," he assured, looking at the door.

Messiah noticed he was jittery. Something was up.

"Is everything alright, Mr. Johnson?" She followed his gaze.

Mr. Johnson stepped closer and whispered, "Your boyfriend asked me to send you home early."

Messiah inhaled deeply. She couldn't believe Shyhiem had interfered with her job but had the gall to be mad at her for helping his kids.

"He's not my boyfriend and I don't care what he asked you, I'm staying."

"Oh, no you're not." Mr. Johnson pushed her back towards the break room. "I don't want no trouble from Goodnight. Just do us both a favor and take the rest of the night off."

Messiah peeped the fear in his eyes. She hated the effect Shyhiem had on him. Mr. Johnson was a kind old man. He didn't deserve to be intimidated and bullied by a man half his age. Repulsed by Shyhiem's irrational behavior, she placed her jacket on and grabbed her purse. If he wanted a fight, she was going to give him one. Messiah stepped out the diner into the cold, damp October air. Shyhiem was right there waiting inside his car with the window rolled down.

"Get in!" He ordered.

Messiah acted like she didn't hear him and kept walking.

"Messiah!" Shyhiem followed her down the street slowly in his car.

Messiah pursed her lips together and continued to tune him out.

"Really? You gon' act like you don't hear me?"

Silence.

"Messiah, I know you hear me talkin' to you."

"What?" She finally snapped.

"I'm not gon' tell you again. Get in the fuckin' car!"

"No! Leave me alone! Go be wit' yo' family!" She waved him off.

"You are my family!"

"Boy, please. No, the fuck I ain't." Messiah placed her cold hands inside her jacket pockets, as puddles of rain splashed beneath her feet.

"Will you stop actin' like a brat and get in the fuckin' car," Shyhiem barked.

Messiah stopped dead in her tracks.

"You got a lot of nerve! You know that? You ghosted me then accused me of tryin' to kidnap yo' kids to get back at you! Do you know how fuckin' stupid that sound? I mean, is that really what you think of me?" Her lips trembled.

Don't you fuckin' cry. You bet not let a tear fall, she held her head back and willed herself not to break down.

"Just leave me alone, Shyhiem." She wiped her eyes and resumed walking.

Shyhiem stopped the car and hopped out. The ice-cold air hit him in the face. Doing a light jog, he caught up with Messiah.

"Hold on. Let me talk to you." He turned her around to face him.

"What don't you get? I don't want to talk to you!" Messiah yanked her arm away.

"Baby, I'm sorry." Shyhiem said with a hint of desperation in his voice.

He felt like shit for coming at her the way he did. His emotions were all over the place. The news that his father was dying had him spiraling out of control. He didn't know what to do with the information or how to digest it. He hadn't reached out to Messiah because he needed time alone to think. For the past few days, he'd been at the loft sorting his feelings out. He never meant to make Messiah a causality of his internal battle but the damage had already been done. He'd taken his frustrations with his father and Keesha out on her.

"You hurt me." Messiah caved in.

"I know, baby, and I'm sorry." He cupped her face with his hands and placed his forehead on hers. "My father is dying."

"What?"

"I just found out the other day. That's why I haven't called."

"Why didn't you just tell me that?"
"I don't know. I just needed a minute. I was gon' get right back to you, I swear." Shyhiem closed his eyes and inhaled her intoxicating scent. "Messiah, I don't know

what to do. I hate him. He treated me and my mother like shit. Now, 'cause he's dying, he wanna talk."

"What will it cost you to hear him out and see what he has to say?"

"My sanity. I don't trust that nigga as far as I can throw him," Shyhiem replied honestly.

If he's anything like your brother, I understand, Messiah thought.

"I'm not gon' tell you what to do, but if I had a chance to talk to my parents again, I would take it in a heartbeat."

"I don't know, man. I'll think about it." Shyhiem gently stroked her hair.

"Don't touch me." Messiah smacked his hand away. "I don't fuck with you like that." She stepped out of his grasp.

"C'mon, Messiah, don't do me like that." He would give anything to hold her in his arms.

Messiah calmed him down.

"You told Keesha I couldn't have kids. How could you do that to me?" She fumed.

"What are you talkin' about?" Shyhiem asked confused. "I would never tell her that."

"How she know then?" Messiah folded her arms across her chest.

Shyhiem thought for a second; then it dawned on him who the culprit was.

"I mentioned it to my brother. He must've told her," he confessed.

What Shyhiem couldn't figure out was why Mayhem did it.

"My bad. I didn't know he'd run back and tell her. I'm sorry. I should've kept it to myself," he apologized sincerely.

Messiah loved having the upper hand, but she couldn't stay mad at Shyhiem forever. He said he was sorry and she believed him. Plus, she didn't want to fight anymore. She'd missed him like crazy the past three days. It would be hard to let go of the hurt he'd caused; but instead of beefing, it was best they go back to her crib. There, in the dark with their naked bodies pressed together, she could show him just how much she forgave him. Shyhiem needed her and she was going to give him every inch of her love until the sun came up.

"It's ok," she sighed. "I forgive you."

"Now, can we go home?" He gripped her waist and bit her neck. "My dick hard as fuck."

"We can," Messiah giggled. "But before we go. Here." She pulled his gift out her purse.

"What's this?" Shyhiem took the box from her hand.

"A gift. I was going to take it back, but you apologized, so…"

"What you get me a gift for? It ain't even my birthday." Shyhiem cheesed like a little kid.

He couldn't remember the last time somebody did something nice for him.

"Just shut up and open it." Messiah wiggled her legs, excited to see his reaction.

Shyhiem tore off the wrapping paper and bow. His mouth dropped open when he found what was inside. Messiah had gotten him a Cannon Powershot SX710 HS.

"Babe," Shyhiem's eyes lit up. "How did you—"

"I used my paycheck from the diner. It's not brand new or anything. It's refurbished. I figured, since you love filming so much, you could start perfecting your craft. Nothing is holding you back from being a filmmaker, Shyhiem. If that's what you wanna do, then go for it. I haven't seen any of your work 'cause you're hella secretive about letting me see the footage, but… I believe in you."

"Damn, I can't believe you did this for me. This is crazy." Shyhiem inspected the camera in awe.

"You like it?"

"Like it?" He screwed up his face. "I love it. I love you." He gave her a big kiss and twirled her around.

Messiah smiled brightly.

"I ain't tryin' to be funny or nothin', but can you afford this?"

"No," Messiah laughed. "I don't care how much it cost. Seeing you so happy makes it all worth it."

"We love Jesus but you done learned a lot from Satan." – Kanye West feat. Rick Ross, "Devil In A New Dress"

#28

Shyhiem

"What you doing?" Shyhiem asked Messiah over the phone.

"Pullin' up to Blank Space." She replied, checking her face and hair in the mirror.

Things between them were better but still a little tense. Messiah said she'd forgiven him but he could tell things were different. She'd closed herself off again. He couldn't blame her. He'd mishandled her trust. Shyhiem had fucked up in the worse way. To regain her trust, he had to be on his P's and Q's.

"Who you wit'?" He inquired, standing on the steps of the apartment building.

"Bird."

"Why you ain't tell me you was going out?"

"I ain't know I had to," Messiah quipped.

Shyhiem's controlling conduct was starting to wear thin. Messiah was a grown-ass woman. She didn't have to answer to him or anyone else. Shyhiem wasn't her boyfriend. Even if he was, that still didn't give him the fortitude to dictate her whereabouts. They were back on good terms, but the way he'd played her to the left still hovered over her like a dark cloud. Pretending like he hadn't went off on her for nothin' was something Messiah just couldn't do. She'd seen a side of him she didn't like.

"I know you ain't have to. I just wish you would've. I was tryin' to get up with you tonight," he clarified.

"You're more than welcome to come kick it wit' me at Blank Space."

Shyhiem wasn't really in the mood to be around a bunch of people. He had to see Messiah tho'. The feeling that he was losing her wouldn't escape him. He had to make sure they were straight.

"What they got going on tonight?"

"Black Spade is performing." Messiah applied a coat of lipgloss to her lips.

"Oh word?" Shyhiem perked up.

He and Spade grew up together in Pine Lawn. They even went to the same high school. He was a dope-ass lyricist and singer. He stayed on some fly shit. Shyhiem always tried his best to support his music whenever he could.

"A'ight. I'm gettin' ready to go check on the twins real quick. I'll slide through when I'm done."

"Ok."

Shyhiem ended the call, feeling even further apart from Messiah than he had before. He hoped and prayed they'd be able to get past this hump. Losing her wasn't an option. Shyhiem placed his phone inside his pocket and went in to the building. He'd FaceTime'd the kids several times since he'd been away from the apartment, but there was nothing like seeing them face-to-face. Enough time had pass. It was time he and Keesha came to some sort of conclusion.

If he didn't take anything else away from learning his father's diagnosis, it was that life was short. Keesha irked his nerves but she wasn't going to keep him away from his children. Shyhiem unlocked the door and walked inside. The place smelled like old, fried chicken grease and spritz. Shyhiem couldn't do nothing but shake his head. The apartment had gone to shit since he'd been gone. It looked like Keesha hadn't cleaned up once since he left. Clothes were strewn everywhere. The dishes were piled up in the sink. The trash was overflowing and there were two, old bags of trash sitting next to the trash can.

When he walked, his sneakers stuck to the floor. Something sticky had been wasted and Keesha hadn't cleaned it up. Shyhiem was surprised they didn't have roaches. He had to get his kids out of there. He wasn't brought up in filth and neither would his kids.

"Daddy!" Shania and Sonny ran towards him at full speed.

"Hey." He lifted them both off the ground and swung them around.

"We missed you. Are you coming home today?" Shania hugged his neck tightly.

"That's the plan," he responded.

"Not if I got anything to say about it." Keesha sauntered into the living room, smoking a cigarette. "Me and you need to talk."

Shyhiem put the twins down.

"Please don't leave again, Pop." Sonny pled, not wanting to let go.

Not having his father around to protect him left Sonny vulnerable to Keesha's wrath. With Shyhiem being gone, she'd been extra cruel to him. She'd whooped him with a belt twice and locked him in his room without dinner. When she played with Shania, she excluded him. If his dad was around, Keesha wouldn't treat him that way.

Shyhiem wouldn't allow it. Seeing the fear in his son's eyes reminded Shyhiem of the night he left. He wanted to promise Sonny that he wouldn't leave again, but when dealing with Keesha, there was no telling what was going to happen.

"We'll see, li'l man." Shyhiem gave him a kiss on the cheek.

"Y'all go sit down and watch TV while me and yo' daddy talk," Keesha ordered.

Once the coast was clear, she sat on the arm of the couch, shooting daggers at Shyhiem with her eyes. He pulled out a chair from the dining room table and sat down.

"Did you check yo' bitch and tell her to stay the fuck away from my kids?" Keesha mean-mugged him.

Shyhiem cocked his head to the side.

"We talked," he replied dryly.

"I'm not playing, Shyhiem. If I catch her around my kids again, I'ma fuck her pretty, little face up. Give her a buck 50," Keesha referred to slicing her face with a box cutter.

"You ain't gon' touch her."

"Oh, I'm not?" she dared.

"Not if you wanna live," Shyhiem threatened.

"Are you really sticking up for this ho after what she did? The bitch is crazy!"

"No crazier than you." Shyhiem said, bored with the conversation. "Look, I thought we were going to talk about the kids. That's what I came here for."

"We are." Keesha bobbed her head back and forth.

"You keep bobbin' yo' head like that it's gon' fall off," Shyhiem scowled.

"Anyway." Keesha rolled her eyes hard. "I don't want you seeing her ass no more."

Shyhiem chuckled and rose to his feet.

"I ain't got time for this shit. You are fuckin' miserable. I feel sorry for you."

"You the one that's gon' be sorry. 'Cause if you don't stop seein' her, you can forget about seeing these kids."

"You out yo' muthafuckin' mind if you think you gon' keep me away from my kids. You must've forgot who the fuck I am." His brown eyes darkened.

"I know exactly who you are. You the same pussy-ass nigga that chose a bitch over his kids. So, since you wanna be wit' her so bad..." Keesha jumped up and went back to the bedroom. "...be wit' her!" She started to throw Shyhiem's clothes into the hallway.

"That bitch so muthafuckin' important, go stay wit' her ass!" She threw his t-shirts, underwear and socks on the dirty floor.

"You gon' put me out 'cause I don't wanna be wit' yo' funky-ass? Bitch, suck my dick! Fuck you! You mad 'cause I don't want you! You's a fuckin' bum! You need to be thanking me 'cause if it wasn't for these kids, I would've been off you!"

"Blah-blah-blah… blah-blah-blah-blah." Keesha mocked him. "Boy, please, save all that tough talk for someone who care. You gettin' yo' ass up outta here tonight!"

"So, I guess you gon' start payin' the rent up in this muthafucka!"

"No, you are!" Keesha grinned devilishly.

"See, that's where you got the game fucked up. I ain't payin' shit if I don't live here."

"Oh, yes you are. I'ma put yo' ass on child support, and please believe the state gon' take more out yo' paycheck then what you give me now. It's a win-win situation for me boo-boo. You the one that's gon' lose. So, what's it gon' be? That bitch... or yo' kids?"

Shyhiem wanted to strangle her for putting him in such a predicament. Keesha had him by the balls and she knew it. He couldn't afford for her to put him on papers. He'd never be able to pay for a place of his own if she put him on child support. On top of that, he'd never risk not being able to see his children. He loved them more than life itself. They were his life support. Without them, he'd have no will to live.

But Shyhiem couldn't continue to live his life held hostage. He'd given Keesha too much say so over his life. She'd used his kids as a weapon long enough. He had to put his foot down and step out on faith. God wouldn't allow her to get away with her dirty work and neither would he. He would have to remind Keesha just how gangsta he was.

"Do what you gotta do." He turned around to leave.

"What?" Keesha said, surprised.

She'd bet money that he'd cower, like always, to her demands.

"You heard me. Make yo' move," Shyhiem smirked. "File for child support and I'ma do some filing myself."

"File for what?" Keesha's heart pounded out of her chest.

"For full custody."

"I ain't even worried about it. Ain't no judge gon' give no convicted felon custody, so try me, bitch." Keesha pointed her finger at him. "Shania and Sonny come say bye to yo' daddy!"

The twins ran out their room.

"Pop, why you leaving so soon?" Sonny asked sadly.

"Yeah, I thought you was gon' stay?" Shania poked out her lip.

"You better hug him real tight 'cause y'all ain't gon' ever see him again!" Keesha yelled.

"Shut the fuck up! Stop sayin' stupid shit!" Shyhiem barked, giving the twins a hug.

"You shut the fuck up! Sonny and Shania, yo' daddy don't love you no more! Him and Messiah gon' start a new family. He ain't gon' never see y'all again."

Unable to take her bullshit anymore, Shyhiem charged at Keesha and wrapped his hands around her neck. He didn't want to put his hands on her but being aggressive was the only thing bitches like her reacted to.

"Get yo' fuckin' hands off me." Keesha gasped for air, as she dug her finger nails into the skin of his hands.

"You gon' quit playin' wit' me." Shyhiem squeezed tighter.

"Daddy, stop!" Shania pulled on his leg, crying.

Hearing his daughter cry made Shyhiem fall back.

"FUCK!" He screamed, punching his fist into the wall, as Keesha fell to the floor.

Plaster crumbled around Shyhiem's hand.

"Shania, call 911!" Keesha coughed, getting up. "Yo' ass is going to jail tonight, nigga!"

Shyhiem had to get out of there - and quick. He would die before he went back to jail.

"Look at what you did to my neck?" Keesha looked at herself in the mirror.

Shyhiem's finger prints were embedded into her skin.

"You gon' put yo' fuckin' hands on me, nigga! For real? That's what we do now? I'm callin' yo' P.O." She cried, snatching her phone up.

Pissed that he'd once again allowed her to take him over the edge, Shyhiem dipped without saying another word. Keesha had all the physical proof she needed to get him locked up. He'd fallen right into her trap. She was a real-life demon. Keesha belonged in the pits of hell with Satan. He prayed that God would forgive him for his brash decision. He never wanted his kids to think physical abuse was ok. He'd tried to keep his temper on one but Keesha had a way of taking him there. She knew exactly what buttons to push to make him explode.

If Shyhiem didn't pull it together fast, he'd continue to let her and the devil reign supreme. The attack on his life was abundant. Everywhere he turned, there was drama. Things weren't good between him and Messiah, his father was dying and Keesha was holding his kid's hostage. If one more thing happened, Shyhiem would either kill himself or someone else.

"Everything I got they wanna take it. My money and my lady, no." – DJ Khaled, Bryson Tiller and Future, "I'ma Be Alright"

#29

Shyhiem

Blank Space was bumpin'. Cars were lined down the street and on the adjacent corners. It took Shyhiem damn near 10 minutes just to find a parking space, which pissed him off. He was already in a foul mood after the throwdown with Keesha. As far as he knew, there was probably a warrant out for his arrest. Keesha was a petty, vindictive bitch. She'd do anything to spite him. He wished he could go back in time and redo the night she pulled up on him in front of the liquor store. With what he knew now, he would've never touched her.

She was a viper. Her only purpose in life was to make him miserable. She was a shitty person and an even shittier mother. Keesha didn't have a motherly bone in her body. The twins warranted a better mother figure than her. If only Messiah could've been the mother of his kids. She'd be the perfect mom. She was caring and affectionate. She didn't fly off the handle and act irrationally. It truly sucked that she'd never be able to have his baby. If he didn't have children of his own, being with a woman who couldn't bear children would've been a deal breaker.

Shyhiem chirped his car alarm and stepped outside into the chilly air. Thankfully, the Pittsburg Pirates snapback, white, Yeezy Season 3 hoodie, satin, blush-colored, bomber jacket, light, denim jeans ripped at the knees and gray, Yeezy 750's shielded him from the fall weather. A swarm of people stood outside Blank Space shooting the shit, eating pizza and drinking. Tricky stood out amongst the crowd. Shyhiem had forgotten all about the dice game and the money he owed him.

"Goodnight!" Tricky shouted, drunk. "My man."
He dapped him up aggressively.

"Yo, chill." Shyhiem drew his hand away and
flicked his wrist.

His right hand was badly scrapped and bruised from
punching the hole in the wall.

"Nigga, you got my money, while you being extra
friendly? Wit' yo' drunk-ass." He asked, in front of
everyone.

"C'mon, Shy, you ain't gotta front me out like that.
I thought we was cool. You like a brother to me, man. You
know I got you." Tricky pulled out a wad of cash and
peeled off four, crisp, one-hundred dollar bills. "My bad it
took so long." He handed him the dough.

"'Bout time." Shyhiem pocketed the money.

"You want something to drink? You look like you
need something stiff in yo' mouth."

"What?" Shyhiem balled up his fist.

"I ain't even mean it like that. You know what I was
tryin' to say. C'mon, let me get you something to drink."
Tricky draped his arm around his shoulder.

"I'm good. I'm just here to see my girl."

"Yo' girl in there? For real? I ain't know you had a
chick. I'm happy for you, fam. Yo' brother in there too."
Tricky escorted him inside.

A sliver of red and blue light shined inside Blank
Space. Shyhiem searched the room for Messiah. Bodies
were everywhere. There was barely any room to get
through. Black Spade was on stage killing it. Everyone was
crowded around the stage, watching him perform. Heads

were bobbin' and hands were clapping to the beat of his latest music. The vibe in the room was crazy.

Everyone was having a good time. The atmosphere reminded Shyhiem of a turnt house party. Black Spade held court in the center of the stage with a mic in his hand. He jumped in the air, hyping up the crowd. A DJ and a band backed him up. His new music sounded great. The song he sung sampled the Biggie lyric *It was all a dream*. Shyhiem wanted to be on everyone else's level, but his heart just wasn't into it. He would much rather be curled up behind Messiah, stroking her slowly. Bogarting his way through the crowd, he found his brother. Mayhem was standing by the bar with a few of his pot'nahs.

"Look who decided to come out." Mayhem gave his brother a one-arm hug, shocked to see him. "Messiah let you off yo' leash tonight?"

"Eat a dick." Shyhiem hit him with the middle finger. "I ain't stayin' long. I'm gettin' the fuck outta here 'fore you shoot up the place. You seen Messiah?"

"Nah, I ain't even know she was here."

If Mayhem knew she was there, he would've pulled her to the side and had a conversation with her. He wanted her out of his brother's life. She was no good.

"I just got here a li'l minute ago."

"Where the fuck is she at?" Shyhiem mumbled under his breath.

He was starting to feel like Messiah was playing games with him. What if she wasn't at Blank Space at all? Then Shyhiem remembered she'd invited him to swing through. She had no reason to lie to him. Shyhiem was trippin'. He was in his bag over Keesha. He couldn't blur

337

the lines between the two ladies. Lying about her whereabouts was something Keesha would do. Messiah was nothing like her. As Shyhiem searched the room for her with his eyes, mad people he knew approached him to show love. He hadn't been out in a minute so people were happy to see his face. Shyhiem shook a few hands when Mayhem leaned over and whispered in his ear, "Aye, ain't that yo' girl?"

Shyhiem followed the direction of his brother's hand and spotted Messiah in the middle of the dance floor grinding all up on some random dude. Technically, she wasn't grinding. She and the dude weren't even touching, but Shyhiem didn't care. To him, dancing with another man was a no-no. Where he came from, it was the ultimate sign of disrespect. The fact that his brother and friends were there to witness her betrayal infuriated him.

To make matters worse, she had on the shortest, skimpiest outfit he'd ever seen her in. It was like 58 degrees outside and she had the nerve to have on a black, wide brim hat, silver, tribal, statement necklace, a white, crochet, spaghetti strap, sweetheart neckline romper and black, suede, over-the-knee- boots. The hem of the shorts barely covered her ass. Shyhiem didn't know what had gotten into her but he wasn't feelin' it. She'd embarrassed the fuck out of him and made him look like an idiot.

"I told you that bitch was a fraud. She just tryin' to get in where she can fit in," Mayhem said vehemently.

Shyhiem swallowed his brother's words. He didn't want to take heed to his warning. Messiah loved him. He had to hold onto that. Tuning Mayhem out, he elbowed his way through the sea of people. Messiah was blissfully unaware of his presence. She was in her own world. Stone-faced, Shyhiem walked up, pushed her to the side and got up in the dude's face. He was an ole light skin, Chris

Brown lookin' ass nigga. He looked to be no older than 22. He had a thick beard and a teardrop tattoo under his eye.

"Fall back, bruh, this me." Shyhiem ice-grilled the guy.

"Who the fuck are you?" The guy looked him up and down, refusing to backdown.

After hours of being in the club, he'd finally built up the courage to step to Messiah. Her soft lips and dimpled chin had him hypnotized. He wasn't about to lose out on her now. He didn't know who homey was but dude had him fucked up. Messiah didn't have a ring on her finger, so in his mind, she was fair game. Before things got out of hand, Messiah stepped in-between them and placed her hand on Shyhiem's chest.

"Baby, calm down. We were just dancing."

Shyhiem continued to stare the dude down. The veins in his temples were thumping over time.

"C'mon, dance with me." Messiah wrapped her arms around his neck and pulled him close.

As soon as Shyhiem took his eyes off the guy and looked down into Messiah's sparkling, brown eyes, his mood changed. His shoulders relaxed and his guard was down. The guy took the hint that Messiah no longer wanted to dance and backed away.

"You are too damn fine to be so mad all the time." She two-stepped from side-to-side.

"What was you dancing wit' that nigga for? You tryin' to make me catch a case?" Shyhiem rested his face in the crook of her neck.

Her perfume had him wanting to peel her barely-there outfit off right there in front of everyone.

"You are so dramatic. Just say you missed me and that I look great." Messiah rubbed the back of his head.

"You always look good, but why you up in here wit' these li'l bitty-ass shorts on?" Shyhiem cupped her ass cheeks like a basketball.

"'Cause it's cute, hater." Messiah closed her eyes and enjoyed the feel of his hands on her butt.

Swept up in the tranquil sound of Black Spade's voice, Shyhiem and Messiah became lost in the music. No one else in the world existed but them. At times, he felt like he was caught up in a strange dream. Shyhiem wouldn't exchange this kind of love for all the riches in the world. What they had was irreplaceable. He'd follow her to the ends of the earth.

All eyes were on them. All the chicks in the spot where jealous that Messiah was the one who had his heart. None of them existed. He only had eyes for her. All the dope boys in the club had a hard-on for her but she only had eyes for him. Niggas loved the way her ass sat up and her legs bowed. Shyhiem was proud to say she was all his. Ever since he'd ran up in her, Messiah hadn't been the same. He'd exposed her to the real. A lame nigga could never get her attention.

Messiah couldn't keep her hands off him. Her tongue roamed his lips as she tugged on his dick. He was so happy she was over her shy girl shit. This was the Messiah he loved. Discreetly, he slipped his fingers in-between her legs and found that she was already wet for him. Shyhiem played in her wetness as she released a soft moan. Visions of him searching her body with his tongue all night invaded her brain.

"Keep touching me like that, you gon' find the roadmap to heaven," Messiah bit his bottom lip.

"That's the point." He winked his eye. "C'mon, let's go home." He intertwined his fingers with hers.

Messiah looked down and peeped the cuts and scrapes on the back of his hand.

"What happened to you?" She inspected the bruises closely.

"Me and Keesha got into it again."

"You didn't hit her, did you?"

"No." Shyhiem furrowed his brows. "Why would you ask me something like that?"

"'Cause Sonny told me you hit her the last time y'all got into it. I just wanted to make sure you didn't do it again."

"Don't get it twisted, I don't go around hittin' bitches. For your information, I punched the wall."

"Is that it?"

"I choked her," Shyhiem stated like it was nothing.

"I don't like the bitch but that's even worse. Let me find out you like puttin' yo' hands on women." Messiah arched her brow.

"I don't know what you're tryin' to insinuate, but Keesha ain't no woman. She's the fuckin' devil."

"You ain't lyin' about that," Messiah agreed.

"She's threatening to keep my kids away since I won't stop seeing you."

"What?" Messiah said in stun.

"Yeah, now you see why I spazzed out. Messiah, I would never put my hands on you. You know I ain't even that type of dude."

"I hope not, for your sake. 'Cause if you ever put yo' hands on me, you won't live to see another day," she warned.

"You ain't gotta worry about that. Like I said, that ain't even me. C'mon," Shyhiem kissed the palm of her hand. "Let's go back to the crib so I can put these 10 inches up in you."

"You so nasty. Let me find Bird so I can tell her I'm finna leave."

"A'ight, meet me out front."

Shyhiem stepped outside. His brother and his crew were posted up, sparking a blunt. A full moon was out. A bad feeling shot through Shyhiem's stomach. He could feel it in the air. Something bad was going to happen. Ignoring his intuition, he reached out for the blunt.

"I'll catch up wit' y'all later. I'm about to head out." He took two puffs off the blunt then passed it back to Mayhem.

"Everything good? What was up wit' ole girl?" Mayhem asked.

"Nothin', they was just dancing."

"You sure?" Mayhem nodded his head towards the door.

Shyhiem turned around to see the same corny-ass muthafucka up in Messiah's face again. Pissed that he'd disrespect him after he told him she was taken, Shyhiem stormed over to them. He could hear the dude say, "Fuck that nigga. He mad pussy. You too damn fine to be fuckin' wit' a lame. Let a real nigga like me, get yo' number so I can take you out sometime."

"Nah, I'm good." Messiah shook her head, spotting Shyhiem coming near.

Her eyes pled with him not to overreact. Shyhiem only saw red. The young bull wasn't even able to get another word out before Shyhiem punched him in the mouth. Grabbing him by the collar of his shirt, Shyhiem proceeded to hit him with a barrage of lethal blows to his face. The guy was so dazed, he didn't even have the opportunity to fight back. All he saw was stars.

"Shyhiem, stop! I can handle it!" Messiah tried to pull him off the boy.

In a trance, Shyhiem reared his arm back and hit her in the eye with his arm. The forceful swat of his arm caused Messiah to fly back into the wall. Messiah held her eye in tears, paralyzed in fear. Shyhiem was no longer himself. He'd morphed back into Goodnight. He couldn't hear her cries. His fist hadn't collided with live flesh in years. The feeling was enthralling. He was tired of people testing him. Muthafuckas would remember how and why he'd gotten the name Goodnight.

It was in his DNA to take niggas' heads off. He lived by the code of the streets. If a nigga tried you, there was no talkin'. You fought and killed for respect.

343

Shyhiem's heart beat like a bass drum. His deathly blows to the guy's face caused the dudes legs to buckle. On the ground, Shyhiem stomped him out. Never one to miss out on pandemonium, Mayhem and his pot'nahs joined in on the fun. They were beating him so bad, Messiah thought he was going to die. Tears streamed down her face. She was distraught. Hearing her friend's cry for help, Bird rushed to her aid.

The display of ghetto dysfunction before her sickened Bird. Shyhiem and his rowdy crew of thugs were pounding a young man to a bloody pulp. She'd seen people get jumped before, but not like this. Shyhiem and his boys seemed to genuinely enjoy tearing the dude apart.

"Shyhiem, stop! You're gonna kill him!" Messiah screamed to no avail.

The man she loved had disappeared. The person in front of her was an imposter. This person was a monster. He didn't care about anything or anyone. All he cared about was inflicting pain. Shyhiem kicked the dude so hard in the face blood curdled from his mouth and onto the gray suede of his shoes. The guy's face was so swollen, he was barely recognizable. The fact that Shyhiem could be so callus and cold towards another human being scared the living daylights out of Messiah.

Shyhiem was no longer a man she could trust. She'd told him she didn't like violence but he got off on it. He liked living in his dysfunction. Her cries didn't make him stop. It was like he'd forgotten she was even there. The sound of police sirens nearing is what brought Shyhiem back to reality. Huffing and puffing, he wiped sweat from his forehead, smearing blood on his face. Splatters of the guy's plasma were all over his clothes.

344

"Did he do this to you?" Bird questioned, incensed, examining Messiah's eye.

"It was an accident. He ain't mean it."

"What you mean he ain't mean it?"

"Bird, calm down. Shyhiem loves me. He would never hit me on purpose. I was a mistake," Messiah wept.

"A nigga puttin' his hands on you ain't no fuckin' mistake. Look at yo' damn eye!" Bird exclaimed.

"You don't understand." Messiah broke down.

Hearing Messiah sob hysterically, Shyhiem turned to console her.

"Uh ah! Don't you touch her!" Bird wagged her finger in his face. "Look at what you did to her face!"

A red bruise circled Messiah's eye. Shyhiem didn't even remember striking her. Shyhiem wanted to die. He'd swore to never put his hands on her and he'd done it.

"What the fuck are you doing, dog?" Bird eyed her friend quizzically. "This nigga ain't no better than Bryson! When are you gonna get that pain doesn't equal love? Look at him!" Bird pointed at the battered man on the ground.

"This shit ain't normal! Does this look like love to you?"

Messiah held her breath. Her best friend had her questioning if she was repeating the same, crazy pattern. Was Shyhiem another negative distraction? At first, she didn't think so, but after what had just happened, she wasn't so sure.

"Yo, on my mama, I ain't mean to do that. You know I would never hurt you." Shyhiem frantically tried to make her understand.

"Really? 'Cause you did." Messiah spat.

"Messiah, I'm sorry." Shyhiem begged, feeling her slip away.

"So am I. Stay the fuck away from me." She cried, leaving him standing there alone.

"At the end of the day, you're still my first."
–Kehlani, "Everything Is Yours"

#30

Messiah

The following day, Messiah went on with life as usual. She couldn't let the brawl at Blank Space stop her from getting a coin. She simply covered her eye with foundation and concealer and went to work at the diner. On the outside, she seemed cool as a cucumber, but on the inside, a battle was ensuing. Shyhiem had been calling her nonstop but she hadn't answered one call. A part of her wanted to hear him out, but the logical side of her told her it was a waste of time. The black eye she sported was evidence enough that he couldn't be trusted.

And yes, he'd done it on accident, but that didn't replace that she had a black eye. Shyhiem's reckless behavior couldn't be tolerated. She didn't want that kind of energy in her life. What he'd done was inexcusable. He could've killed that man; and for what? All because he tried to holla at her. The fight was unnecessary and it was childish. It all could've been avoided if he would've just calmed down and let her handle the situation. Yet and still, once again, Shyhiem had let his anger get the best of him.

Messiah took into consideration that he had a lot going on. His father, who hadn't raised him, was dying, Keesha was trying to keep his kids away from him, his six-year-old son was gay, and little did he know, but his baby mama was fuckin' his brother. The man had a shit load of drama. Messiah just didn't know if she could handle it all. She didn't know that to give him strength, she'd have to give up pieces of her own. Messiah had her own demons to deal with. She needed every morsel of her sanity to survive.

Loving Shyhiem was hard. He came with too much baggage. It was starting to become clear that she and him were two, broken individuals who'd found love and solace in one another. But their horrific past and people around them kept tearing them apart. Maybe being with him wasn't where she needed to be. They'd taken a leap of faith and fallen flat on their faces. *This is what you get for moving so fast,* she thought, bussing tables.

Messiah took the dirty dishes and cutlery back to the kitchen to be cleaned. It was almost time for her to leave. A hot bubble bath and Stevie Wonder's song *Love's In Need Of Love* were calling her name. She needed to decompress and figure out what her next move would be. Something needed to change. She wanted a change in scenery. She hated St. Louis and the people in it. She had to get out.

A change in profession would make her happy. Working at Charter in the Call Center and being a poorly-paid waitress wasn't where it was at. Messiah had too much talent to be wasting her life away. There had to be more to life than living paycheck to paycheck.

Getting back into ballet was her main goal. She had Shyhiem to thank for that. If he wouldn't have pushed her to dance that day at the studio, she would've never realized how much she missed it. Messiah loved ballet so much that she wanted to resume taking classes. The goal was to brush up on her skills, become a teacher and open her own studio. Messiah loved working with children. It would be an absolute delight to teach other young boys and girls the legendary art form.

"Messiah, you have a customer at table four." Mr. Johnson got her attention.

"Yes, sir." She pulled out a pen and pad and headed over to the table. "How may I help you?" She asked, not paying attention to the gentleman's face.

"Messiah, it's me." The man said.

Messiah looked up from her notepad and found Bryson. Stunned, she steadied her balance so she wouldn't fall. For weeks, she begged God for this day. She begged God to let her hear his voice again. Now that he was there, sitting alone at a booth, she wasn't so sure she was happy to see him. His eyes were bloodshot red. It looked like he'd been crying nonstop for days. His clothes were disheveled and mix matched. The man was a wreck.

"What are you doing here?" She finally found words to speak.

"I know you probably don't want to see me, but you're the only person I can talk to." Bryson replied, somberly.

"Talk to me about what? You haven't been wanting to talk to me."

"I know and I'm sorry. The way I did you was fucked up. Maybe that's why God is punishing me," he sniffed.

Bryson looked like he was on the verge of death. Messiah tried not to care. She wanted to revel in his pain but that wasn't who she was. She never wanted to see anyone she cared for in agony. Slowly, she slid into the booth and placed her pad down onto the table.

"What happened?"

Bryson gazed blankly at his shaking hands. Messiah had never seen him so shaken up. Something terrible must've gone down.

"Is it your parents? Are they ok?"

"They're fine." Bryson wiped his nose and sniffed again.

He could barely look Messiah in the eyes.

"What it is then?"

"It's Kenya," His voice cracked. "She lost the baby."

Messiah's eyes grew wide. She couldn't believe her ears. Kenya was halfway through her pregnancy. Once again, life had repeated itself. Bryson had lost another son. Messiah felt her heart contract. The feeling that she'd caused this crept into her psyche. She'd wished death on the baby when he broke up with her. *This is all my fault,* Messiah thought, placing her hand over her mouth. Words held weight and power. She'd spoken death over an innocent baby's life and killed it.

"Bryson, I'm so sorry." She reached across the table and held his hand.

"Messiah, it hurts so bad." He choked up.

Tears clouded his eyes. Messiah placed her head down and shed a tear too.

"Don't cry. I've made you cry enough." He lifted her chin and wiped her tears away.

Staring deeply into her eyes, Bryson cupped her cheek with his hand. Messiah placed her hand on top of his. The heat from his skin radiated into the palm of her hand. The love they shared was still there. She could see it in his eyes as he looked at her. She wanted to hate him for what he'd done, but the six-year relationship they shared wouldn't allow it. Maybe Bryson showing up unexpectedly with such tragic news was a sign from God that she was moving in the wrong direction.

"Here." He reached inside his pocket and slid her engagement ring across the table. "This belongs to you. I shouldn't have ever taken it in the first place."

Messiah glared at the ring then back up at his face. Was he asking her back? Did he wanna try again? At the end of the day, he was her first. Bryson knew her in and out. She couldn't erase what they shared. A million thoughts flooded her brain. She could hear her heartbeat through her ears.

"What does this mean?" She asked, breathlessly.

"Yeah, what does it mean?" Shyhiem questioned over her shoulder.

"What do you do when you love her but you know she love somebody else?" – Mack Wilds, "Explore"

#31

Shyhiem

Messiah quickly turned around in her seat and looked at him. Shyhiem wanted to go off but turning up had gotten him in the predicament he was in now. He'd come to the diner to talk things out and tell her he was sorry. He had to make Messiah see that she had no reason to fear him. Despite her anger and disappointment, she knew deep down how much he loved her. Shyhiem wasn't willing to lose her. They could start all over again, if she'd give him another chance.

Love wasn't easy. It would be such a shame if they'd part. They were on the cusp of greatness. She had to know that. The fact that God had brought them together wasn't by chance. It was written that they were meant to be. She was his Ruth and he was her Boaz. Their love was real and pure, but Messiah had always had one foot out the door. The nigga sitting across from her, holding her hand was the thing holding her back.

Shyhiem couldn't understand why he had such a hold on her. He'd fucked her over in the worst way. He would never leave her for another chick. He was devoted to her. Messiah had to make up her mind. Either it was him or Bryson.

"Who is this?" Bryson asked.

"A friend of mine." Messiah heard herself say.

"Oh, that's what I am?" Shyhiem said, taken aback.

Messiah had just shot him, pointblank, in the heart.

"A'ight, Messiah." He turned to walk away.

Messiah sat and watched him leave, unable to breathe. She didn't know what to do or say. Her future and her past were staring her right in the face. Which one was she to choose?

"I'll be right back." She rose from the table and raced out the door.

Shyhiem was halfway to his car by the time she made it outside.

"Shyhiem!" She race-walked down the street.

"I'm your fuckin' friend?" He barked over his shoulder. "That's all I am to you?"

"No! Just let me explain!" She caught up to him.

"Explain what? That you love me but you love him more?" Shyhiem spun around and faced her.

"I don't know how I feel!"

"Yes, you do." Shyhiem called her out on her bullshit. "You know exactly how you feel. It's cool to kick it with the li'l hood dude, but as soon as college boy comes back, all bets are off."

"You know it's not like that." Messiah said, offended by his words.

"What the fuck is it then, Messiah?"

"'Don't act all innocent, Shyhiem. You're no angel in all of this. You left me hanging for days then accused me of kidnapping your kids!"

"I thought we got past that?"

"I lied, I'm still hurt. As soon as I opened up to you, you let me down. That let me know that this is nothing but a game to you. You saw something you liked and you went after it. You don't love me for real!"

"Bullshit! You know I love you!" Shyhiem stressed at the top of his lungs.

"Why?" Messiah's whole body began to shake. "We never said what this was. Everything just happened. We got caught up in the moment, in how we made each other feel, 'cause it felt good at the time. But none of this is real. Who's to say this is supposed to last?"

"Is that how you really feel? You think we got caught up?"

"We both knew what it was. I never said I was your girlfriend. Nor did you ever ask me to be."

"A'ight, so here it is." Shyhiem's voice shook slightly. "I love you. You love me. The last month and a half have been the best few weeks of our lives. I want more. I want you. Do you want me?"

Messiah pursed her lips together and willed herself not to scream. Hot tears scorched her cheeks like they'd been set on fire with gasoline. She wanted to run and hide. If she cried one more tear, she was sure to combust.

"Messiah, I love you." Shyhiem cupped her face with both his hands. "I love you. I love you. I love you. I love you. I'll say it a billion times. I love you." He closed his eyes.

"I knew it the second I saw you. You're brave, you're beautiful, you're generous and you're kind. You're the woman I've been praying my whole life for. Do you know why I come to the diner sometimes twice a day? It's so I can see you, breathe you, be around you. Seeing you, sometimes, is the highlight of my whole day," Shyhiem confessed.

Messiah held her head down. The emotions swarming inside her belly were nauseating. Shyhiem made her face him and placed his forehead on top of hers.

"Remember what you said to me that time I took you to the loft? When we were siting underneath the stars. You said nobody ever chooses you. Well, here I am choosing you. I've chosen you time and time again. Baby, you just have to choose me too," he urged. "You have to let me in. Baby, I wanna know everything about you. I wanna know why you listen to Stevie Wonder every time you're in a bad mood, what you dream about when you have nightmares. Messiah, I love you and I wanna be with you. That's what you want too. Isn't it?"

Messiah stood silent.

"Isn't it?"

"I don't know," Messiah replied, truthfully.

"What you mean you don't know? Fuck him! Come home with me!"

"I can't!" She yelled.

Shell-shocked by her response, Shyhiem let go of her face and stepped back. Nothing else needed to be said. The cranes in the sky had fallen. She'd made her choice. Their love wasn't set in stone. It wouldn't withstand the odds. He'd played the game of love and lost his heart to her.

Messiah stood in the freezing cold on the sidewalk. Her heart was telling her to run after him and confess her undying love, but her mouth told her to keep her mouth shut. She didn't want to sell Shyhiem a dream. Her feelings were all over the place. She couldn't give herself to either him or Bryson. For the first time in her life, Messiah had to choose herself.

Shyhiem got in his car and sped off. He wanted to cry but his pride wouldn't let him. Fuck love. A nigga like him wasn't supposed to give his heart to a woman anyway. Females played too many games. The allure of loving someone was over. Shyhiem was jaded. It was time to put his feelings to the side and get back to business. If Messiah didn't want him, then he'd choose the one thing in life that had never let him down. Lighting a blunt, he called his brother. Mayhem answered on the first ring.

"What up?"

"I'm in."

To Be Continued

Made in the USA
Middletown, DE
01 August 2017